I0612623

THE BULARI SAGA

# TRAVEL GUIDE

JESSIE KWAK

First edition October 2024

*Cover art by Dusty Crosley*

*Cover design by Jessie Kwak & Robert Kittilson*

*Edited by Kyra Freestar*

*Map by Jessie Kwak*

www.jessiekwak.com

# CONTENTS

PART 4
EPHEMERA

# PART 1

## WELCOME TO BULARI

To the Maraka Valley

N
W E
S

Geordi Jimenez
Space Terminal

Jet Park

Casinos

Downtown

To Julieta Yang's

Dry Creek

Altamira
(Blackheart territory)

Tamarind District

University of Bulari

Carama Town

## LETIZIA DIAMANTE PRESENTS:
## BULARI

*WHETHER YOU'RE HERE TO DANCE THE NIGHT AWAY in an exclusive nightclub, discover a new favorite artist in one of the many museums, or sample your way through Bulari's incredible food scene, this once-ignored city has something for everyone.*

---

Welcome to Bulari!

These days, the capital city of New Sarjun has thoroughly transcended its reputation as a hard-scrabble mining outpost to become a hotbed of culture and cuisine. You don't have to look too hard to see the roots, but scraping out a city this impressive in a climate so harsh was no small feat, and the citizens of Bulari are understandably proud.

It's a city of many contradictions, and travelers with an adventurous spirit are sure to find a thrill in the myriad of experiences available. Whether touring the stunning natural desert landscape, shopping your way through the Tamarind, or rubbing elbows with celebrities at one of many exclusive restaurants, Bulari has plenty to offer.

## When to Go and Weather

Prized for its mineral-rich hills rather than its climate, the Bulari Valley varies from uncomfortably warm to soul-meltingly hot. For that reason, most tourists visit sometime between the first of the fall thunderstorms and the last of the spring desert bloom. If you have time, escape the heat with a romantic getaway to the southern New Sarjunian town of Alusina for a weekend of wine tasting, art galleries, and river cruises.

## Neighborhoods: Central Bulari

### The Tamarind

Surrounding a lush swath of park blocks just east of the downtown core, the Tamarind is a paradise for shopping, dining, and people watching. The towering eucalyptus, oak, fan palm, and tree aloe ward off the worst of Bulari's heat, creating a pleasant place to while away the afternoon with a cup of tea or a glass of Alusinian cinsuat in one of the many parkside cafes. Most of the better hotels, such as the Blue Falcon, are located in this neighborhood.

. . .

*Downtown*

The business heart of Bulari, the downtown area is clean, crisp, and cutting edge. Expect a well-heeled crowd of young professionals on their way to the top of the corporate ladder, with plenty of sophisticated dining options to impress potential clients. The neighborhood quiets down in the evenings as night life fires up in the Tamarind, but a robust security presence keeps the streets feeling comfortable for out-of-towners.

*Government District*

New Sarjun's seat of power is also home to many of Bulari's most interesting museums. Stroll the People's Plaza for a good example of the early colonial architecture typical to the city, and be sure to visit National Museum for an in-depth exploration of the city's history. Visitors are also welcome inside the lobby of the capitol building, where impressive columns showcase the famed local sandstone and rose salt. The international embassies are all here, too, if you run into any issues.

*University of Bulari*

This gorgeous Hypatia Educational Facilities Corporation campus is just up the bluff from downtown, and offers a beautiful view out over the city. The University's biology programs are particularly well-known, and plant lovers will delight in a stroll through the campus's botanical garden to explore the extensive collection of local flora.

## Neighborhoods: North Bulari

### Casino District

A trip to Bulari isn't complete without a visit to the spectacular Casino District. Try your luck on the develier tables at the venerable Orveto's Thousands, or sit in on a game of mystix at the newest jewel of the drag, the Lorelei. After dinner at one of the many exquisite restaurants, catch a show at Ayisha's Palace. The gorgeous music venue's namesake, Ayisha Amadule, performs regularly and puts on an incredible show. Top off the night with one of Phaera D's signature cocktails at the exclusive Devil's Table before retiring to your high-rise hotel room at the Aterciopelado to admire the view of downtown Bulari.

### Geordi Jimenez Space Terminal

While you may be tempted to spend as little time as possible transiting the space terminal, it's worth a second look. This busy hub is more than a transit center, it's the lifeline of New Sarjun, and a great spot for people watching. If you find yourself with some extra time before your shuttle off-planet, catch a bite to eat on Levels A or B. The kitsch travel-themed watering hole Le Comptoir Darna in particular is worth a stop. And if you need a last-minute gift (or a quick prosthetic repair), you'll find something unique at a little repair shop called Hallelujah It's Fixed run by the charming Hallelujah Oni.

*Travel advisory: While Levels A and B are perfectly safe, it's best to leave the terminal's Level C to the locals.*

## Jet Park

There's not currently much of note in Jet Park, but rumors have it the space terminal's nearest neighborhood is on its way up. There have been some significant investments lately from local business owners, including the gentech-focused Juvex Spa Center, and a brewery venture backed by Willem Jaantzen, the controversial owner of Downtown Bulari's culinary jewel, the Jungle.

## Neighborhoods: The Fingers

*Travel advisory: It's best not to visit the Fingers without a local guide.*

## Dry Creek

This formerly working class neighborhood has been in steep decline over the last few decades as violence between local gangs made the neighborhood quite dangerous. Bottom line, avoid Dry Creek.


### Altamira

Once a wealthy settlement in its own right, Altamira's fortunes were reversed after being swallowed up by Bulari proper a little over a century ago. Now, Altamira is one of the nicest of Bulari's Finger slums, in part due to the iron rule of a local criminal organization led by one of recent memory's most infamous Bulari citizens, Thala Coeur. The street gang boss turned former mayor continued running the neighborhood from exile, and is rumored to have retaken her throne. Altamira is safe enough if you have an escort.


### Carama Town

The smallest of Bulari's Finger ravines spilled out long ago to create the largest of the town's slums, spreading into the plain south of Bulari's downtown. Carama Town is a largely working class neighborhood where new immigrants tend to cluster in regionally-influenced micro-neighborhoods that each have their own flavor. If you have time to kill and a good driver to guide you, a trip through Carama Town's famous traffic can be a thrill.

Of course, most tourists don't go any farther than Anjali Lumaban Boulevard, a stunning monument to one of the city's founders. On weekends, you'll find a vibrant farmer's market in the plaza, which is a good place to buy souvenirs and taste the local street food. And don't miss the various culture and music festivals held on the plaza throughout the year.

## Where To Eat

Bulari is a city of immigrants, and they've all brought their most impressive recipes. No matter your favorite dish back home, you're sure to find a restaurant in Bulari that makes it better.

### The Jungle

Topping every epicurean traveler's must-visit list, the Jungle's reputation is certainly fueled by the notoriety of its owner, Willem Jaantzen. However, the dining experience lives up to the hype. There are no bad tables at the Jungle! Incredible living foliage creates a private retreat at every table, and exquisite white-glove service makes every guest feel like royalty. Only the luckiest guests can secure an invitation to the exclusive Golden Orchid room in the back of the restaurant, where Bulari's elite conduct business over chic cocktails and appetizers.

Be sure to make your reservation well ahead of time, or prepare to wait for hours for a seat at the bar.

### Jade's Finest Coffee and Chicken

At first glance this hole-in-the-wall downtown diner may not look like much, but don't be fooled. You may not see anyone sitting at the tables, but Jade's does a brisk business in takeaway — it's a local favorite both for residents and business people on their lunch break. Don't miss the chicken in black bean sauce!

## The Oasis

The Oasis is the best place in Bulari to try the city's most famous local dish, korris. Any of the dishes on the menu will delight, but if you're in a group, do yourself a favor and let the owner, Ajesh Paiman, choose a feast for you. Oh, and if you believe the rumors, the Oasis is also the place to catch a glimpse of some of the biggest players in Bulari's seedy underbelly. Be warned that the korris here is spiced for locals, not tourists, so ask for a milder version if you're not accustomed to New Sarjunian heat.

## The Devil's Table

Buy-ins at the high roller's tables here may cost as much as your shuttle ticket back into orbit, but anyone can enjoy a cocktail or dinner at the bar. Be aware that the dress code is strictly enforced, but even if you didn't bring evening wear it's worth a shopping spree in the Tamarind for a glimpse inside this exclusive experience and a chance to set eyes on the proprietor. One of Bulari's rising darlings, Phaera D also owns the Lorelei

Casino and has been scandalizing the press lately with rumors that she's stepping out with the notorious Willem Jaantzen.

*Lucky's Palladium Coast*

If you need to get away from the always-on energy of the Casino District, Lucky's is the place to go. A few blocks off the main drag, patrons don't visit Lucky's for the food so much as the camaraderie. It's a great place to drink with the locals! Sit at the bar and you're just as likely to run into a great gambling legend as an off-duty dealer. Keep an eye out, and you might just spot some of the most powerful names in the casino business doing business over mediocre noodles.

THANK YOU TO OUR SPONSORS!

THE DEVIL'S TABLE

# PART 2

## SHORT STORIES

# TIMELINE

*Exploring the Bulari Saga has been like solving a puzzle, with every book or story I write shining a light on another small portion of the world.*

*I did not write things in order. I apologize. My brain does not work in a linear way when telling stories. ⁻\\_(ツ)_/⁻*

*Ultimately, I recommend approaching the Bulari Saga world by starting with Double Edged, followed by the rest of the books in the Bulari Saga. Then, explore the constellation of character-specific novellas and short stories that shine a flashlight on fascinating parts of the picture that aren't within the scope of the main series.*

*Of course, some readers disagree with me. They say it's best to start with the prequel novellas* (Starfall, Negative Return, *and* Deviant Flux), *then move on to* Double Edged.

*If you haven't read any of the books, you can always dive in with these short stories. Some are set before the books (or outside of their storylines), so contain no spoilers. Others will definitely spoil parts of the Bulari Saga.*

*You do you.*

*This timeline is my attempt to guide you through where the stories and scenes you're about to encounter fit within the larger story arc.*

*Note that all the following short stories and deleted/alternate POV scenes (bolded) are included in this volume. I've organized them chronologically within their sections.*

*Enjoy!*

## Before

40 years ago:  **"Rogue"**
20 years ago:  **"Meeting Toshiyo"**
               *Negative Return* (novella)
               **"Bad Intentions"**
15 years ago:  *Starfall* (novella)
12 years ago:  **"Storm Warning"**
10 years ago:  *Deviant Flux* (novella)
9 years ago:   **"Girls' Night"**

## Now: The Bulari Saga

*Double Edged* (Book 1)    **"Trouble"**
                           **"Phaera at Leone's Party"**
                           **"Beto Makes the Call"**
                           **"Coeur at the Greenhouse"**
*Crossfire* (Book 2)
*Pressure Point* (Book 3)    **"Deathtrap"**
*Heat Death* (Book 4)
*Kill Shot* (Book 5)

(a few months later)    **"Holiday"**

# ROGUE

*This is one of the earliest short stories I wrote set in the Bulari Saga universe, and it's also our first glimpse of the couple who eventually got their own book series (The Nanshe Chronicles): Raj and Lasadi Dusai.*

*This story was originally published in* Space Cocaine Vol. 1.

NORMALLY WHEN A JOB STARTS TO GO THIS BAD, it's a logistics issue. Somebody didn't think through all the options, one thread snags, and then the whole plan unravels into a mess.

That's something Willem Jaantzen can deal with.

But this time? Someone on *this* job is deliberately snagging threads.

If Jaantzen's learned anything in his first, rough, twenty-four years of life, it's that survival is all about watching your own back and having an exit plan to get out with your fair share when things go sideways. Problem is, Jaantzen normally takes jobs down on solid ground where he can melt back into the city. He's not used to this space pirate shit. Being trapped in a tin can hurtling through the skies above New Sarjun with another — smaller — tin can as his only way home is not his idea of a good time.

But a job's a job.

And damned if he's going to die in space.

Dez is pretty fast with his knife, but Jaantzen is even faster with a gun — even with this lightweight electric piece Amita insisted he carry instead of his usual pistol with the hull-tearing large-cal bullets. His first electric bolt hits Dez square in the temple, and though it may not pack a big punch — Jaantzen has been shot with one plenty of times before — it'll fry someone's wires if you hit them where it counts.

Dez's been hit where it counts.

The other man goes still, but he doesn't fall, just floats in the zero G of the luxury yacht's cargo hold, all loose joints and slack jaw, a patch of flesh on his pale temple singed bubblegum pink and carbon black and stinking with smoke.

"Not today, asshole," Jaantzen mutters, shoving the

electric pistol back into its holster and giving Dez a gentle push to float him out of the way.

Jaantzen shoulders Dez's bag as well, then pushes the heavy rubber crate awkwardly out of the cargo hold and into the corridor. One silver lining of the head-spinning weightlessness on this docked yacht? Down on New Sarjun he'd be screwed getting the goods back home after shooting his partner.

Still, the rubber crate is ungainly, bumping off Jaantzen's shins and scuffing the immaculate cream lacquer of the walls. Even in the lower deck, the hall-way's handholds are gold plated. Pry one of these off and Jaantzen will eat well for a month. Pry all of them off and he won't have to work for Amita any more. He could start his own outfit, maybe. Choose his own jobs.

Think of the Devil, and Amita's voice crackles in his ear.

"Dez, Will. What happened?"

"Dez tried to double-cross us," Jaantzen answers. "I've got the goods."

A pause. He pictures the face Amita's probably making at this very moment: one eye narrowing, lips quirked to the side as she decides who's bullshitting her. She made that same face ten years ago when she found Willem Jaantzen fresh from breaking out of the orphanage, lost in the wrong gang's territory. He'd been just some soft kid trying to convince her he'd be worth keeping alive, that he'd work out to be more than just another mouth to feed.

Amita's pause is brief; she didn't fight her way to the top of her crew by making slow decisions.

"Copy that," she says. "Let's get out of here."

Jaantzen awkwardly ricochets into a ladderway and propels the crate up toward the docking bay.

Time to get off this boat.

And to find out who else on the crew Dez was working with.

---

It would be a simple job, Amita had said. A luxury yacht, the *Dahlia Regina* with a cargo hold full of drugs — raw Indiran snow. Real, not synth, she'd said with a gleam in her eye that said she'd tried both and knew the difference.

Jaantzen just understood it would fetch a better price. Even if he could afford it, he wasn't interested in the baggage that came with tasting that honey.

The yacht's owner would be down on New Sarjun brokering a deal with one of the nightclub owners in Bulari's Tamarind District, Amita had said. No real security on the boat, on account of nobody would be stupid enough to try to hit it while it was in orbit.

Amita'd smiled as she'd said this last. She's not stupid, but he suspects she thinks he is. Her own hunk of muscle with no ambition of his own, at her beck and call whenever she needs somebody with a gun for one of her many jobs.

Jaantzen's not stupid, either. But he's broke, and he's worked with Amita on enough jobs to know she doesn't go in without an exit plan. The trick to working for her is making sure you're part of that plan.

"Just me and you?" he'd asked.

She'd shaken her head. "I've got a pilot, a tech, another gun, you, and me."

"Five?" Jaantzen hadn't liked five. Hell, Jaantzen doesn't like jobs that require more than two, tops, but the paydays are only so big when you're working on your own. Sometimes you gotta trust somebody else not to shoot you — at least not until closer to the end of the job.

Amita'd given him that half smile, golden-brown eyes locked on his, the look that says, *I know you're going to do it, I'm just waiting for you to say yes.*

And Jaantzen had just shrugged. What the hell. He'd never been in space.

Might as well see if it's everything it's cracked up to be.

---

Turns out jobs with Amita in space are just as messy as jobs with Amita on solid ground, only with a side of terrible, gut-curdling weightlessness.

Jaantzen pushes the crate up the last ladderway and bites out a curse.

Dez was the other gun, and Beetle was the tech, all

wiry and lean, tawny brown skin and a shock-purple hair done up in a mass of skinny braids.

Currently, Beetle is dead at the console in the bridge, quivering droplets of blood pearling away from a knife stuck in his spinal column. Since he was supposed to hack the security settings that would get them off this boat, this is not a good sign.

It wasn't Dez, since Dez never left Jaantzen's side. His gut says Haruko, the pilot, but Jaantzen isn't trusting enough to rule out Amita. Could be she brought along a crew she thinks is disposable.

Willem Jaantzen is not disposable.

"Amita, come in," he says.

Jaantzen activates his grav boots beside the console, stumbling briefly as the magnets catch. Beetle's floating face-down over the control panel; Jaantzen shifts him gently out of the way. The tech's hand trails behind him as he floats out of the chair, leaving a smear of sticky blood on the console's glass.

Computers aren't Jaantzen's thing, but the green outlines around the docking clamps that have hold of their shuttle looks like all systems go. Hopefully Beetle got through the security before getting knifed — but that's no longer their biggest problem.

A proximity alert is blinking in the corner of the screen. Jaantzen swipes it open and growls with frustration. It's an Alliance cutter, making a beeline directly toward them.

Amita still hasn't answered. Jaantzen's got the

goods, so there's no way she took off without getting a payday. Why isn't she responding?

"Amita."

But there's something off in the silence around his voice. The connection's been cut.

Jaantzen whirls just as a pop from a handheld electric barb sounds. The barbs zip past him and clink off the console, wires flailing.

He blocks the electric barb with enough force that it goes flying from his attacker's hand, then punches them in the jaw before they can react. Jaantzen's ready to grapple, but he's unprepared for the *Dahlia Regina*, where his grav boots suck at his feet like mud and his assailant — a woman with a thick braid of blond hair — goes flying out of reach from the force of his punch, crashing against the navigation array.

She's not alone. Her companion takes aim.

For such a big ship, the yacht's bridge is cramped: the nav console takes up a third of the space with its chrome plated panels, and a pair of chairs — one of which is taken up by Beetle's body — are bolted to the floor. It's not nearly enough space for the three-person shootout Jaantzen's attackers seem to be planning, but it's perfect for a brawl.

Jaantzen can brawl.

He launches himself at the second assailant — a tawny man with long, wavy black hair — and catches him around the midriff before he can fire. They crash into a wall panel; there's a shriek of metal hinges as the panel's thin metal door crumples under the impact.

The man's tall and lithe, but what he knows about fighting in zero G isn't a match for Jaantzen's bulk and strength. With his opponent securely pinned against the wall, Jaantzen clocks him in the jaw — once, twice — and then his own head rings with a blow from behind.

The woman's caught him with a flying kick, ricocheting gracefully to catch herself on the ladder and crouch like a cat ready to spring.

When she does, Jaantzen locks his grav boots and twists, using her companion's back as a shield to deflect her. But he's not expecting the man's effortless weight. He almost loses control, then the man is grinning as he corkscrews deftly in Jaantzen's hands, breaking free. His knee catches Jaantzen under the chin as he spins away.

Toward the electric barb, which is floating near the ceiling.

Jaantzen launches himself after it, and what he lacks in zero G grace, he makes up for in size, catching the man once more and locking his grav boots to the ceiling, using his mass to pin the man in place beneath him.

He pulls his electric pistol, and lodges it between the man's eyes.

The man moves slowly, lifting hands above head and slowly releasing the electric barb he's just caught, sending the weapon floating out of reach. A smile spreads across his face, rakish through bloodied lips.

"Not a bad fight for a grounder," he says. His accent, that brash lilt: he's from Durga's Belt. "But it looks like we're at an impasse."

His black eyes twinkle, then roll meaningfully to Jaantzen's right.

Jaantzen spares a glance to see the woman aiming her own gun squarely at his own head; a faint, familiar whine fills the room as the weapon warms to her palm. It's not an electric stun pistol like what Jaantzen has. Jaantzen's will do serious damage to the man at this range, but hers will tear through the hull if she doesn't aim true.

That calm look in her eyes says she tends to aim true.

For a moment, Jaantzen fights pure vertigo as he realizes they're on the ceiling, the woman standing on the floor with Beetle's body drifting beside her. He focuses his attention back on his captive before he loses it.

"Did you kill my tech guy?" Jaantzen says.

"No," the man says. "It was a tall guy, pale. Black buzz cut?"

Haruko, the pilot. Jaantzen feels a thrill of fear for Amita, chased by the realization that Haruko could possibly be working on her orders and she's planning on double-crossing Jaantzen, instead.

Whatever the man sees on Jaantzen's face causes him to smile sadly. "Another one of yours, then? The crew you run with is a mess."

Jaantzen's not in a place to pick who he works with, and he's not about to have a heart-to-heart with this asteroid-belt pirate. He needs to get rid of these two, schlep the cargo back to the docking bay without Dez or Beetle to help, and either sweet talk Amita into not ditching him in space or help her fight Haruko, depending on the situation.

And he needs to do it fast.

Because that Alliance ship he noticed earlier? It's hailing them.

*"Dahlia Regina,* this is the Alliance patrol vessel *Andaluz.* We're receiving a distress signal, and will board if we receive no reply."

"This was excellent choice of target, if I do say so myself," the man says. "If unfortunately executed on all our sides. But I think we can still salvage the day. Pirate's honor, spoils go to the victor. Particularly when it's the victor's home turf."

Jaantzen frowns at him. "What do you mean?"

"We raided a resupply ship heading to the Arquellian embassy on New Sarjun just a few days ago, and we picked up quite the feast in Arquellian delicacies. We'd be happy to give you dinner and a ride back home on the *Nanshe.*"

At the name, Jaantzen's eyes widen. He may not pay much attention to what happens off New Sarjun, but the exploits of the *Nanshe* get around.

"You're Raj Dusai."

"At your service." Raj gives him another bright

smile. A thread of blood drifts from his nose. "Allow me to introduce my wife, Lasadi."

Lasadi tips her chin in greeting, but her aim doesn't waver.

"You give me a ride planetside? And what do I give you."

"For starters, you take that gun away from my head, and we get a move on so we can get off the ship before the Alliance catch us. We stand here — excuse me, lay here — bartering much longer, we're all rotting away in prison."

Jaantzen doesn't move.

"You can trust us," Raj says. "Of course everyone says that. But if you know who I am, you know the Dusais keep their word."

"Nobody keeps their word."

Behind him — below him — Lasadi laughs. "Maybe you've just been running with the wrong crew."

"*Dahlia Regina*, this is the Alliance patrol vessel *Andaluz*. We're now attempting to board. Be aware that we will treat anyone on board as hostile."

"I let go of my weapon and your wife shoots me," Jaantzen says.

"Where's the honor in that?" Lasadi says. "But I guarantee if you harm Raj, your brains will be a fresh coat of paint on this gaudy-ass ship."

"It could use some redecorating," Jaantzen says, but he finally sits up, and slips his electric pistol into its holster at the small of his back. He risks another look at Lasadi Dusai, and his stomach clenches once more with vertigo at clinging to the ceiling while she stands on the floor.

Lasadi holsters her own weapon, and Jaantzen releases his grav boots, pushing off Raj's body gently in an attempt to get his feet right on the true floor. He's overspinning, but Lasadi rights him effortlessly despite being half his size. Raj pushes from the ceiling gracefully as a cat.

Jaantzen lets out a string of curses.

The cargo — the payday — is gone.

"Amita!" he yells, knowing for sure the line of communication is cut. It's a yell of frustration and rage, equal parts fear for her safety and fury at the possibility she's betrayed him.

In response he hears a blood-curdling scream of pain. The voice is distorted and raw, but Jaantzen would recognize it anywhere. It's torn from the throat of the person he's known longer than anyone in his life: Amita. He pushes himself up the stairwell toward the docking bay at the rear of the *Dahlia Regina*, forgetting the notorious space pirates behind him.

"Kid, wait!" he hears Raj shout.

Amita's floating in the docking bay when they arrive, limbs sprawled like somebody's forgotten doll, the ozone scorch of an electric pistol still lingering in the air. Her eyes are blinking rapidly — Jaantzen knows that look of someone who's been stunned, her nervous system overloaded and shut down. But she's still alive.

Haruko is loading the cargo onto their shuttle, a piece of trash that barely looks spaceworthy on its own, let alone in comparison to the gleaming yacht whose docking bay it currently fills.

The blast from Haruko's electric pistol just grazes Jaantzen's arm. He feels the flash of heat, the sharp bite of electricity in his bicep spidering out through his body. His hair stands on end, his fingertips tingle. If the shot had hit him square on, his arm would be useless.

Jaantzen fires back, but zero G is shit for proper footing and the shot goes wide to hit the doorway to the shuttle. The doorway arcs a moment with flickering blue. Jaantzen curses himself: one wrong hit and the shuttle's dead.

"C'mon, kid," Raj says beside him. "It's not worth it."

The shuttle door is closing, Haruko mashing at the controls beside it. If Jaantzen launches himself now, he might just make it through, might just be able to catch Haruko and, what? Put a gun to his head and force him to fly them both home? Leaving Amita floating there for the Alliance to find? She'll likely turn on him someday, but apparently today was not that day. He'll defend himself when that day comes, but he won't be the first to turn.

"I bought us a few more minutes," Lasadi calls. She's been furiously typing commands into the control panel by the bay airlock.

"*Dahlia Regina*, this is the Alliance patrol *Andaluz*. Release control of the docking doors immediately, or we will respond with lethal force."

The shuttle's engines rev.

"He's getting control of airlock," Lasadi yells. "If we don't get out of here immediately we're spaced." She pushes herself away from the control panel, rocketing toward the far end of the docking bay, where a panel in the wall has been pushed aside. "Raj, now!"

"You coming or you dying, kid?" Raj Dusai asks Jaantzen.

"Not without my crew." Jaantzen pushes himself over to Amita, catches her in midair; she's struggling to swallow, eyes wild and limbs stiff. She's impossibly light.

"Let's go then."

A warning begins to sound as the depressurization sequence begins. Jaantzen isn't sure where Raj and Lasadi are parked, but he knows that the Alliance like to have a scapegoat — especially when they've been pissed off. He fires his electric pistol at the shuttle's docking clamps, then again at the engines. A net of blue electricity crackles over the shuttle, and the docking mechanism convulses once then sticks open, clinging to the floor of the docking bay. The engine whines and begins to smoke.

Through the glass panel, Haruko is screaming something Jaantzen can't hear. Jaantzen lets him scream, grabs Amita by the shoulders and maneuvers her over to the far end of the docking bay where Raj

Dusai is waiting to help pull her through the passageway.

It's a short glide to the hole Raj and Lasadi have lased in the hull of the luxury yacht. Lasadi's there already, smearing the edges of the cutout section with a golden goo.

"Try not to touch this, big guy," she says as Jaantzen passes Amita through to her. Jaantzen doesn't have Amita's slight build, nor Raj's, nor Lasadi's. But he manages to get his wide shoulders through without disturbing the goo — mostly. He helps Lasadi maneuver the plate back into place, and the two edges fuse together with a fizzle. Through the airlock, and Lasadi points him to the cramped cockpit where Raj has already strapped Amita into a seat.

Nobody says anything as they release the airlock and Raj shoves off from the *Dahlia Regina*. The outline of the yacht fills the viewscreen, all gold-and-green paint and stylish lines. They float a moment nose-to-nose with the yacht while Jaantzen's fingers curl around his armrests. They should be flying out of here as fast as possible, not sticking around. What are they doing?

Hiding from the Alliance cutter, he realizes. The docking bay doors are on the far side of the yacht, and the Alliance won't have visual on them while they're docking. Nor will their proximity sensors be triggered while the *Nanshe* is merely drifting.

"They're in," Lasadi says. She taps a sequence

into the console in front of her. "I overrode the *Dahlia's* quick release; they're not going anywhere for a bit.

"Love it," says Raj. "Strap in, kid."

Lasadi pivots the *Nanshe* and hits the thrusters, the force of the movement pressing Jaantzen into the seat as gravity suddenly shifts in yet another flush of vertigo. And either the Alliance cutter doesn't see them, can't undock in time, or ignores them in favor of Haruko trapped in his shuttle with crates of raw Indiran snow.

Whatever the reason, they're home free.

After a time, the pressure lets up, and Jaantzen is weightless once more. Raj is humming absently into the silence; Amita's breath comes ragged and slow.

*Your crew's a mess*, Raj had said. And, yeah. Sure. It is. But where the hell are you supposed to find people to trust? He's known Amita almost half of his life, but he's still not sure she won't sell him out the minute things go south.

"I guess you didn't get your payday," Jaantzen says. Neither did they, but at least he and Amita got out of here alive. He can only hope Amita was pulling this job on spec, rather than with the backing of a potential buyer.

Jaantzen can see only the curve of Lasadi's cheek lit by the instrument panel, but there's no missing that slow smile. "We got what we came here for," she says. "The cargo would have fetched a good price, but secrets? That's where the real money's at." She turns and her gaze slides past him to Amita; the smile fades. "Check on your friend."

Jaantzen disentangles himself from his harness and lets himself float over to Amita. She has a burn sear on her right collarbone, the wound blistered and weeping. But her breathing is more or less normal, now. She blinks, focuses on Jaantzen.

"You almost got yourself killed for me," she whispers, voice coming harsh through raw vocal cords. "Why?"

"It's what crew does," Jaantzen says. What crew *should* do, anyhow.

Amita's gaze cuts down, hands tight on the armrests. Jaantzen doesn't like the half-guilty way she's trying not to look at him, so he turns away to see Raj and Lasadi leaning together over the controls. Not just crew, but partners. Lovers. Family. They're not talking as they navigate together. Like their fighting style, they're perfectly paired without having to discuss it.

Lasadi leans companionably over Raj to flick a switch on his console, and Raj's body responds almost unconsciously to accommodate her, a small smile on his lips as he brushes a hand over her thigh.

Jaantzen clears his throat.

"You're going to drop us off?"

"It's not safe for us to hit surface at the moment," Raj says. "Not with the Alliance out there looking for scoundrels like ourselves. Let's give this some time to quiet down before we attempt to land you."

Lasadi stands and stretches. "I'm famished," she

says. She glances at Amita. "Let's get something on that burn, then we'll meet you two in the galley." She's gentle as she helps Amita with her harness, guides her out of the cockpit.

Raj unstraps himself as well. "Nothing like a wild adventure and a meal to bring together new friends." He grins and swivels his chair to hold out his hand; his face is still bloody from their earlier scuffle. "What's your name, kid?"

New friends? Jaantzen's last real friend died the night he escaped the orphanage and met Amita. Since then he hasn't met anyone he trusted enough to use that word for — including her. He's just assumed friends were something you left behind in childhood along with toys and getting shoved around.

Raj is watching him with an expression Jaantzen can't quite put a finger on. The other man seems amused, but there's no hint of a hidden agenda. He senses it from Lasadi, too: she could take you or leave you, but she's not going to bullshit you.

There's something about these two he implicitly wants to trust.

*We'll see*, he thinks. *We'll see.*

He holds out a hand. "Willem Jaantzen."

"Nice to meet you, Will," Raj says. "Your girl's going to be okay."

"She's not my girl," Jaantzen says. "I'm in her crew."

"Then I'd be looking for new work if I were you.

Las and I are always looking to take on good people. You ever consider space piracy?"

Jaantzen laughs, surprised, then shakes his head. "If I never come to space again, it'll be too soon."

Raj claps him on the shoulder. "Suit yourself. Now, I hope you're hungry. I promised you a feast of Arquellian delicacies, and I've got a feeling we'll have a lot to talk about."

---

*Want more Raj and Lasadi? Head to jessiekwak.com/ nanshe to pick up a free copy of* Artemis City Shuffle.

# BAD INTENTIONS

*When I started writing* Double Edged, *I thought Coeur would die at the end. I figured I might give her a bit of a redemption arc, let her die saving someone's life. But the more I wrote her character, the more she grew on me — and I seriously loved how her presence forced the rest of my characters to confront their own demons.*

*So when I was asked to write a story for an anthology about Villains, I knew I wanted to write about Coeur.*

*(Plus, I killed off Naali Hinoja at the beginning of* Double Edged, *so none of you got to see how cool she actually is. I wanted to write something that would let her shine a bit.)*

*This story takes place at the same time as*

Negative Return, *and is essentially Coeur's take on the events of that novella.*

*Enjoy!*

---

THE KID'S HUNGRY; THALA COEUR LIKES THAT.

He doesn't pull his punches, not even for her, and the blow whips past Coeur's guard and cracks her on the jaw. She grins. Feints with a double jab, then skips the cross he was expecting and tags him in the temple with a left hook. She lands a couple of body shots while he's off guard, then dances back as the bell rings.

She acknowledges the shouts of "Blackheart!" from the handful of onlookers with a flash of a smile and touches gloves with the kid.

"It was an honor, Blackheart," he says, panting.

"Better luck next time," Coeur answers.

Naali Hinoja is waiting for her outside the ring, leaning shoulder against post, arms and ankles crossed. Coeur's lieutenant's flame-red hair is piled on top of her head, a vivid contrast to her pale skin, white suit, and black silk shirt.

"I like the new kid," Coeur tells her. He's in a

crowd of young ones on the other side of the ring now, riding high with new cred: He got in the ring to spar with Blackheart and didn't entirely get his ass handed to him.

Naali shrugs one shoulder. "I like that he's not afraid to land a punch on his boss."

"He's ambitious," says Coeur. "Set him up with Axel, he needs some more muscle."

"Will do."

Coeur sets her gloves in her locker and catches the towel Naali tosses to her. Another pair has already taken the ring, and the rest of the people in the gym are either watching them spar or absorbed in their own workouts.

She loves this energy.

Over the past decade, Thala Coeur has painstakingly carved out her own little piece of the city of Bulari. This gym, which takes up the entire first level of an old colonial-era church, is its beating heart. Shouts and squeaking shoes and the thud of flesh hitting mats — it's the perfect soundtrack of ambition and self-improvement for a neighborhood like Altamira.

Altamira is Coeur's territory, the second of the five Finger ravines fracturing the bluffs west of Bulari proper. It had been its own settlement, back in the early days of colonizing the planet of New Sarjun, a sort of posh escape from the rough-and-tumble mining town Bulari had originally been. As Bulari's fortunes changed, though, power concentrated in the center of the capital city, attracting the rich to it like a flame. Once proud Altamira had become at first unfashionable, then a forgotten slum.

Until Blackheart enforced some rules.

This deep in the ravine, no one can touch her — and it's been ages since anyone tried.

Now you could call Altamira comfortable. Quaint, even. Lately, though, this modest slice of Bulari has been fitting Coeur's ambitions a little too tight, like a perfectly tailored jacket after you start upping your weights game.

"You see any of the fight?" she asks Naali. Her lieutenant is following her up the stairs to the second level of the church, where Coeur's office overlooks Altamira's bustling central plaza.

"You're lagging on your slips," Naali says, dress boots sharp on the metal stairs. "Left side. The kid tagged you twice when you should have been paying attention. Anybody who saw that move will be trying it on you next."

Coeur palms the biolock on her office, holds open the door for Naali. "Anything else?"

"Your last combo needs work. You got lucky and he was tired."

"Maybe I was tired, too."

But Naali's mouth is set in a firm line as she settles a hip against the window, looking down over the lunch carts and ball-playing children on the plaza; she's not here to critique Coeur's boxing skills.

"Sylla Mar has become a problem," Naali says.

Coeur frowns at that. "What'd she do?"

Sylla runs a crew in Dry Creek, the Finger ravine north of Altamira. The region's a wasteland of warring street crews, and though occasionally one of them tests Coeur's borders, she doesn't worry about them much. She's always thought of Sylla Mar as benign.

"She sent a headhunter after Willem Jaantzen night before last."

Coeur can't help the laugh that escapes her — this complication is too rich. Jaantzen must be alive still or Naali would have led with the fact that Coeur needed to hire another showrunner, stat. That would have been disastrous, given they're on the eve of a job she's been working on for months.

"Does she know he's working for me?"

"Unclear," says Naali. "She might have spies with us or with him. But taking Jaantzen out doesn't get her any more territory; could be she's got a grudge against him for some other reason." Naali taps manicured nails against her pale chin. "The other option is she didn't intend to kill Jaantzen at all. The headhunter she sent was some Carama Town kid, real green. She could've been trying to get the kid out of her hair."

"Well RIP."

"Jaantzen didn't kill him."

Coeur lifts an eyebrow.

"Word is he hired him for our job."

Coeur curses under her breath. "Sylla Mar sends a kid to take out my showrunner two nights before this job, and Jaantzen puts him on the crew?"

"Doesn't seem likely the kid is meant to be a mole. Everyone knows Jaantzen's reputation."

Sylla had tried to provoke Jaantzen into taking care of her dirty work, and god knows why but the notoriously brutal street butcher went soft and let the kid live. So now Sylla's sweating real hard, under the probably correct assumption that Willem Jaantzen knows who ordered a hit on him and will punch back with devastating aim.

"Wouldn't want to be in Sylla's stylish heels right now," Coeur says. "Jaantzen's gotta be making plans to destroy her."

"He tends to do that," Naali agrees. "Which is why I'm going to reiterate this one more time: If you're still planning to stab him in the back, you make sure the knife hits the heart."

"Always do."

"I'm serious, Thala. My job's to keep you from doing shortsighted shit, and crossing Jaantzen could be fatal."

"You don't think he's gone soft?"

"Because he let the headhunter live?"

"Because of everything lately."

The man's been pulling back from some of his more violent revenue streams, leaving his usual dregs of humanity behind and collecting strange strays to his crew — including a newly liberated Giaconda Áte, the meddlesome Sulila doctor Coeur thought she'd taken care of for good by getting her shipped to the Alliance's Redrock Prison.

"It's that sweet tail he's shacked up with," Coeur says.

"Gia?"

"Nah, the waitress. Tae. Maybe he's found some religion between her legs."

Naali purses her lips. "I don't want to be the one to test it."

Coeur grins and gets to her feet. "My aim's good, Naal. Let me hit the shower and call Ximena. Time to head down and check in. I'll take Sarah."

"You bring in Sarah by herself, Jaantzen's going to think she's a nanny."

Coeur cracks her neck, thinking. Sarah's one of her best, and Coeur wants her there to keep watch on the job. But Naali's probably right, as usual. Probably best to come at it from the side.

"Get me another body, someone disposable," she says to Naali. "What about that slab of muscle who's been scratching around for jobs lately?"

"Jaxie?" Naali's lips quirk to the side.

"What."

"You know Sylla's the one sent her scratching."

"Did she?" Coeur laughs. "Two birds, then. Go tell her it's her lucky day."

She calls her half sister when Naali leaves; Ximena Nayar answers brusquely as always. In the hologram she's wearing her Alliance uniform, black hair coiled tight in a military bun where Coeur has hers woven into a crown of gold-capped braids. Beyond their coloring, Coeur's never seen the resemblance between them. Ximena's only a few years older, but her severe temperament sketched lines in the red-earth skin between her eyes years ago. Her spine's ramrod straight and there's not a hair out of place, but Ximena is as crooked as they come. She's just grifting the Alliance from her position as a requisitions officer at Redrock Prison instead of running a Bulari crime empire like Coeur.

"Hey, sis," Coeur says. "We all set?"

"The delivery's still on target." Ximena frowns, taking in Coeur's disheveled appearance. "Are you at the gym? This is important."

"And I've got important people on it."

Ximena takes a sharp breath. "I'm going out on a limb to help you," she says. "If this falls into the wrong hands . . ."

"Mine aren't the wrong hands?"

"Thala. You keep telling me you want to move beyond the small time. If you want to run for mayor of Bulari — and win — you need to take things seriously."

Coeur rolls her eyes. "I am."

"Because sometimes it looks to me like you're just getting bored. You get greedy when you're bored."

Hardly anyone but Ximena gets to see Coeur's angry side, because only Ximena can get under her skin like this. But Coeur's not going to let her sister goad her today.

She leans back in her chair, casual. "You know what I see out my window right now, Mina? Kids playing ball in the plaza. Old folks going for a lunchtime walk. Not a single boarded-up window in sight, and nobody sleeping in the alleys. You tell me Altamira isn't better off since I killed McTiernan and took this place over."

"Altamira is, for sure," Ximena agrees. "But Altamira is a slum. Bulari is — "

"The capital, I know. But Bulari is eighty percent slums, and everyone at the top ignores that. They come from the glitter, they rule for the glitter. They make deals with Arquellian corporations and the Alliance and toss the rest of us out on the trash heap. I'm gonna help them remember whose blood built this city."

"So you're being selfless, is what you're telling me."

Coeur winks. "Everybody at the top is selfish. I'm selfish with the little guy in mind."

"Be careful," Ximena says. "That's all I'm asking."

"I got it, sis. You let me know if anything changes on your end."

Coeur cuts the connection and pinches the bridge of her nose. There's no one else she'd trust enough to steal this sensitive Alliance tech for her, but she could do without her sister's lectures. Let Ximena worry, though. Thala Coeur may come from the Finger slums, but once she's diverted this shipment into her own hands, she'll have the key to unlock any door in Bulari.

The light in her office has become unnaturally dim of a sudden. Outside her window, the sky is washed a pale orange. A gust of wind whips the branches of the ancient eucarix lining the plaza and tears at the fan palm, whistles against the church's roof. Coeur frowns at the horizon: A dust storm's rolling in for the evening.

Good. The heat and the dust storms are the city's two great equalizers; from the highest downtown tower to the lowliest shack, everyone in Bulari will be battening the hatches tonight.

And Blackheart's light shines best when the city's dark.

---

Jaantzen's operation is bare bones, as uncomplicated and brutal as the man himself. He's set up in a warehouse in Jet Park, near the spaceport, a half-dozen cots scattered throughout the echoey space, a single desk that's probably older than Coeur. She's given him plenty of money already to finance this show — hopefully he wasn't as thrifty with guns as he was with the accommodations.

A few of the crew are gathered around the desk when she walks in. She already knows Kai, Jaantzen's right-hand man, and Naali's sent her profiles on the rest.

A couple are pretty standard hires for Jaantzen: the driver with the gambling problem, the Arquellian special operations agent turned mercenary. But Jaantzen's new strays are among the mix. The medic, Giaconda Áte, whose expression darkens at Coeur's bright smile. The strange little ops tech, Toshiyo, who Jaantzen scooped out of a Ruby Basin mine.

And there, walking back in from the balcony with Willem Jaantzen, is the wiry headhunter Jaantzen let live.

The young man's name is Manu Juric, said the slim file. Dark skin, lean muscles, and an apparent flair for fashion with his acid-green hair and manicure, the brilliant blue eyeliner. He watches her with a wary respect, returns her nod of greeting without hesitation.

She likes his confidence, likes the easy way he holds himself. Likes how hungry he looks — if Coeur knows one thing about Sylla Mar, it's that she threatens easily. A kid like Manu coming bold into her organization hunting for a place, she might have hung him out of instinct. The kid took this gig for Jaantzen, but if he's as ambitious as he seems, she might have a place for him herself once the smoke blows over.

Jaantzen, predictably, does not look happy to see her.

"I wasn't expecting a skeleton crew, Willem," she says brightly. "Or do you have others hiding in the closet?"

A muscle twitches in his jaw. "This is the crew," he says. "They'll get your job done."

Coeur shrugs, the gold caps on the ends of her braids sliding off her shoulder. "Then it's a good thing I brought reinforcements." She jerks a thumb at the two women who followed her in. "Sarah. Jaxie."

Sarah's a masterpiece of ink and tech, a combination of prosthetics she picked up in the military and a penchant for body modification. She's loyal and smart, but the thing Coeur likes most about her is the prosthetic right eye she's agreed to let Coeur patch in to for this gig.

Jaxie is muscle without brains, her head topped with mass of skinny brown dreadlocks, her eyeteeth lacquered in turquoise and trimmed with gold. Thing Coeur likes most about her is that she'll probably take a bullet when shit hits the fan, and Coeur won't have to see her hanging around her gym anymore.

The others are watching her newcomers warily. Kai gives Coeur a mildly wounded look, like he's worried she's bringing her own people in to watch him. She is. It's not that she doesn't trust Kai in particular, it's that she doesn't trust traitors in general. The fact that Jaantzen's right-hand man is willing to sell him out works in Coeur's favor, but it's not exactly a shining endorsement of character.

Jaantzen does a careful once-over of Sarah and Jaxie, but, "It would have been nice for them to be here for the initial planning," is all he says before gathering them all around the desk and asking the scrawny ops tech to lead them through the plan.

The plan's a basic smash and grab on the delivery driver, and Coeur listens with half an ear, evaluating the ops tech, Toshiyo, as she talks. Toshiyo's got a sweet Ruby Basin drawl, a slight hesitation like she's not used to being around all these big-city criminals. Because of course she's not, if Jaantzen hired her out from some mining operation. Why recruit so far afield, Coeur wonders. Maybe he's burned too many bridges with people he could have hired in town.

Best this way, in the end. Ops tech is most likely going down with Jaantzen, and Coeur'd rather it not be anyone she knows and likes.

Giaconda is watching Coeur more than the presentation, a fiercely protective glare when she catches Coeur's gaze on Toshiyo. Coeur gives her a slow wink. *Don't worry, sugar, I'm not going to eat the cub. The Alliance will — but then you know all about that.*

The delivery's scheduled for tomorrow morning, so as soon as Toshiyo finishes her rundown, the rest of the crew spread out. To get some rest maybe, or just giving her and Jaantzen a wide berth like they're worried about getting caught in the crossfire if they stick around.

"Willem," Coeur says when they're alone. "How's the missus."

"You told me I had complete control of the crew," Jaantzen says.

"Changed my mind. A lot of my money's on the line."

"So you don't trust me."

"I don't trust anyone, and neither do you." Coeur flashes him a smile, gets an unimpressed look in return. Tough crowd. "Though I've never hired someone who literally tried to kill me."

Across the warehouse, Manu's been cornered by Jaxie; seems like he's telling her to piss off, which is a good sign he knows Sylla set him up to hang. Jaantzen follows her gaze.

"I appreciated his sense of style," he says.

"I didn't figure him for your type. Too much eyeliner."

Jaantzen doesn't rise to the bait — he never does, probably never will.

He's always been irritatingly serious, but lately something's shifted. Where he used to be a fracture-prone stony shell over a molten core, now he's quietly grounded. Calm. Coeur's told Naali he's gone soft, but that's not entirely it. And even if he had, that's not why he's dangerous.

Thala Coeur is about to make moves. She knows how to buy off the rest of the small-time crooks and gang lords running the Bulari underground. She can call in their debts of favor when it matters, if necessary. But Jaantzen? She no longer knows what makes him tick, which is a problem.

That's what makes this job so perfect. She gets a fall guy and removes an unreliable piece of the Bulari underground, all in one fell swoop.

"How'd he do it?" she asks.

"Hornet tags," Jaantzen says. "Seeded the Bronze Room with them, then came at me when everyone was distracted by the explosions."

"Flashy."

"Didn't work."

"Well, I'm glad the kid is a bad headhunter, or I

would have been buried in sand without a showrunner," says Coeur. "You know it was Sylla sent him?"

"I know."

"And?"

"I'll take care of it."

"Good, because I'm not interested in dealing with low-level drama." Coeur gives him a tight smile and he nods, message received. She's paying him an incredible sum, far more than he usually earns. It could launch him out of Sylla's bargain-basement league, and a year ago Coeur would have seen that as a positive. Now, though, this strange new and improved Jaantzen isn't who she wants to rely on when she makes her own moves.

"Uh, guys?"

The cub at the desk — Toshiyo — is hunched over her hand terminal.

"What is it?" Jaantzen calls.

"They're on the move." Toshiyo's eyes go wide. "It's showtime."

"Now?" Kai asks. And again, more forcefully when Toshiyo frowns at her hand terminal, cupping a hand over her ear to help her hear: "Now?"

"Let her work," Manu snaps, and Kai rounds on him.

"Let her work," Coeur orders before all this testosterone sparks a brawl at the most inopportune time. Kai's mouth snaps shut, chin dropping.

Coeur sighs. She's promised him a good gig after this, but that may not happen. She's got more important things to do than constantly bring him to heel. Her comm chimes and she slips it out of her pocket, not surprised to find a message from Ximena: TIMELINE MOVED UP, IT'S HAPPENING RIGHT NOW.

"The courier company's moving the package," Toshiyo says.

"Have they changed routes?" Jaantzen asks.

"No, boss. Just delivery times."

"Why?"

"Not sure. Could be because of the storm coming in."

"You find out, you let me know."

"Yeah, boss."

"Then the job's still on as discussed," Jaantzen says. "Kai, Oriol, you're with Sarah in the truck. Manu, Jaxie, you're with Beni."

Coeur steps back to let them gear up, propping a shoulder against the wall by the door and thumbing through her comm to make her own preparations. She sends a quick thanks to Ximena. Checks that Naali's waiting for her outside. Double-checks she has the right address for this warehouse to send to the Alliance in that perfect window after her people have secured the package, but before Jaantzen and Toshiyo have made it out.

She slips her comm back into her pocket as a figure appears in her peripheral vision.

Manu.

Coeur lifts her chin for him to approach.

"Wanted to say thank you for the opportunity," the

kid says, and Coeur turns her full attention on him, not hiding the fact that she's evaluating.

He waits out her scrutiny with feigned nonchalance, not quite hiding his nerves. He's scared of her, but confident in himself, which she likes. She thinks back to the sparring match in the gym this morning, her jaw still aches in a good way from the blow the new recruit landed on her. She likes the fear — people should be afraid of her — but it's not useful in people who work for her.

Then there's Manu's shocking green hair, the matching manicure, the eyeliner. The quick self-deprecating comments to break the tension and get others to laugh. Some of the others on Jaantzen's team seem to be writing him off as a jokester, but the act's deliberate, which means he's one to watch. The fighter who looks like they're not taking the match seriously is the one who beats the shit out of you in the ring because you thought they were clowning.

Never let your guard down around someone who's trying to get you to underestimate them.

This one has potential.

"Good to see new talent," Coeur finally says; Manu's shoulders straighten slightly. "You and me, we'll talk when this is all over. I like me some fresh blood from time to time."

That twitch of the corner of his mouth: He's trying to play it cool, but he's thrilled.

"Sounds good," he says, inclining his head in respect.

Coeur shines on a smile. "Good luck," she says and means it. She lifts a hand to Jaantzen — last time she'll see him, she supposes — and leaves the warehouse with a jaunty swing in her step.

Naali's scarlet Taosa ViX is parked out front; she sprang for self-polishing paint, but even that can't quite hold up to Bulari's infamous dust storms. The faint haze building up over the city will probably provide good cover for the smash and grab, though it'll wreak havoc on the spaceport and the traffic. And maybe the comms, but they'll burn that bridge when they come to it.

For now, Naali's got the feed from Sarah's prosthetic up in the spinner when Coeur lets herself in to the passenger seat. Manu fills the frame as Sarah asks him a question.

Naali purses her lips at the holo. "He going to break our way?"

"Kid's an opportunist," Coeur answers. "He jumped Sylla's ship for Jaantzen's as soon as he got a chance, and he's got ambition. He'll be on our side once he gets which way the wind's blowing."

"We don't know what kind of offer Jaantzen made him. Kid might feel some sort of loyalty."

Coeur laughs. "What kind of loyalty could Jaantzen inspire? The kid's got personality, and have you even seen Jaantzen smile? Nah. Kid's a good bet."

Naali's quiet a moment. "How much a good bet?"

"I'd put a hundred marks on him."

"I hope you're right." Naali drops the Taosa into

gear. "If not, I'm taking myself out to a very nice dinner with a view at the Blue Falcon once the dust storm clears."

———

"I like this girl," Coeur says. "The ops tech." They've been driving in silence too long, the only sound Toshiyo's clear, unharried instructions over the ops channel.

She and Naali aren't following her instructions, of course, they're heading to the alternate rendezvous, the one Coeur set with Kai and confirmed with Sarah — it's a dive bar one street past the respectable part of downtown Bulari's business district. Neutral territory, far enough away from the scene of the crime, close enough to the safety of Altamira. Plus, on the slim chance Jaantzen slips past Alliance security, she doesn't need him knowing where she and the goods are meeting up.

Coeur leans back in Naali's passenger seat, listening. The cub sounds unexpectedly confident over the comms considering how jumpy she'd been in person. "She's sharp. I'm almost regretting burning her."

"What do you need an ops tech for?" Naali drums her fingers on the spinner's controls, listening. "Mayors run committee meetings, not heists."

"Why not both?"

That gets her side-eye; her lieutenant's patience is

wearing thin today. "Thala. Honey. You need to take this seriously."

"You're starting to sound like my sister."

"I thought that's why you keep me around."

"Fair."

Coeur likes to think of Ximena — and now Naali — as her off switch.

She's never had much self-discipline on her own, never been good at boundaries, and that's what's allowed her to soar. She's not any more powerful than the small-timers like Sylla Mar and Willem Jaantzen, but unlike them, she's got no regulator on her ability to imagine another future. Why stop with Altamira when the entire city of Bulari is calling her name?

Ximena calls her greedy, but greed implies taking more than what you can handle.

Coeur's not greedy. She's hungry.

But she's watched plenty of ambitious people burn out bright and fast because they didn't have their own voice of reason, or the smarts to seek out people like Naali who weren't afraid to fill that role.

"He just reached Pioneer Plaza," says Toshiyo over the ops channel. "Turning left on Mahti Drive."

"I see him," Sarah responds, and Coeur leans forward to watch. Sarah's feed shows the view from the driver's seat of her vehicle; she wrenches the controls violently as the unmarked transport van in front of her screeches to a stop in an attempt to miss the second team's spinner.

Kai and the Arquellian merc — Oriol — blow open the rear of the van while the second team takes care of the driver.

"I have visual on the cargo," Kai says. "Moving it now."

Naali glides the Taosa ViX into an alley behind the rendezvous point; Sarah's feed flickers and goes snowy with pixelated static for three heartbeats before stabilizing again.

"C'mon," Coeur mutters. This is not the time to lose comms. "Sarah. You've got it? Get out of there."

"Yes, ma'am, we have the crate," Sarah says; her voice comes through in fits and starts. "Heading — second rendezv— now."

Coeur presses Send on her message to Ximena: *Now.*

"Don't be smiling yet, Thala."

Coeur grins at Naali. "I'm not." But her people have the cargo, and Ximena's sending the anonymous tip to the Alliance containing the address of the warehouse where the man who stole their cargo is waiting for his crew to return. Ximena's got a guy on the team who owes her a favor, and he'll make sure Jaantzen is killed resisting arrest. Some nice payoffs and threats for the crew — nothing should link Coeur back to this job.

"We've got a little problem," Sarah says.

From the driver's seat, Naali lifts an eyebrow at Coeur: *I told you so.*

"Tell me."

"I can't raise Jaantzen's other driver, Beni. He took off and left his passengers, he's not answering his comm."

"So he's heading back to the warehouse?"

"Most likely."

Then he'll get swept up by the Alliance, too. Not a problem — and good riddance, Coeur hadn't liked the looks of the twitchy bastard. She checks the feed she set up on the warehouse, but no one's gone in or out since the team left. Any minute and the place will be swarming with Alliance special ops — no matter they're not supposed to be able to operate on a non-Alliance planet like New Sarjun. The assholes do what they want.

Might be convenient for Coeur now, but it's one of the things she'll work on putting an end to when she's mayor.

"Can't raise Gia either," says Sarah.

Now there's another loose end, one Sarah is meant to wrap up. Giaconda Áte is too much of a wildcard to leave alive — even with Jaantzen out of the picture.

"Should have had your sister take care of that bitch while she was at Redrock," Naali says mildly, but her tapping on the spinner's controls has gotten sharper, more tense.

Naali Hinoja likes plans. Maps, charts, clear order. Coeur likes chaos, and this is one of those days where wrangling Blackheart is going to push Naali to her limits.

"I tried," Coeur says. Ximena may be crooked as all

hell, but she's got some moral lines Coeur finds incredibly inconvenient. "Where's she at, Sarah — you put a tracker on her rig."

"Still at the crash site," Sarah says, puzzlement clear even as her voice breaks up. Her next vicious curse comes through the comms just fine. "We checked the crate," Sarah says. "The goods are gone. Beni is in the crate."

The other driver, who they assumed was heading back to the warehouse.

"Which means Gia's probably driving Beni's spinner?" Coeur asks, getting an affirmative grunt from Sarah.

Naali swears. "With the goods. Which means Jaantzen was planning on betraying you this whole time."

Which means if he gets taken out by an Alliance special ops team, Coeur's never getting her hands on that shipment. She lets out a snarl of frustration and opens a channel.

"Willem," she says when he answers. "Get out of there. The Alliance got tipped off."

His response is dry: "Did they."

Naali shoots her a sharp look; Coeur ignores her.

"Is our deal still on, Thala?" Jaantzen asks. She's trying to listen to the background noise, trying to gauge if he's left the warehouse. "Because I have the item you asked me to steal for you, and I intend to deliver it in exchange for the fee we agreed on."

"Course the deal's still on."

"Excellent. Because you know I'm good for my word."

"Counting on it, Willem. I'll meet you — and Giaconda — at the backup rendezvous. Oh, hey." She waits a beat; she can still hear his breath on the other end of the line. "The case is rigged to blow. Shoulda told you that earlier."

She cuts the connection and slams her hand into Naali's dashboard.

"Gods-fucking-*dammit*, Thala." Naali hits a button on the dash. "Axel? I need a team at the old shipping center on 137th. Now."

And she peels out of the alleyway.

---

"You're exceptionally lovely when you're furious."

Naali ignores her, hands over an extra magazine, which Coeur slips into her jacket pocket. She's already wearing a pair of pistols, a comforting presence in the small of her back.

"You get flushed," Coeur says. "Really sets off the green of your eyes."

"Axel will be here in three," Naali says.

Coeur winks at Naali and opens a channel to her security chief. "Axel, hey. We lost Sarah's feed twenty minutes ago, but here's what I know. The good guys inside are Sarah and Jaantzen's man Kai. Bad guys are definitely Jaantzen and Giaconda Áte. The rest are mercs. Not sure how they'll land, but there's a kid who might break our way. Black skin, green hair, too much eyeliner. Can't miss him."

"Copy that, boss."

Naali unbuttons her white suit jacket and checks her own pistol in its shoulder holster, then slings a pulse carbine over her shoulder. Pulls down the pair of green optical lenses nestled in her flame-red hair and blinks a few times while they sync.

Coeur cracks her neck, massages the sore spot on her jaw.

Axel's van emerges from the haze at the end of the street, headlights cutting swaths through the twilight dust storm; his team pours out and approaches, merely silhouettes against those lights. Still, Coeur knows them. She knows everyone who works for her; she trains beside them, spars with them.

Axel's bristling with weapons, long silver hair swept back from his brown face in a loose bun. She clasps his hand in greeting, lifts her chin to his team. "Priority number one is getting the goods," she tells them. "Priority number two is Willem Jaantzen doesn't walk away, understood? Let me do the talking and watch for my signal."

Her security chief nods and gestures to the bay doors. Two of his team flank the doors, rifles drawn, another two step up to lead her in. Naali's at her shoulder with her pulse carbine in her hands, Axel taking up the rear.

Coeur follows her people through the door and a half-dozen guns swivel uncertainly in her direction.

Well, isn't this a nice little tableau.

She's arrived at the end of a standoff — the electric tension has the room lit up like a casino. That and the stench of blood and plasma give clues to what's happened.

Jaantzen, Jaxie, the Arquellian merc, and Manu are still standing; the crumpled bodies in the middle of the floor belong to Sarah and Kai. She can't see where the twitchy getaway driver or the ops tech cub are, but the rear doors of the cargo van are open. Are her goods inside? Or with Giaconda, who is still missing from the picture?

"Willem," Coeur says, waving her guards and Naali back so she can step into the center of the room. She scans the little group, meeting each person's gaze in turn. Neutral steel from the Arquellian merc. Puzzled confusion from Jaxie. Ready resolve from the young headhunter, Manu — she lifts an eyebrow and he nods faintly, his stance shifting ever so slightly to cover Jaantzen more than her.

And Jaantzen, whose face is almost impossible to read.

"I thought we had a nice plan," she says. "Didn't you think so?"

"Up until the part where you were planning to hang me up for the Alliance."

Coeur shrugs. "Sorry about that, Willem. I apologize for underestimating you."

"I don't expect you'll do it again."

She won't; ideally she won't have to estimate him at all after this. She scans the room again, letting the pieces fall into place. Someone's breathing heavily, as though injured, but it's not anyone she can see. Sounds like a woman. Toshiyo the ops cub? Gia?

"I misjudged your ability to inspire loyalty," Coeur says.

"Money can do that." Jaantzen glances at Kai's body. Money can do amazing things, it's true. She'd bought his right-hand man out from under him, and it hadn't even cost her much.

"Speaking of money." Coeur holds out a hand, reaches slowly for her comm in her pocket, shows him what she's doing as she calls up the transaction. Presses Send on the transfer. Two breaths later Jaantzen's own comm chimes. "You've got your cash, so bring in your gal and let's do some business." She juts her chin at the bodies on the floor. "What do you say, we're even — looks like we both lost people on this one."

"I'm not sure Kai was one of my people. But I would say we're even, Thala. I was in it for the job, you were in it for the goods. We've both gotten what we came in for. Except you didn't get a fall guy to distract the Alliance."

"That's fine. I have a plan B."

"Glad to hear you'll end up all right."

"My goods, Willem."

She stretches fingers along her left thigh, ready to

signal the instant she has the goods in hand. This has gone on too long.

"Ms. Ravi," Jaantzen says, and there's a corresponding shift from the cargo van. So that *is* where the ops cub is hiding. She'll trust Axel has noted the same thing. "Can you please ask Ms. Áte to join us?"

But Gia's been waiting right here all along. A boot heel clicks on concrete, echoing through the warehouse.

"Got your goods, Thala."

Gia's voice comes from the doorway that leads into the warehouse's offices. She appears there a second later, pushing a wheeled cart with Coeur's case perched on top.

Coeur grins. "Thanks, sugar," she says, and is rewarded by a murderous glare.

"We'll be on our way, and you can have your goods," Jaantzen says. "As you suggested, I think we can say we're even. But please take me off your list of available contractors in the future."

"I'll be taking a few people off my list," Coeur says. Her gaze sweeps the small crew again, landing on Manu with a question: *Are you in?* This kid wants to be a headhunter, here's his chance to take out Jaantzen and get in with one of the best-paying crew bosses in the city.

He nods again. Excellent.

"You're free to go," she says to Jaantzen. "You have my word. Pleasure working with you, Willem."

"Wish I could say the same."

Jaantzen lifts his chin to Gia, who gives the cart a kick. It glides across the cracked cement floor, straight towards Coeur.

Time slows. Coeur's right hand closes over the handle while the left signals her team, and she rolls, expecting the coming firefight.

She's not expecting the entire place to explode around her.

A hail of gunfire erupts from the outside, shattering glass and splitting her team's attention between their targets and defending their backs.

Coeur draws and fires — and icy pain slashes through her shoulder. In shock, she registers that the bullet came from the headhunter, Manu, who's covering Jaantzen's exit rather than taking the man out. She snarls a curse and fires again, but the searing pain in her bicep drags her aim off track.

"Thala, let's go!"

Naali's pulling her back, Axel's blocking her in, and she wants to tear at them both but they're just doing their job and making sure their boss gets out alive. Keeping her from flaming herself out in the heat of battle.

"Priority one is the case," Naali growls Coeur's own words back at her; Coeur turns and sprints for the door as a bullet shatters the pane of glass above, showering her in razor-edged hail.

Coeur ducks into Naali's Taosa ViX with a grunt of pain; Naali throws her pulse carbine in the back seat and slides behind the controls.

"You're hurt," Naali says as the engine roars to life. "How bad."

"I don't know, gimme a sec." It's a measure of how worried Naali is that she doesn't even toss off a "Don't bleed on the upholstery, boss." Coeur palms open a channel. "Axel, report."

Something combusts within the warehouse; the concussion thrums through Coeur's chest even as Naali peels away from the curb.

"Axel."

"I'm here," he says. "But they're gone, boss."

"Your team?"

"Gilly got hit but she'll pull through. You?"

Coeur finally turns her attention to the blazing fire on her left bicep. There's a bloody tear in her jacket, instead of the puncture she'd expect if the bullet had gone in. "Scratch," she says. Naali lets out a sharp breath; her right hand slips from the spinner's controls to squeeze Coeur's knee in relief. "They had rein-forcements?"

"No, it was hornet tags," Axel says.

Fucking hornet tags?

"See if you can track that van, then head back to base." She cuts the connection and leans back in the seat, smoothing her fingers over the case in her lap as if that'll soothe the rising fury. "Hornet tags," she says finally.

"Same thing the headhunter used to bust up the Bronze Room when he tried to hit Jaantzen," says Naali.

Coeur probes a finger at her bloody arm, hisses at the pain. "Bastard tried to shoot me, too."

"Guess that means you owe me a hundred marks."

"I'm bleeding and you're trying to collect a bet."

"Bet's a bet, Thala."

"What's he called again? Manu Juric?" Coeur rolls the syllables over her tongue; they're sweet as blood.

"I'll put his name out."

"I want him alive," Coeur says. "Got something special in mind for him."

"Course." Naali's gaze cuts from the road to the case in Coeur's lap. "You get what you need?"

Coeur types in the code Ximena gave her; the case unseals with a soft whir. She eases the lid open and grins.

"The future's bright, Naal," she says.

The corner of Naali's mouth tugs into a smile. "I believe it."

Coeur seals the case once more, pressing her palms flat on the smooth surface and staring out the window as the streets of Bulari pass by in a dusty haze. Right now they're heading back to the safety of Altamira, but soon there'll be a day when every street's hers to build up and protect.

The dust storm is already blowing itself out as they climb into Altamira ravine, and Coeur catches the occasional glimpses of Bulari's glittering downtown through Altamira's crowded, colorful townhomes. From up here in the Fingers, the city sprawls into the valley like a welcome rug.

Jaantzen's out there in the tangle of lights some-where, but even he can't stop her rise now. Let him hide. Let him get cocky and comfortable with his new home life and his clutch of strays.

The city of Bulari is calling Blackheart's name, and that's a call she's gonna take.

# STORM WARNING

*When you write a 5-book saga with a rather large cast of characters, you're likely to hear from readers that you should have written more about so-and-so.*

*One of those characters is Detective Timo Cho of the Bulari Police Department, who spends some time investigating our heroes and learning some truths of his own about how the seedy underbelly of Bulari works.*

*I loved Cho, and loved being in Cho's point of view for his scenes. Because his storyline is a bit separate from the rest of the characters — he is investigating them, but not physically interacting until the end of the book — I actually approached his storyline in Pressure Point as though I was writing a short story. The end result was a fun noir detective subplot mixed in with the rest of the adventure. (Complete, of course, with a femme fatale.)*

*I'd wanted to revisit Cho's story for a while now, so when I saw a call for submissions to a sci-fi crime anthology called NOIR, I knew exactly what I wanted to write.*

*"Storm Warning" is the story of Detective Timo Cho doing what he does best: asking too many questions.*

*It's set in Bulari, but is completely apart from the events of the Bulari Saga, so it stands on its own. If you've read the Bulari Saga books, you'll find another fan favorite character makes a cameo. If you haven't read the Bulari Saga, no worries! "Storm Warning" is meant to be just plain fun.*

*This story was first published in NOIR in 2022.*

---

When Detective Timo Cho watches the replay he doesn't pay attention to the body. He focuses on the killer's eyes.

They're a deep, after-sunset blue with a thin ring of silver around the pupil, narrowed with intense focus though the lines around the eyes are relaxed — this surgery is complicated, but routine. The timestamp on the footage says they're around the three-hour mark, but it's not just the demands of the morning's work threading the surgeon's sclera with glints of red. The irritation could be from the lens he wears, the faintly shimmering assistive tech floating over delicate eye tissue — but Cho guesses the surgeon also hasn't been sleeping well. There are bags under his eyes. The outside corner of the right eye is inflamed.

And, there.

That's the moment when things go wrong. A flurry of sudden blinking. The pupils flare, the brows draw in, the corners of the eyes crinkle in sudden confusion. One of the capillaries in the sclera of the left eye bursts, glazing the eye with a wash of red just before the surgeon begins making the fatal cuts.

Ten seconds later, both eyes widen in horror. And squeeze shut — Cho turns the replay off. He's seen what comes next enough times.

A Sulila-trained surgeon — the elitest of the elite — deliberately killed a patient in the middle of surgery and then slit his own throat.

Cho leans back in his chair in the Bulari Police Department's least-malfunctioning investigations cube, cracks his neck. Studies the patterns of water leaking into the ceiling, layered over the years like a topographical map. If only he could read that to understand what happened here — and how to proceed on this case without pissing off his supervisor, the public, or Sulila corporation.

Cho's supervisor, Major Ngara, would say start by making Sulila happy and keep the public from knowing why they should be angry. In fact, he'd given Cho step-by-step instructions, handed down from Sulila: review the hologram, declare the surgeon had a mental breakdown, write up a report that absolves Sulila of responsibility and reassures the public that their hospitals are safe.

Cho digs his mechanical left fingers into a hard knot of muscle in his right shoulder, lets the front legs of his chair clatter to the floor, and skims the replay back to the beginning. This time he lets his gaze go soft as the hologram plays around him, only half-watching the murder, waiting for something to ping his subconscious.

Getting to see the moment of a murder is rare, it definitely eliminates the *who*. Just leaves Cho with the *why*.

The holograms he usually works with are done after the fact, meticulously recorded by Hallie Bachelet and her crew of crime scene techs, body blanks programmed into the scene so detectives can play them like puppets and puzzle through what might have happened. This recording, though, is surgery room footage, supplied by Sulila. The quality is amazing — way better than the tech the Bulari Police can get. Cho halfway expected the rich file to crash the BPD's system when he loaded it in the scenario desk.

Provided by Sulila means censored by Sulila. A few things are blurred: proprietary surgery tools, the patient's medical data, and the assistant's face — Cho's not allowed to talk to them. The Sulila PR team has provided the BPD with a transcript of the assistant's testimony to "protect an innocent person's identity."

Cho pulls out his comm; Hallie Bachelet answers almost immediately. "You around?"

"Depends." From the distant clatter of voices and ringing comms in the background it sounds like she's in the office. "You got something happy and uplifting to show me? I just got back from a pretty rough scene."

"It's all puppy dogs and flowers in this investigations cube. I'm on the Sulila case. Can you help me with this footage?"

She'd say yes anyway, but a chance to muck around with proprietary Sulila footage sweetens the deal. Hallie swears under her breath.

She's there by the time he has the scenario desk reset, slumping into the seat beside him with a sigh. She's still dressed for a crime scene in silver-gray scrubs and an appropriately somber hijab, a touch of mascara smudged in the warm brown skin under each eye.

"Bad day?" Cho asks. Hallie waves him off.

"Same old. What's your question?"

He lets the footage run, pausing about ten seconds before things go wrong. This time, he's not looking at the footage at all. He's watching Hallie's reaction; her attention darts immediately to the blurred parts.

"Any way to repair the blurring?" he asks.

She scoots closer to the scenario desk. "Maybe. Super easy if it's just a filter the PR team slapped on." She types for a few minutes, then hits Play once more. The blurring is gone. "Who's a hero?"

"You are."

Cho leans in to study the now-unblurred assistant as Hallie plays it again from the beginning, but he stops it before it gets to the murder — he did promise her something happy.

Hallie waves away his hand. "The day I've had, Timo, nothing else can faze me." She frowns through the murder-suicide, then stops. Replays it.

"I thought you were looking for a cheer-up," Cho says.

"Shush." Hallie leans in, hits Pause. "There."

Cho frowns at the body, at the surgeon, at the frozen horror on the assistant's face. "What?"

"There's time missing in the recording," Hallie says.

"Can you get it back?"

"That'll be tougher than just clearing a filter, but I can get one of my techs on it. But Timo."

Cho turns to meet her gaze.

"I thought you were supposed to have an easy solve on this."

"Don't you want to know what *actually* happened? Justice shouldn't — "

"Have compromises, I know. You say it all the time. Just promise me you won't make any mistakes here."

"I promise." He seals the promise with a wink. "Can I thank you for the help here with dinner tonight?"

"I thought there was a storm warning."

"That's not until tomorrow."

Hallie's smile tilts to the side. "Then sure. So long as we don't talk about work."

"Done."

Cho switches off the hologram when she leaves, does a fast search for the assistant's profile, then wipes the search and logs out of the scenario desk. He's got a few hours before dinner, and he doesn't owe Sulila's PR team a report until tomorrow. Still time to ask a couple of questions.

---

Cho eases his stiff shoulder as he walks through the door to the Sulila hospital, watches the nurse at the reception desk clock his gloved left hand and the awkward way his sub-par prosthetic pulls at the sleeve of his pale blue suit. Nice prosthetics, you can barely tell — but Cho's working with a detective's salary, and the arm's been missing long enough that the cheap chipped plastic and faulty wiring feel like part of his own body.

"You have an appointment?" she asks.

"I'm here to see Dr. Su-Jin Anand."

The nurse swipes up a screen, dainty eyebrows drawing together as she checks. "Oh? I'm sorry. Dr. Anand isn't in today."

"No?" Cho feigns surprise, lets her worry about disappointing a patient. "I thought she would be here."

"She's not. She — "

And now the nurse isn't just apologetic. She's genuinely confused.

"Where is she?"

"I'm sorry, but who's asking?" Polite, but pointed.

It's a question Cho gets a lot, usually barked out gruffly by some young tough in the Fingers. He could lie now, but he goes on the hunch that Sulila's PR team assumed the BPD would play along, and didn't bother warning the staff not to talk to any detectives.

"Detective Timo Cho."

The nurse's eyes go wide, but she shakes her head and opens up a screen. "I haven't seen her, but this is her usual shift. Let me check . . . hm. Su-Jin is on extended medical leave."

"How can I reach her?"

"I'm afraid you can't. She's been sent back to Arquelle."

"Must have been quite the emergency."

"Yes . . ."

But Cho's only got surprise on his side for so long. That stitch between her eyes, the nurse is starting to put two and two together and realize why a BPD detective might be asking for Su-Jin Anand, who only yesterday was assisting a tragic surgery.

Someone else was faster than the nurse. The sharp click of a heel sounds on the reception room's tile, the steps angling toward Cho like a heat-seeking missile; the skin between his shoulder blades pricks. Maybe someone put a flag on the BPD system for any searches for Anand, maybe they put a tag on Sulila's security for

Cho's face, or any BPD badge ID pinging through the entry.

"Excuse me, detective . . ."

"Cho." He turns with a smile and his good hand outstretched. "Timo Cho."

The woman before him has long, shimmering black hair with blue highlights, skin pale as Cho's, but with warmer undertones. She doesn't introduce herself. He knows who she is. Cecily Adams, Head of PR.

The smile Adams gives him is knife-sharp, dangerous. But Cho's spent earlier beats of his career in the Fingers, in Altamira, facing down gang members with switchblades and plasma carbines. Sulila's PR team may objectively be more dangerous, but this woman in the smart suit isn't going to knife him in the hospital's lobby.

"Are you here to deliver your report? I thought I asked your supervisor to send it to me directly."

"No, ma'am. I just had a few questions for Su-Jin Anand."

"We sent you Dr. Anand's testimony."

Cho smiles easily. "Always follow-up questions in this business. Just trying to get to the bottom of this."

"And we're grateful." Adams holds out a hand to the door. "But Dr. Anand's not available. You can ask me any questions directly."

The heat of Bulari hits him like a sandbag when Adams ushers him out of the building, and beads of sweat immediately prick on the surface of his skin.

Well. He'd been wondering if Sulila knew the *why*

of this case, and now he's pretty sure the answer is yes. You don't work this hard to keep a detective from the truth unless you know you should be afraid of it.

He missed a message from the coroner; he calls her back on his walk to the train station, listens to her shoot down his possible solves one after the other. Nothing in the surgeon's bloodstream, he didn't have a stroke, no physical indication of what happened. Raised cortisol levels and a sudden high-stress response right before the end, but no apparent reason for it.

"Quick question," the coroner says when she's done. "I think I can guess, but what hand did he hold the scalpel in?"

"His right."

"Got it."

"Why?"

"Strange thing, but the incision looks like it could go either way. Like he slashed one way, then went back and cut the other."

"That's impossible." Cho didn't see that in the hologram; was it in the missing time?

"I'm not here to speculate. Just telling you what I see."

He meets Hallie Bachelet at Chavela's, a nondescript restaurant on Twelfth and Eucarix with cracked vinyl seat cushions and bad lighting; when Cho suggested it, he'd been thinking about the food more than the ambiance.

"Nice place," Hallie says.

"Food's better than it looks. Best korris you'll find without going into the Fingers."

She's cleaned up since the office, ditched her tech scrubs for a casual tunic over leggings and a silver-edged hijab. She's done her makeup, he realizes. She was definitely expecting a better restaurant.

Next time.

"I got lightly kicked out of the Sulila hospital today," Cho says once they've ordered.

"I thought you said you weren't going to get into trouble."

"I wasn't looking for trouble. I just wanted to talk to the assistant."

Hallie straightens. "You weren't supposed to know the assistant's identity. If they trace it back — "

"Your name's not on this, don't worry. How was your day? Did it get any better?"

"Yeah, after that DV — " Hallie cuts herself off. "We weren't talking about work."

"Sorry."

Cho's gratified to see Hallie's dubious expression shift to delight as the food is delivered; she leans forward to breathe in the rich spice, spears a bit of chicken with her fork.

"So," Cho asks. "How *else* was your day?"

Hallie closes her eyes, enjoying the bite. "I had a nice shower," she says. "Fixed a janky cupboard door in my kitchen without having to call the building super. You?"

"I came straight from work."

"Well, what do you do when you're not at work?"

Cho shrugs. He wanders the city, mostly, keeping a finger on the pulse. A lot you can learn in the way a corner kid looks at you twice, in the washing tides of graffiti. You can tell what gang's cleaning up what intersections, who's taking control, who's losing the edge.

It's not just the gangs he's keeping an eye on, though — he also likes walking the downtown, the government district, the tourist strips. Millions of lives flicker in and out of this city; Cho is curious about each and every one of them. Helps him do his job better.

They're not talking about work.

"I like to stay in shape," he says. "Walking. Working out."

"Thrilling." But her gaze did dip. The lines of his left arm are sculpted metal and wiring, but he's proud of the work he's put into his right, and his abs. Maybe one of these days they'll stop saying good night after dinner's over, and she'll find that out.

Hallie takes another bite. "Okay, I'm dying to know. What did you find out about the assistant?"

"She's on a ship back to Arquelle. Medical leave."

One of Hallie's eyebrows shoots up. "Not suspicious at all."

"She saw something. I need that missing footage."

"My tech's still on it."

"Ask them if they can find anything after the official end of what Sulila sent, too." He tells her what the coroner said about the extra cut. Hallie frowns.

"No one needed to help him finish the job, he wasn't going to make it."

"Exactly." Cho helps himself to another scoop of chicken korris. "Since we're talking work anyway, are you doing okay? You said you had a tough scene this morning."

Hallie sighs. "This must be why I keep going out to dinner with you. I can't tell this to another guy."

"Hopefully there are other reasons."

"Maybe." Her mischievous grin fades quickly. "It was a domestic violence call, couple of students up at the University. He attacked her in their apartment, really tore into her, then started after himself. They're both at the hospital now. The girl doesn't want to press charges, though. She says it was an accident. You don't accidentally stab your girlfriend three times with a knife."

"That's fucked, I'm sorry. Do you know what started it?"

"She says they were just studying, then he started blinking weird and attacked her. She thought maybe he'd been drinking and she didn't know it."

"Blinking? The surgeon did something similar." That second before his eyes widened and the capillary burst. That second before things went wrong.

Hallie frowns. "What are you thinking?"

"About not making compromises when it comes to

justice," Cho says. Hallie presses her lips together. "Who's handling the university students?"

"Lopez," she says without hesitating. "I can call her right now."

The back of Cho's neck pricks; when he glances back, a man in a suit is perusing a menu. His gaze slides up from the menu to meet Cho's for a second too long.

"What's wrong?" asks Hallie.

"Nothing. But don't involve yourself anymore. Let's enjoy our meal, I'll give Lopez a call in the morning."

---

And this is why they shouldn't talk work at dinner; by the end of the night both Cho and Hallie are too haunted to do more than say good night. Not that his shitty apartment is a good place to bring someone home.

One of these days, though.

Cho keeps an eye out behind him as he walks back from the train, but he doesn't catch another glimpse of the man in the suit. Cho has been followed more than once. The gangs in the Fingers are less subtle about their intimidation attempts, but he recognizes one when he sees it.

He locks himself in and calls Detective Ada Lopez; she's still at her desk, long dyed-blond hair scraped back in a high pony tail, medium brown skin, gold studs in ears and nose. She gives him a flat, tired look.

"You still working?" Cho asks.

"Of course. What the hell are you doing?"

"Same, I suppose. I had a question for you on the case you picked up today."

"The Coruscan salesman who strangled his husband half to death or the corporate exec who shot her lover because he wouldn't leave his wife?"

"Neither. Couple of university students?"

"Yeah." It's affirmation and permission rolled into one sharp syllable.

"The girl said right before the attack her boyfriend started blinking rapidly? Any idea what that was about?"

"Being a trash abuser?" Lopez sighs. "You want to interview the victim? She'll talk to you — she'll talk to anybody about how her boyfriend's innocent." There's exasperation in Lopez's tone, just a touch. But her job is to keep victims safe and put their attackers away, not to find out what went wrong. "Or you want to talk to the attacker."

"They're both still at the hospital?" Lopez grunts affirmative. "Then no. Lemme send you a couple questions to ask, if you don't mind."

A long pause. "You're on the Sulila case," Lopez says. "Even in DV we've heard you're supposed to let this one drop."

"Wouldn't mind finding out what happened first."

For a second he thinks Lopez will say no, but she takes a sharp breath. "And I don't mind you owing me a favor. I'll call you tomorrow."

No men in suits the next day — or at least none that don't belong strolling through Bulari's downtown core on their lunch break, craning their necks to study the sky for signs of the incoming dust storm.

Cho's digging into noodles from a passable stand on the corner when Lopez shows; she's got a cup of coffee in one hand despite the rising heat of the day. She sits at the other end of the bench.

"Am I supposed to pretend not to know you or what?" she asks, hooded eyes narrowed at the passing crowd. "I don't know how to do the spy games shit."

"Makes a nice break, though, yeah?"

"If it doesn't come back to bite me in the ass."

"I'll keep your name out of it."

"Thank you. I asked the attacker about the blinking," says Lopez. "Took some cajoling, but we got a deal, and you've got your information. You were right, there was something else going on — they've got him in surgery right now."

Cho tilts his head. "What do you mean?"

"Amphetamine implant. Same sort the military uses to keep soldiers awake, apparently it's all the rage for students at Hypatia." She shakes her head. "Better than developing a silver addiction and having to hit up a shady dealer once a week."

"Where'd a college kid get military implants."

"I didn't say his implant was military," says Lopez.

"Once surgery's over I'll take it in for evidence, but let's just say the kid didn't go to a pro."

"Still, can't be cheap."

"He wouldn't say where he got the money. Willing to talk about almost anything but that. But he's indentured to Starward Logistics, so he gets a basic living stipend while at the university. He could have saved up."

"Can you take a look into his finances? See if he got a big deposit sometime around when he would have gotten the implant?"

"Why not. Anything else?"

Cho shakes his head, standing. "How many more students you think have something like this?"

"I don't know." Lopez's expression is dark. "But I find another kid in the hospital because of this, I'll take apart every illegal mod shop in this town myself."

"I'll keep you in the loop." Cho starts to walk away, then stops. "That implant. It's in the neck?" He touches the side of his neck, just under his ear. Right where the extra cut on the surgeon's neck was.

"Exactly there," Lopez says. "How did you know?"

"We didn't find an implant on the surgeon. And I'm pretty sure I know why."

He can feel Lopez's gaze on his back as he walks away; maybe someone else's, too, but he doesn't give them the satisfaction of turning around to look. Instead, he pulls out his comm and enters a number by heart. A familiar voice answers: Hallelujah Oni.

"Detective Timo!" says the tinker, rich voice wrapping around Cho like a comfortable whiskey glow. "How's the arm, mon ami?"

"All good, Louis." Cho flexes the fingers on his prosthetic out of habit, but everything's been working perfectly since Louis did his last tune-up. "Got a question for you, actually. You have a minute?"

"For you, always."

"I'm trying to track down an illegal gentech mod shop. Specifically, amphetamine implants."

"I wouldn't know anything about that." Louis sounds offended; Cho frowns. "You think I know people like that?"

"Just thought you might have heard something."

"Not my crowd, detective." Tone sharp, end of conversation. Cho can't think of another time Louis shut him down so fast.

"Of course not. Thanks for your time."

"Detective."

Cho's fingers pause over End Connection.

"When are you coming to get your servos replaced?"

"Servos?"

"Detective," Louis chides. "I've had these servos on my shelf for months. You ask me to special order and then don't come in? Are you seeing another tinker?"

They did the servos last time, and Louis has an encyclopedic knowledge of every repair he's ever done in his storied career, whether a simple household rehydrator or a prosthetic arm.

"I'm sorry." Cho drips apology in his tone for

whoever might be listening in. "You got time this afternoon? I've hit a dead end on this case anyway."

"Of course, of course." Louis sounds delighted. "I'll see you then. Best come fast before the storm hits."

"Thanks, Hallelujah."

Cho slips his comm into his pocket and stops to check for train times out to the spaceport terminal where Louis's shop is located. When he turns to scan behind him, two men in suits have stopped a half block away. This time, they don't care that he sees.

---

Cho takes the long way to Geordi Jimenez Space Terminal, circling in until he's as certain as possible there are no men in suits on his tail. Louis' shop is on the B level of the terminal, a cheery pair of picture windows with displays of repaired electronics and trinkets for sale, a sign over the door with a cartoon choir of angels floating above the words, "Hallelujah It's Fixed!"

Louis Oni is sitting behind his workbench as always, what looks like a traffic drone broken down and neatly laid out on the mat in front of him. He grins when Cho comes in.

"Can I help you with something, stranger?"

"Good to see you, too." Louis clasps Cho's arm when he comes in for a handshake, no surprise in his face at Cho's metal left bicep. Louis has worked on it plenty of times. "How are you, friend?"

"Can't complain," Louis shrugs. "Durga's still shining and New Sarjun's still turning. Those servos are in the back." He touches a switch under his workbench and the open sign in the window flips to "Be back in a moment." The door's triple bolts slide shut with a sharp *snick*.

Visiting any other one of his sources, the sound of a door locking behind him would send a chill through Cho's spine. Louis, though — Cho trusts him with his life. It's not that Louis is on the right side of the law, not exactly. He's just a tinker in a busy public place who hears plenty and is willing to share it with the few people he trusts. Cho knows Louis doesn't just talk to him — he's got friends in the underground crime organizations, too.

In the early days, Cho didn't understand Louis Oni's motivations. Eventually, he realized Louis simply has a finger on the pulse of the city's constantly brewing storm of troubles, and is invested in making sure that trouble misses his shop and the people he cares about.

"You asked me a question earlier." Louis fixes Cho with a look. "I don't know the answer and I don't care to find out. You understand?"

"I understand."

"Good." Louis sighs. "If you had been the only one to ask me this question, I would be a happier man. But now?" He pushes aside the curtain to the back.

The back room is where Louis does bigger repairs,

and where he works on the human patients who come attached to the prosthetics he services. A man is leaning awkwardly on the work bench, pink flush to his pale skin, bloodshot gray eyes. He straightens when Cho enters, runs his hands down his thighs to dry the palms. No obvious prosthetics, but then he's not here to see Louis, he's here to see Cho. That gold chain at his throat, the iconic symbol polished and gleaming. He's a Sulila doctor.

"See, mon ami," Louis says brightly to the doctor. "The detective came."

Cho holds out a hand. "Detective Timo Cho."

The man meets his handshake but doesn't give his name; it doesn't matter. Cho's got a good eye for faces, and there's no such thing as an undercover Sulila doctor. He'll find out who the man is when it's time to know.

"Jacket off," Louis says to Cho. "Up in the chair."

"My arm's fine," Cho protests.

"On the house. Idle hands find mischief, mine more than most. Don't make me sit still while you two talk."

Cho shrugs off his jacket and rolls up his sleeve above the elbow, and Louis settles in with a hum to unscrew the panel in Cho's forearm. "Our doctor friend refers me patients," Louis says by way of introduction. "He's doing good work."

"I thought Sulila had their own prosthetics center," Cho says.

Louis runs Cho's fingers through a diagnostic

sequence, each metal digit curling and flexing, glinting dully in the light.

"Not everyone can pay Sulila prices," the doctor says. "Louis came highly recommended a few years back, so I started sending people here off the record. He's been a godsend."

"Hallelujah," Cho says with a smile. "What do you know about amphetamine implants?"

"They're more common than I wish they were. Sulila has exacting standards, and I'd be lying if I said I hadn't taken something to help myself along. Most of us abuse caffeine, of course. Pills — basic stuff. But sometimes someone goes looking for a more permanent fix. Performance review comes back, they start threatening to send you out to a mining colony in the belt or tacking more years on your indenture."

"Is that what happened in this case?"

"I don't know why my colleague went looking, but I know what he found. A black market implant."

"How do you know that?"

"Because I'm the one that cut it out of his neck."

"You were supposed to make it look like part of the initial cut."

The man nods.

"Who asked you to cut it out?"

"Our supervisor."

"So they've seen this sort of thing before."

"Not like this. Normally it takes years to build up that type of intolerance and reaction — this was a bad batch."

"Do you know who's selling them? One of the gangs?"

Louis makes a *tsk-tsk* with pursed lips. "Organized crime, you mean? Organized from the very top." Louis fixes the doctor with a look over the top of his heads-up set; the doctor nods imperceptibly.

"Sulila is selling them," Cho guesses. "And not just for use by their own doctors."

"It can't be traced to Sulila. But they've been supplying the tech to a series of local underground shops operating out of little holes in the wall like this — no offense Louis."

"None taken."

"You get a bad performance review, it might come with a recommendation to take a little R-and-R, maybe go see a shop in Jet Park and lay low for a few weeks before coming back to work."

"You have any proof?"

The doctor stiffens. "You won't find any."

"Sulila's cleaning house," Cho says; the doctor nods. "So why come to Louis about it? Why agree to talk to me?"

Cho can feel the doctor shutting down. Feel him second-guessing, and Cho can't afford for him to start thinking too much about the consequences.

"A patient is dead because of this," Cho says, leaning in. "How many of your colleagues might have gotten a tainted implant?"

"Sulila will know," the doctor says. "They'll take care of it."

"It's not just your colleagues." Louis and the doctor both frown at him. "Domestic violence case: Engineering student at the Hypatia University of Bulari with no history of anger problems. He put his girlfriend in the hospital after getting an implant."

The doctor gnaws his lower lip. "I can get you a recording."

"Ah, that's good," Louis murmurs — he could be talking about the doctor, he could be talking about Cho's arm. "Rotate your wrist."

Cho does, and the doctor stands. "I can't come straight to you," he says.

"Send it to me with your next referral," Louis says, not looking up from Cho's arm. "Slipped in an ankle joint or sealed in a hip plate." He smiles at that and clicks the cover back into place.

"You don't need to get involved any more than you already are, Louis."

"Someone's giving tinkers a bad name," Louis says. "And I have my own ways of hunting."

Whether or not he'll share what he finds with Cho doesn't matter. Take down one underground gentech mod shop and another dozen will pop up in its place — so long as corporations like Sulila and Hypatia keep creating the need.

Cho leaves first, his comm chiming almost as soon as he's out the door. His supervisor, and it's not the first time he's called.

"Where the hell have you been?" Major Ngara

growls. "I've got Sulila's PR team in my office, and no report from you."

---

It takes the right kind of swagger to walk into a "where the hell are you" meeting with the boss almost a half hour after getting the call. You don't want to show up out of breath, but you don't want it to seem like you dawdled. Either way, Cho figures, he's deep in the shit and he might as well walk in with some dignity.

He splurged for a taxi and spent the ride back laying out everything he found to send to Ngara. Major Ngara won't share anything until Cho is back — and the fact that he's willing to make the Sulila PR team wait is a testament to how badly he wants to be able to throw Cho under the bus on this one.

Cecily Adams is sitting in front of the super's desk; a spiky, electric current sours the air, like she and Ngara have spent the last hour exchanging excruciatingly polite barbs about the weather forecast.

"Hot out, yeah?" Cho says when he strolls in. He's got a tray full of coffees — not from the BPD's shitty coffee maker, but from the New Manilan stand across the street. He sets them on Ngara's desk with a smile. "Dust storm's definitely brewing for this evening."

"Where the hell have you been, Cho?"

"Chasing leads," Cho says, handing a coffee to a startled Cecily Adams. "Cream? Sugar?"

"I don't know what kinds of leads you think you found," she says, recrossing her legs. An emerald heel flashes in the band of sunlight slipping through the super's window. "But I assure you we've got this handled."

Cho raises an eyebrow at Major Ngara; Ngara's glare says shut the hell up and let him handle the mess, so Cho leans back in his seat. Sips his coffee.

"We have bad news," Ngara says. "We believe your surgeon had an illegal amphetamine implant that caused him to lose control."

"And we don't believe it was an isolated incident," Cho says, ignoring Ngara's icy stare. Cho's not going to bring up the fact that Sulila was trying to cover it up — he's smarter than that. Almost. "You'll want to clean house."

"*We* will?" Cecily Adams lifts an eyebrow. "This city is full of these marketplaces."

"Because the demand's there," Cho points out. "We've been dealing with black market gentech mod shops for a while, but as soon as you smack one down another ten pop up."

Adams turns to Ngara. "Send us your notes and we'll take care of it."

A muscle jumps in Major Ngara's jaw, roping veins pulse in his temple. Cho keeps his mouth shut. Handing over a detective's notes to a corporation is absolutely not how this works. But it is exactly what Cho expected; and after a moment of internal struggle, it's exactly what Major Ngara does. Call Cho paranoid, but he keeps his notes clean and sparse. There's nothing in there about Louis, Lopez, Hallie, or anyone else who might have helped him.

Cho schools his expression into chastened as Cecily Adams knifes out in emerald heels. Railing against Ngara might lose him his job, but railing against Cecily Adams and Sulila could cost him a lot more.

He waits until the sound of her heels fades.

"That's it?" Cho asks Ngara. "Your grandma's next on the operating table, some asshole slices her up, and the corporation responsible gets away with it?"

"What do you expect me to do? Sulila's an Arquellian company. Alliance."

"And New Sarjun isn't part of the Alliance, but we still have to bend over backwards."

"I'm going to hear about this," Ngara says. "What the hell was I thinking, giving this case to you?"

"You were thinking I ask too many questions?" Cho guesses. And that he knows people in dark corners Ngara can't be seen in.

That jumping muscle again; Cho's instinct is spot on. Ngara wanted to know what had happened, even if he knew they'd never get a solve. Finally, Ngara sighs. "What made you think of the implant?"

"I watch too many of those body mod competition shows," he says.

"Those shows will rot your brain. You need a hobby. A girlfriend."

"And what do you and the missus watch in the evenings?"

Ngara shakes his head, snort of laughter. "None of your goddamn business."

Cho's comm chimes: Lopez. *Found out how that college kid paid for his implant. Got a big loan from Hypatia, right after a bad review. Anything else you want me to look into?*

Of course the loan was from the University. Can't have kids flunking out, that's bad for business — Hypatia has a reputation of churning out busy worker bees to the specifications of other corporations. Cho frowns at the message, an inkling of an idea forming out of smoke.

Ngara doesn't ask what the message is. He swipes open his desk and fixes Cho with a look. "You've got a plan?"

Cho shrugs. Ngara doesn't really want to know.

"Then get out."

Cho doesn't go back to his desk. He messages Lopez to let it drop, then takes his coffee and walks. That storm brewing on the horizon is breaking the usual heat of the afternoon; it looks like a bad one by the dark smear to the south. By dinner the sky will be choked with sand and the streets will be impassible. Nothing you can do to stop it from sweeping through and leaving the city in rubble, just like there's nothing you can do to stop the Alliance corporations from doing the same.

Only, sometimes, there are anomalies in the atmosphere. Competing weather patterns disrupting the path of the storm.

His comm chimes: Hallie.

"I just stopped by your desk," she says. "You on your way home to get ahead of the storm?"

"Something like that." Cho stands on a train platform, debating whether to catch this train out to the bluffs, or leave well enough alone and head back to his apartment.

"Timo, what are you doing?"

"Making a compromise," he says. The train to the bluffs shudders to a stop. Cho slips his comm into his pocket and steps inside.

Hypatia Corporation runs the University of Bulari, along with one of the city's two technical colleges. They own half the city grade schools, too — they brag that they educate more students in the city of Bulari than they do in their home country of Arquelle. Cho knows what that means. Arquellian kids have the money not to take on an indenture for their education. Kids in Bulari are easy pickings.

Still, the grounds are gorgeous. Towering eucalyptus and oak, fan palms and tree aloe, bright-faced and determined students scurrying through the pathways. A few of them might be there free and clear because their parents had the money to buy them a good job, but most are bankrolled by whatever company Hypatia's agreed they'll spend the next ten to twenty years working for.

Cho climbs the steps of the administrative build-ing, dwarfed by vast columns and sweeping doors, an environment shield glimmering in place to protect the building from the coming storm. He slips through the shield, ignoring the tingling against his skin and faint ache in his shoulder plate, and heads into the marble entry. He doesn't have an appointment, but that doesn't matter once he flashes his badge. Unlike Sulila, Hypatia Corp must not be in the middle of covering up an active investigation. Good for them.

A few minutes later, he's seated in the university president's office. She meets his handshake easily.

"I'll get right to the point so we can both get home before this storm," Cho says. "The BPD has been trying to shut down illegal body mod shops in town, and it's come to our attention that some of your students may be visiting them to get amphetamine implants. Are you aware of the incident yesterday?"

The president nods. She's somber, but there's a current of anxiety beneath; she knows exactly what Cho might find out about Hypatia's supplemental loan program.

Cho had hoped she would be ignorant, or at least that she'd let him believe she was. But she knows her students are going into even more debt to get illegal amphetamine implants — and that Hypatia's funding it. Maybe they're holding books instead of scalpels, but still. A girl is in the hospital.

Cho can't take both corps down, though. Hell, he

can't take either of them down. But sometimes one brewing storm can shove another aside.

"We're going to be looking into all this," he lies. "We wanted to give you the courtesy to do some investigation on your own. As a sign of respect for the Alliance, of course."

He smiles and waits for the pieces to click into place.

"I'm horrified," she says. "We'll do anything we can to help you shut these operations down. Where do you think the implants are coming from?"

"Oh," Cho says brightly. "A rival Alliance corporation, actually. I'm happy to share everything I have."

---

Cho's apartment isn't expensive enough to have windows, but on nights like this, when the building's rattling in the storm, that's not a bad thing. Plenty of sand and dust is already bleeding through the building's faulty air filters, and he'll find a fine layer of grit over everything when he wakes up in the morning.

Cho pushes Send on the files Louis sent over, the ones that prove Sulila's been supplying the bad batch of implants. The University of Bulari's president will forward them to her bosses higher up in Hypatia Corporation. The reporter Cho sent them to will publish an expose if they can get it past their own bosses. The chief of staff at the mayor's office — one of Cho's regular drinking buddies — will go over it in hushed tones with her wife and try to decide if she's going to bring it to the mayor of Bulari.

That's all Cho can do.

The ledge between his prosthetic thumb and forefinger makes a perfect bottle opener; he cracks open a cider and takes a long draught, washing away the sour taste of the day.

It's far more than he was supposed to do, but it still isn't enough.

He's wrapped up a case and no one's coming to justice. Not the people responsible, anyway — not Sulila, not Hypatia. The kid who put his girlfriend in the hospital will lose his guaranteed indenture, but not his debt load, which means he'll probably get picked up for a shitty, poorly paying contract in the mines. Maybe the behind-the-scenes pressure Hypatia will put on Sulila means the next surgeon who gets an amphetamine implant will get a better quality one. Maybe it'll lead to reform of some sort. Maybe it'll lead to Cho's own government putting pressure on Alliance corporations not to sweep in and use the city of Bulari as their own personal playground.

Most likely it'll lead to a darker storm.

Cho turns up the music and turns down the lights, leaning back on his couch and taking another long drink of his cider. The building thrums around him, shivering in the gusts of the storm.

Offworlders complain about the dust storms, but you need them to chase the chaff out of the streets from time to time. And they're just another of the many reasons Cho loves Bulari.

# GIRLS' NIGHT

*When I was writing* Double Edged, *I hired a Deaf editor to advise me on my representation of Starla.*

*She gave me wonderful feedback. (Including the advice to treat sign language like I would any other language, and put it in normal quotes; in the draft I sent her, I had italicized any signed speech.)*

*But one of the biggest things she commented on was that she hoped Starla had a community of deaf and USL-speaking friends where she could just be herself.*

*Simca and El Anahoy show up in* Double Edged, *but I hadn't much explored Starla's other friendships. The editor's comment inspired me to ask what Starla does when she's just out being herself. Where do she and her friends go for fun? What is she like when she's not being badass?*

*We get more of Starla, Simca, and Letizia Diamante in later books of the Bulari Saga — and Toshiyo even joins in the clubbing fun. But when I was putting together this short story collection, I wanted to write something that was purely girls being girls.*

*And, of course, I needed to find out what the history was between Starla and Luc Chevalier, who shows up and stirs up so much emotion in* Kill Shot.

*If you've read the epilogue to* Kill Shot, *you know I'm eventually going to explore what they get up to together. If you haven't, you can download it at jessiekwak.com/bulari-epilogue.*

---

THIS IS HOW MUSIC IS MEANT TO BE EXPERIENCED: rippling through a sea of bodies slick with sweat and bright with gaudy colors, jeweled eyebrows glittering and glowing neon filaments whipping in their hair, lights and movement pulsing in time to the beat hitting Starla's chest.

The DJ plays the crowd like an instrument, drawing out tension and building up anticipation in a flurry of discordant tremors that agitate the sea of dancers. Spotlights wash them in light and plunge them into dark as the vibrations become more rhythmic, more insistent, more all-consuming until the DJ finally drops the beat and every single person on the dance floor breaks.

Heavy bass thrums through Starla in a feverish pulse. Her hands shoot into the air and she screams as the rest of the crowd open their mouths in primal passion, losing herself to movement with the bodies around her in the one place she still feels safe in this city.

This crush of bodies should worry her. Enemies could be anywhere — and it had once felt that way. When she was fifteen and just fallen from the stars to land on New Sarjun, the gravity of the planet and the mass of so many strangers weighed her down. But now the gravity grounds her. The anonymous pressure of so many strangers uplifts her.

She couldn't collapse here even if she wanted to — the dance floor won't let her.

She drifts in the music until the balls of her feet and her calves ache and the sensation of thirst becomes impossible to ignore, then politely extracts herself from the person who's most recently become her dance partner, signing that she's going to get a drink.

Not in USL, of course. This person wouldn't understand her if she did. She uses the sign language of the noisy club, miming taking a swig and pointing in the direction of the bar, followed by a wave good night so her dance partner doesn't misconstrue Starla's gesture as an invitation. She didn't need to worry. They're still vibing with the music and simply shift their focus to the next closest willing body in the crowd.

Starla pushes her way through glowing, parti-colored dancers, scanning for Simca and Leti. Simca's already leaning against the wall with her high heels dangling from one hand. Her gold minidress bares brown thighs and shoulders rippling with muscles toned in the amateur wrestling circuits, and every inch of exposed skin gleams with sweat and glitter.

Starla catches Simca's attention and raises a hand in Leti's namesign, eyebrow lifted to make it a question.

Simca stabs a finger towards a shadowy corner; Leti's unmissable in her chartreuse suit, her sleeves rolled up and black silk blouse unbuttoned well below the lower edge of her lacy orange bra. She's been making new friends, her arm slung around the bare waist of one girl while the other leans in to giggle something in her friend's ear, cleavage aimed at Leti.

Starla waves an arm until Leti looks up from the show. "I need a drink," she signs, in USL this time. "Ditch the club trash."

Leti doesn't argue, of course. This night is for having fun with old girlfriends, not making new ones, and with a suave move and a mimed promise to come back later, Leti extracts herself and leaves the two club girls disappointed in the corner.

Starla and Leti wedge into their favorite booth

while Simca heads to the bar — it's her round — and Starla leans down to rub her heel.

"I'm out of practice," she signs when she straightens again. "But it's nice to be back dancing."

"I'm glad your godfather let you out of your gilded cage." Leti accompanies that with a wink to let Starla know she's just teasing, but there's a bite of truth in it. It's been over two years since the civil war in Bulari's underworld ended with Blackheart ousted into exile, but only a few months since Starla's godfather, Willem Jaantzen, has relaxed enough that she feels comfortable coming out.

She doesn't blame him. It had been a bad time, the usual undercurrent of tension between neighborhood street gangs boiling over until the violence spilled into the lives of everyone in the city. Bodies in parks, bodies in the streets, and Manu —

No. She's not thinking about her shattered family tonight. It's girls' night.

"Speaking of out of practice," Leti signs, "if you're ready to brush up on your bedroom skills, that sweet snack in the corner has been eyeing you."

Starla turns, curious, to spot a man sitting alone at the bar. He's darker complexioned than even Leti, and with that charcoal suit, he should be drinking in the light and obscured in shadow. Instead he radiates a magnetism that draws attention, especially in this gaudy crowd. Something about the cut of his suit seems foreign; gold flashes at his unbuttoned collar and in his earlobes, glints on his wrist as he sips his drink.

He catches her looking and winks.

"He was watching you on the dance floor, too," Leti signs. She accepts a cocktail from Simca, who sets the other two on the table and tumbles into the booth beside Starla.

Simca steals a peek over her shoulder. "The loner in the black suit?" she asks, then gives Starla a wicked look. "Delicious."

Starla makes a face. "Go for it, then. I'm not in the mood."

"Suit yourself." Simca pretends to leap at the chance, her long black braids whipping across Starla's chest. She laughs as Leti grabs her arm and tugs her back into the booth to fall against Starla, who shoos her away in unfeigned protest. She's going to be washing Simca's glitter off for days.

"Traitor," Leti signs. "It's girls' night."

"And who have you been dancing with?" Simca points out.

Leti arches an eyebrow. "Girls." Her gaze shifts past Simca's shoulder and Starla follows it. The gorgeous man lifts his glass in greeting. Starla rolls her eyes and pointedly turns away, club sign language for *Not interested, buddy*. "He's still watching."

"You want me to go tell him to fuck off?" Simca signs. Her fingers are as agile and quick as Leti's or Starla's because she grew up with deaf parents, but she and her brother, El, are hearing. Her smile grows conspiratorial. "Or do you want to have a good time tonight? Seriously. Nobody will stop you."

"I might," signs Leti.

"Last thing Starla needs is another overbearing masc in her life," Simca retorts, and Leti sticks out her tongue. "Jaantzen's not here. Manu's not here. Oriol's not here." Simca nudges Starla. "Unless they put a tracker on you."

Not technically, no. Both her godfather and Manu can check her location via her comm, but that's just for emergencies and she doesn't need the others ribbing her about it. And she'd love to pretend she can just ignore their paranoia for the night, but the truth is, if she goes home with the eye candy in the corner she'll send Manu a message to let him know where she is so Jaantzen doesn't flame into war crisis mode.

She wishes she could call it overreaction. And with the city this peaceful — thanks to Jaantzen's brutal ending of the civil war — she's probably not in any danger.

But friends are dead. Manu still walks with a cane. Jaantzen's broad face is still gaunt and haunted from the people he's loved and lost, and she's not going to add her own weight to his shoulders.

"Not tonight," Starla signs. "Anyway, he's probably a creeper. Just ignore him."

He'll lose interest, eventually. Most do, once they see the girls conversing in sign. There aren't a ton of perks of being deaf, but shrugging off strangers who can't follow the conversation when the three of them are out clubbing is a big one.

"Nice to see the place so packed," Leti signs,

mystery man forgotten. "I think business is finally starting to pick up again in this city."

Leti's in PR, and many of her firm's clients are in the entertainment industry. So many clubs have been doing poorly these last few years, with locals and tourists alike first worried about Blackheart while she was still here, then worried about the instability now that she's gone — though that's bullshit. She was the one making everything so unstable.

"People are ready to do something fun," Simca points out. "Like go see Veyda. How's that going anyway?"

Leti scrunches her eyes shut in frustration. "A nightmare."

"The show? I thought it was sold out?"

"The show's sold out," Leti confirms. "It's *Veyda* who's the nightmare. It's her first time in Bulari and she wants to go out on the town before her show. Won't take no for an answer. My boss thinks it's a great idea — show how safe Bulari is these days. But Veyda's refusing to let us hire a security service because she doesn't want to feel babysat." Leti winces. "And if some off-planet pop star gets kidnapped at the Maxa Club? Horror show."

"Don't take her there," Starla signs in alarm. "That's a Sixth Fingers bar."

"I know, I know." Leti lifts her hands in a shrug. "But that's my point. She doesn't know Bulari."

"Then she doesn't need a security service, just some local bodyguards," signs Simca. She elbows

Starla. "Who can blend in to the club scene but also won't let shit through to her."

Leti laughs. "And these bodyguards, I'm guessing they want backstage passes to her sold-out show?"

"Naturally," Simca signs. "Plus the usual rate."

Leti turns to Starla, who shrugs.

"Why not?" Starla signs. "Sounds fun."

And it sounds easy enough. She and Simca have worked security for Leti's VIPs a few times in the past. Normally that just involves bouncing drunks who want to say hello. Simca may be petite, but she can take someone down in a second flat, and Starla's height is intimidating. That, and enough people know who she is in this town. She doesn't love falling back on Jaantzen's name, but sometimes it's the thing that works.

"You're hired," Leti signs. "Meet us at the Horus tomorrow afternoon."

Simca claps her hands together. "We're going to meet Veyda! Is she as glamorous in person?"

The question launches Leti into an anecdote about the pop star that gets Simca snorting laughter and pokes holes even in Starla's uneasy mood.

Veyda is from one of Bixia Yuanjin's moons, with an ethereal pale beauty and a voice people say sounds like it's drifting gently through the stars. Starla doesn't know her music well, though. Veyda's released some solid club remixes, though the dreamy cadences of her originals are lost on Starla.

Still, the idea of meeting someone from the remote

Bixian moons is intriguing. She's always dreamed of seeing the swirling colors of the gas giant in person, of floating through the glittering ice fields and dazzling light shows.

When she was a child on a remote station in Durga's Belt, she'd listened to her parents' stories of adventure and travel with the certainty that she would soon join them and see the farthest reaches of the system. But she'd barely left Silk Station, only to be torn away by the Alliance when she was fifteen and dumped on this planet to be rescued by her godfather. Now, seven years later, she's still on New Sarjun. Still in Bulari.

Maybe it's time for a change.

She risks another glance at the bar to find the man in the foreign-cut suit still watching her, and wonders where he's from. Leti's right. He looks extremely pick-up-able, were she in the mood to play out a fantasy of ditching this sand-blasted city with an attractive drifter and soaring out among the stars where she belongs. The girls would rib her about it, and they'd forgive her.

But, no. She can dream about that later. Tonight, more than anything, she needs the company of her girl-friends. She's about to give Handsome the universal sign to get lost when he sets his glass down and lifts his hands.

"You ladies want another round?" he signs in USL. The corner of his mouth curves into a smile when her jaw drops. "This 'snack' is buying."

Starla's pale cheeks flush in horror at realizing he

could understand everything they'd just said from across the room. On the other side of the table, Leti throws herself back in surprise, cackling so loud she attracts startled looks from other patrons. Simca — whose back is to the bar — frowns at them both. "What just happened?"

"The snack just asked if we want a round," Leti signs, still gasping for her breath through laughter. "In USL."

"Well then, yes." Simca whirls in her seat and signs their drink order. The man inclines his head and turns back to the bar. He's speaking aloud to the bartender, Starla notes, nodding and replying when the bartender asks him a question. So what's a hearing man who speaks USL doing here tonight?

He approaches their table with fresh drinks a moment later, correctly matching the new drinks with empty glasses. Starla expects him to ask to sit beside Leti — not that she's made any motion to invite him — but he stands casually back.

"I'm Luc," he tells them, giving a namesign along with the spelling. "I saw you chatting and wanted to say hello. It's my first night in town."

"In town from where?" Starla asks. Something about him seems familiar, but she knows most of the few USL-speaking men who frequent the club scene. She'd remember this one.

"Everywhere." Luc smiles, a dimple highlighting his dark cheek. The copper flecks in his eyes catch the light like starbugs.

"You're a drifter?"

His shrug is elegant, liquid, implying fine muscles Starla can't help but wonder about.

"I suppose so." He bows, a gesture that's faintly Arquellian; Starla makes a note to ask Simca if she heard him talking and caught an accent. "It was nice to meet you all."

At his surprise leave-taking, Leti relaxes her bulldog stance. "You can sit if you want," she signs, but Luc shakes his head.

"It's girls' night," he signs. He tilts a nod to Starla. "Maybe I'll see you around."

And he heads out the door, into the night. All three women watch him leave.

"He didn't put anything in the drinks," Leti signs after a stunned minute. "I was watching."

"Well then," Simca signs. "To the good ones, cheers."

Starla smiles at them both. "To girls' night."

Starla's late and bleary-eyed walking into Cobalt Tower's lobby the next morning. One of the perks of living in the tower was that she used to be able to stumble down the stairs in minutes, rather than rushing the fifteen-minute walk from her new place.

But Jaantzen and Manu can't check the security logs in her building to see what time she got home last night, or who with. And that's worth everything.

The lobby's filled with incoming office workers who are employed either by Jaantzen's restaurant supply business, Rosco Kudra Enterprises, or one of the other companies that rents space here. Cobalt Tower could be any office building in downtown Bulari with its double-height glass facade, trendy couches, potted trees, and polished cream marble floors. Only its notorious owner sets it apart.

Buying a prestigious downtown tower was a power move for a kid who grew up on the streets of Bulari, Starla knows. It's a visual reminder to everyone in town of how Jaantzen pulled himself literally out of the gutter to become a businessman this successful, and while his early revenue streams may not have been very legal, the wealth that bought Cobalt Tower came relatively honestly.

Jaantzen's RKE supplies some of the biggest restaurants and hotels in Bulari. Partly because of his extreme reliability — vendors and street gangs alike know better than to disrupt Jaantzen's supply chain — and partly because the city's elite owed him an enormous debt after he removed Blackheart from power. He didn't take their bribes, but he proudly took their business — and took advantage of the depression in downtown real estate values to buy two prime pieces of property: Cobalt Tower, which he made the base of his operations and living quarters, and the Jungle, which he turned into an absolute knockout of a restaurant.

Starla pulls on her jacket as she walks through the doors, waving to Nadhi at the reception desk. She'd normally walk around the desk to the private lift, heading to the fourth floor to check in with Toshiyo. But a familiar face catches her eye.

Absolon Chevalier is sitting on the bright orange couches on the far side of the lobby.

Starla throws up her hands in greeting and diverts her path to meet him, throwing her arms around him for a hug.

"What are you doing here?" she asks.

"A meeting with Jaantzen," Absolon signs, with a wave of his hand that means, *It's just business, nothing you need to worry about.*

Because of course it's nothing for her to worry about.

Starla's used to being shut out of secretive meetings with Bulari elites and foreign allies like Absolon alike. During the civil war she'd been a teenager, and they'd been trying to keep her safe. Now that she's in her twenties, and most of Jaantzen's business is truly and absolutely boring, the patronizing pats on the head land harder and harder.

And anyway, Absolon isn't here to sell Jaantzen new refrigerator units. The gadgets he peddles tend to go boom in interesting ways, and ever since Maribi Station, when Starla first saw the arsenal inside Absolon's ship, she's been dying to get her hands on some.

"Are you talking shop?" Starla signs. "Because I'd love to join you."

"Later, later." Absolon gives her a gentle smile,

then his gaze shifts past her shoulder and the smile goes proud. "I'd like to introduce you to someone. My nephew."

When Starla turns, heat rushes to her cheeks. It's the snack from last night, the one with the gorgeous cheekbones and familiar copper-flecked eyes.

Luc grins at her.

"Hi, Starla," he signs; he knows her namesign though she didn't tell him.

"Hi, Luc." She spells it; let him wonder if she's already forgotten his.

Absolon glances between them both. "I see you've already met."

"At a seedy club last night." Starla's gratified to catch a stitch of concern between Absolon's brows. "Luc was buying strangers drinks." Or, hell. Another theory dawns on her. "Unless you knew who I was and you were spying on us."

Luc holds up his hands in protest. "I guessed who you were eventually," he signs. "But I swear. At first I was just checking you out like any hot-blooded man would."

"Luc," Absolon snaps aloud; Starla's lens transcribes it "Look." He turns back to Starla. "I apologize for my nephew."

"He was a perfect gentleman," Starla signs. Part of her wants to be irritated with Luc, but it's hard to stay mad when that dimple flashes.

"Not that I would be anything else to Jaantzen's goddaughter," Luc signs, and the irritation flares anew.

Because of course — whether they're buying her drinks, avoiding her attention, or checking on her whereabouts, every person in this town sees her only as someone Jaantzen is protecting.

Before she can retort, though, the energy in the room shifts. Even the worker bees in their casual lobby meetings and co-worker chats know who owns the building, and the combination of furtive glances and studied disinterest can only signal one thing: Willem Jaantzen has entered the lobby.

Starla notes the flicker of shock on Absolon's face as she turns to greet her godfather and his lieutenant, Manu. She knows what Absolon sees. Jaantzen's regained some of the weight he lost over the last few years, but his cheeks are still hollow. And one of the main reasons for that haunted look is standing beside him.

But the key word is standing. Manu may still use a cane, but he's relying on it less and less, and the thick ropes of scars along his left hand and arm have gone from angry magenta to a pale pink against his dark skin. He's even begun dyeing his hair again, this time in shocks of electric blue.

Through it all, though, Manu's grin never faded. Even when he first came out of the regen tanks, he was cracking jokes and smiles; that smile widens as he reaches out to shake Absolon's hand with his unscarred right.

"Morning," Starla signs.

"Morning." Manu winks at her. "Just getting in, yeah?"

She's long stopped trying to slide anything by the man she's come to love like a big brother. "Girls' night," she replies.

"You oughta let me come next time. I can be one of the girls. Flirt with all the boys."

"Oriol wouldn't like it." And Starla doesn't need a babysitter.

"He's out of town." Manu grins at her, then turns his attention to Absolon and Luc. The men exchange verbal greetings, then slip back into USL mixed with speech for Starla's benefit as they make plans for the day's worth of meetings.

Manu's a good study, so he's nearly as adept as Simca at speaking and signing together, his hands having regained most of their agility though his left is still stiff. Luc and Absolon both become more stilted in USL as they try to mix it with speech. And Jaantzen — well. Starla loves him, and loves that he's trying his best.

His USL is barely passable in the best of circumstances, and since she got a lens that can transcribe speech more or less accurately, he's been using that as a crutch. Today, he's clearly sticking with USL out of pride.

"The meeting, do you need me at it?" Starla asks Jaantzen; he shakes his head.

"It's nothing," he signs woodenly. "It's okay. For you, it's nothing."

"It's not about RKE," Manu clarifies. "Nothing that interesting. We can fill you in later."

"I could be helpful."

"I'm sure you could," Manu signs; it's not an invitation. "Enjoy your day, though. Life's too short for meetings. You can meet up with us for lunch at the Jungle after."

Normally Starla would jump at the chance. She loves Jaantzen's restaurant, though she still has trouble reconciling the cautious, reserved man with the gaudy, extravagant restaurant. It seems to feed something in his soul, though. And Manu has said in passing that Tae would have loved it, which makes Starla think the Jungle must be some sort of tribute to the wife and children Jaantzen lost to Blackheart. The wife and children Starla never had a chance to meet. Jaantzen's grief is long locked away, though, and until Starla can find the courage to broach the subject, she suspects the restaurant's inspirations will remain shrouded in mystery.

As will the subject of this meeting, apparently.

Starla shrugs like she doesn't care. "I can't do lunch," she signs. "I have work."

"You have work?" Manu's repeating it aloud for Jaantzen's sake, Starla knows. "What kind of work?"

"A gig. It'll go late." And when Manu quirks a questioning eyebrow at her, she just shrugs. "It's nothing that interesting," she signs, throwing his own words back at him.

And to Manu's credit, he just laughs at the fair play.

"The gig doesn't start until afternoon," Luc signs, and she shoots him a glare. He grins back at her. He'd clearly been eavesdropping on their conversation from across the bar.

Manu turns to him. "Help a man out with a hint, then."

Luc looks scandalized. "A gentleman never tells tales," he signs with a fluid shrug. "You'll have to ask Starla." Luc gives her a look. "I wasn't invited to the meeting, either."

He wasn't? Well, this day may have just gotten more interesting.

"Then let's go," Starla signs. "I could use another pair of eyes."

That tension jumping in Jaantzen's jaw, the way Manu's scarred fingers flex — but "Stay safe" is all Manu signs, a wink to soften the big brother caution. He shoots Jaantzen a look that seems to say *It's okay, we're all okay,* but Jaantzen doesn't look okay.

She gives Manu a hug. "Always do." She leaves Absolon and Jaantzen with hugs, too — Jaantzen always seems pleasantly startled by physical affection — and hooks a thumb at Luc to follow her.

If they're not going to invite her into their business, she'll go make some of her own.

By the time they get to her apartment, the back of Starla's shirt is soaked through and Luc's face is gleaming. It's far too hot to do this job on foot, which is why they've come here. The building's door opens automatically for Starla's biosign, letting them into a double-sealed entry that serves two purposes: keeping the building cool, and giving the human monitoring the gate time to make sure the entrant is actually supposed to be here.

She'd audited the building's security herself before she moved in, to ease her own mind and Jaantzen's. Only the absolute pinnacle of security would convince her godfather it was safe for her to be on her own.

"Where are we?" Luc asks.

"My place." Starla ignores his suggestive eyebrow. "We need wheels." She palms them into the lift down to the garage, then turns to Luc as they descend. "What are they meeting about back there?"

"The usual." He shrugs. "Weapons. Security systems. Uncle's got a new Teguçan supplier and your godfather wanted to check out the merchandise."

Weapons and security systems? Nothing interesting, indeed.

Starla clenches fingers tight against a complaining reply, tries to tell herself she understands Jaantzen's caution. He's hinted more than once that he failed her by not sending her to Bulari University when she was the right age, even though it would have been dangerous for her back during the civil war, and she's too old for a traditional education now. Not that she wants to become an accountant or a lawyer, or whatever else he seems to think she should do. She wants to do something useful. Something with her hands. Something that helps people, and keeps her solving interesting new problems. Not sit behind a safe little desk.

Luc seems to sense the soreness of the topic, because he changes the subject. "I thought your gig was security. Stand around, babysit a pop star."

"Yeah, but I like to know the lay of the land before I go in. Leti gave me a list of places Veyda wants to go, so I'm — *we're* — gonna scope them out."

"Leti is suit? Or braids and glitter."

"Suit. Glitter is Simca."

"Got it."

He follows her down the rows of parked spinners. Some of them are quite nice — an apartment building this secure doesn't come cheap — and Starla's ride is parked at the end of the row. A gleaming chrome al-Jurjani Torment.

"GX5," Starla signs proudly to Luc; he frowns at the moto like he's never seen one before. "It's no Trespass, but it's as close as you can get since the Trespass was outlawed." When he shrugs in dutiful yet uninterested appreciation, she tosses him a helmet from her locker. "Hope you like to go fast."

He passes test one with flying colors by putting on the helmet and climbing on the seat behind her without complaint.

Test two goes well, too. His chest is solid yet light against her back, his body comfortable and compliant, and as they head out of the parking garage and ease into the flow of traffic, his hands on her hips and weight shifting easily with hers, she thinks this day might not be such a waste after all.

Veyda is performing tonight at the Horus, down in the Casino District. Simca will meet them there — she's busy at her real job, which has something to do with customer service at a bank downtown. Starla can't remember much about what Simca actually does for money between her amateur wrestling bouts and security gigs, because her talk of stock portfolios and investments always bounces right off. The main point is that Simca hates it, and that sitting behind a desk all day doesn't suit her any more than it would Starla. But unless the prize money she wins at the amateur level starts getting a lot more lucrative, that's probably what she'll end up doing for the rest of her life.

The first spot on Veyda's must-visit list is a trendy revitalized cocktail lounge on the respectable edge of Bulari's downtown business area. It straddles the border between the streets most Bulari civilians will go and the slums that climb the cliffside surrounding downtown, a wasteland of boarded-up windows and suspicious street life.

Starla parks the Torment outside the cracked window where she can keep an eye on it. Luc holds the door open for her, which would strike her as sweet if she wasn't so distracted by how outdated the lounge's security system is. The door scanners are practically as old as Starla herself is, and she happens to know from firsthand experience that particular model hasn't been supported for at least five years. Which means that whatever system they're running these scanners on is either equally outdated, or they're just blinking for show.

A blinking light won't be much of a deterrent if anyone wants to rob the place — especially if they have a basic knowledge of security systems. Starla leads Luc to the bar, where Luc orders a lager and Starla gets a coffee with spiced cacao. She doesn't drink alcohol that often anyway, she definitely won't be drinking right before this job.

She clinks glasses with Luc anyway.

"What's your deal?" she asks when she sets her drink down.

"My deal?"

"Yeah. Your uncle, you travel with him?"

He shrugs and takes a sip of his lager. "I help my uncle with his business."

"Just the two of you? You weren't there when I met him at Maribi Station a few years back."

A complicated emotion flickers over Luc's features. Starla tilts her head in question.

"It was sometime just after that," he signs. "At least, that I came to live with him for good. But I've stayed with him off and on my whole life."

"Your parents, what happened to them?" Starla doesn't care if this is indelicate. She's an orphan herself, she's earned the leeway to ask.

Luc flexes his fingers, thinking. "My mom is kind

of a mess," he finally signs. "When she's great, she's great, but . . ."

"She's not always great."

"And my dad, I'm pretty sure she doesn't know who he is. Uncle Absolon has always been there for us." One of Luc's fingers drifts to the collar of his shirt and unearths a pendant on a gold chain. Hammered gold wire cradling a gleaming black stone.

"She made this, though. She's an artist."

"It's beautiful."

Luc smiles. "Yeah. Like I said."

"When she's good, she's good."

"Exactly."

His expression is pained, so Starla shifts the conversation. "The places you've been, it must be amazing. Where's your favorite?"

"Artemis City," Luc signs without hesitation, but then his smile becomes rueful. "But that could be because it's the only place we ever stopped long enough for me to make friends." He takes a long draft of his beer, then sets the bottle down. Already beaded droplets of condensation are tracing paths down the glass. "So how about you? What's your story?"

Starla shrugs one shoulder. To somebody else, she might say that she works in her godfather's business, just like Luc told her he works in his uncle's business. But no luck trying to pass that off today, because she was clearly not invited to their meeting. Despite her best attempts to find a place at RKE, Jaantzen seems determined to shut her out.

And her story? Absolon knows it so she assumes Luc does, too. Goddaughter of the infamous crime boss Willem Jaantzen. Daughter of the notorious pirates Raj and Lasadi Dusai. Still no name for herself yet.

"I don't have a story," Starla signs.

"What do you do for fun around here? When you're not out dancing with your girlfriends."

Starla bites the inside of her lip, uncertain. "I tinker," she finally answers; it sounds so boring but it's true. "I like gadgets."

"Uncle told me all about your escapades on Maribi Station. He called you a genius."

Starla feels her pale cheeks warming and hides her pleased surprise by taking another sip of her spiced coffee. "It's something I've always done."

One of the projects she's proudest of is, in fact, the Jungle. Jaantzen's restaurant needed to be a place where he could conduct business safely, and the byproduct of Starla's work is that all his allies know the place is equipped with state-of-the-art security — which makes it a good place to take their own clientele. The booths are all individually soundproofed, the kitchen has all the latest gear, and the whole building is airtight.

Not like here.

Starla studies the outdated scanner blinking by the door and the broken camera above the bar, then types out a request on her gauntlet. The words ping onto her comm; she slides it across the counter towards the bartender.

*Is the owner in? I'm bringing a VIP by here later tonight and have some questions about security.*

Thirty minutes later, Starla's wrapping up an impromptu meeting with the owner, who'd confirmed her suspicions that the place is in vital need of a security refresh. He knows it, he told her through Luc, who she'd conscripted as a relatively competent interpreter to save the time she usually spends typing on her gauntlet. He's been meaning to get around to it for ages, but the walk-in freezer went out, they found a colony of bats in the roof, and it's just been one thing after another. Despite the bar being broken into three times in the last few years, upgrading the security hadn't risen to the top of the priority list.

Starla's suspicion that the door scanners weren't actually working was correct, but reconnecting them is just a matter of updating the firmware with an off-market patch. It'll coax the antique equipment into some semblance of functionality for now, Starla tells the owner, but the only real long-term solution is to replace them with something built in this century.

"Have you heard of Almasi Industries?" Luc asks them both. "Top-end scanners, my uncle has one of their sample kits with him. Might even be able to get it here and installed by tonight." He smiles at the bar owner. "At a good deal."

The bar owner doesn't look like he's ready to drop the cost of a new scanner set right now, but he *does* look intrigued. Starla channels her inner Leti. "The revenue boost you'll get if Veyda walks through these doors tonight?" She puts an extra bit of emphasis on *if*, hopes Luc passes it along. "It'll pay for itself by the weekend."

The guy nods slowly, then sticks out his hand for Starla to shake. "Let's do it."

"I'll get ahold of our team back at the docks," Luc says and signs with a grin.

---

The next place on Veyda's list doesn't have so pressing a need, but Starla finds a few bugs to patch on her pro bono systems check and leaves the owner her information to have a conversation about security at the second location they're opening later in the year.

The third place is a complete shithole, the manager a surly woman who refuses to make eye contact with Starla and only talks to Luc. As they leave, Starla messages Leti to tell Veyda that the bar is sadly closed for repairs today. They won't be able to visit.

"Where to next?" Luc signs when they're back in the bright sun.

Starla checks the time on her gauntlet. They don't have time for another stop before picking Veyda up at the Horus, but, honestly, Veyda won't have time to hit the half-dozen places on her list before she needs to be back for her show anyway. If they finish up at the first two places early, Starla can always take her to the Golden Orchid room at the Jungle.

Still. She's been enjoying this afternoon with Luc. The banter, the gentle teasing, the quickly developed in-jokes and the feel of his shoulder brushing against hers. She isn't looking forward to others intruding on their rapport.

"Time to meet a pop star," Starla signs with a sigh.

"Ah, well," he signs back, his gaze lingering, reluctant, and Starla's gratified to know he's been enjoying this time, too.

She can't help but find herself charmed by the refined smile, the graceful hands, the easy anecdotes about places she's only ever dreamed of visiting. He's been to Bixia Yuanjin, he's told her, and to nearly every country on Indira, and all throughout Durga's Belt, and as Starla slips her helmet on she finds herself imagining it's the helmet of an EVA suit instead, that Bulari's dust and traffic and skyscrapers have vanished to be replaced by inky blackness and asteroids and stars.

A girl can dream.

The Horus is in the heart of the Casino District. It's a newer venue aimed at a younger audience, and it's brought some life back to a drag of road known for stodgy stalwarts with aging decor and seedy shows. Starla herself would never come to the drag if not for Simca, who competes regularly at the amateur wrestling night at Herran's.

She parks her al-Jurjani Torment near the Horus's backstage loading dock, scans her ident card for the burly security team at the door, then wanders in to find preparations for the show still underway.

Leti is watching from the wings at stage right, wearing a bold blue suit and matching fedora, the collar of her gold blouse popped up to frame her throat. She waves Starla over, giving Luc a handshake and a long, suggestive evaluation.

"Well played last night," she signs to him with a wink; Starla had messaged ahead of time to let her know he was coming. Leti waves a hand at the stage. "The dry run, they're just finishing it up."

Leti glances past Starla, where Simca is coming through the backstage door. Today she's dressed for work in a dark top and trousers, her black hair in twin braids. All trace of the club glitter has been washed off, though she's still sporting silver eyeliner and a neon-green choker with matching hoop earrings. She grins at Luc with delight, but her attention today is all for the woman on stage.

Starla's been intrigued by vids of Veyda's unearthly gossamer performances, too, but she's less interested in the waifish pop star than in the tech that enables her act.

The star's entire persona revolves around being an ethereal princess from Bixia Yuanjin, swimming through the air as she sings, her diaphanous chiffon dress swirling improbably around her. The effect comes from a clever harness and hidden fans, of course, though Starla suspects she'll continue wearing the harness during the entire show.

She'll need it. Veyda doesn't look like she keeps up any sort of training regimen, and New Sarjun's gravity can be brutal for those who haven't prepared for it. It had taken Starla months before basic exercise wasn't exhausting, and she'd been an active teenager who also trained regularly on Silk Station with her parents. She doesn't fault Veyda for using props to get through a performance in this gravity.

Right now, Veyda's floating mid-stage like a goddess over her moon-sprite subjects, spotlights illuminating pearly mist that wafts around her chiffon dress while a dozen dancers frolic below. A vast crescent moon slides out from stage right; from Starla's vantage point in the wings near the rear of the stage, she can see the scaffolding that allows dancers to climb up and appear at the top, leaping and tumbling in their own harnesses to land gently on the other side of the stage.

The last dancer takes flight, and Veyda must be finished holding a long note because the hearing people around Starla and Leti start to clap. Veyda's arms drift down with fluttering fingers, eyes closed as if in ecstasy.

Her entire demeanor changes the instant the operator lowers her to the stage floor. Veyda snaps fingers at a stagehand, yelling something Starla's lens doesn't transcribe. The stagehand scurries away looking worried.

"She's been like this all afternoon," Leti says with an eye roll.

"A diva?" Starla asks.

"Yep." Leti flashes Starla and Simca a grin. "Good luck tonight."

A tall woman with a glossy black bun and square jaw strides out from stage left, still clapping, and Starla recognizes Angeliq Shaw, the owner of the Horus. She's too far away for her lens to pick up the conversation between Angeliq and Veyda, but body language says the casino owner is gushing and the pop star is complaining about the fit of the harness. Angeliq beckons over another stagehand, who begins to help Veyda out of the many buckles and straps.

"Luc and I checked out some of the spots on Veyda's list," Starla tells Leti and Simca. "Security is good on the first two, but that divey atmo bar off Sixth is out. Sketchy as hell."

"And the owner is an asshole," adds Luc.

Leti glances between them, a faint smile on her lips. "Glad you two had a good time," she signs. "And no worries about the atmo dive. Veyda, she's real slow. After every place she's going to want to refresh her makeup and make a bunch of vids for fans — and she changes her mind constantly. You'll be lucky if she makes it to the first spot."

"I promised the first spot the bump in traffic would help pay for the new door scanners we sold him."

"Look at you." Leti grins. "Well, I'll make sure the whole city hears the rumor that Veyda is *supposed* to be there. No one cares if it's true, they'll flock in regardless."

On stage, Veyda's still arguing with the stagehand

about her harness. She swats his hand away, working the buckles herself.

Suddenly she jerks up and out of the stagehand's grasp, dangling a meter above the ground like a rag doll on a string. Angeliq and the stagehand both lunge for her, but Veyda is swept up again, out of reach.

Only this time, she's not snugly tethered in her harness. The buckles around her hips and thighs have been undone, and although her arms are through the straps, she's sliding out. She doesn't have the upper-body strength to support herself in this gravity, and if her slender form slips out of the harness and crashes to the stage floor from that height, it could break every fragile bone in her celestial body.

Starla's not going to wait for that to happen.

Veyda's wild ascent has her swinging back and forth, so before Starla can overthink her plan, she sprints for the crescent moon platform and scrambles up the scaffolding until she reaches the top. She stretches for Veyda's hand, misses as the woman swings away. But Veyda's flailing gives her swing even more arc, and this time when she gets close, Starla hooks a knee around a support and reaches out as far as she can.

She grasps Veyda's frail hand in hers, reeling her in.

*Please hold*, she prays to anyone who might be listening, as the stage prop platform sways underneath her efforts. *Please hold*.

She scoots herself back on the platform, one hand

finding a support while the other draws Veyda closer; the moon sways, but it's more solidly built than it looks. With one last tug, Veyda is shivering on the platform beside Starla.

"What the fuck just happened," the pop star yells to the world in general, close enough now that Starla's lens can transcribe. Maybe she doesn't know USL for *thank you*, Starla thinks uncharitably. Probably doesn't know how to say "Thank you" aloud, either.

Veyda shrugs off Starla's arm and turns to grip the moon platform's railing. "What the fuck just — "

And her eyes widen.

Starla turns to follow her gaze.

A handful of shadowy figures are standing in the wings at stage left. Starla had been so focused on helping Veyda, she hadn't seen them enter. She doesn't recognize the ringleader, a man with dyed red hair pushed up in short spikes, but she recognizes the intimidation in his grin and the casual way his crew holds their weapons.

Trouble has arrived.

From center stage, Angeliq Shaw squares her shoulders to face him.

"Moses," she says, clearly enough that Starla's lens catches it. "Get your ass out of here. We have an agreement with Dry Creek."

"And that agreement stands," the man — Moses — says. The name doesn't ring a bell to Starla, but he must be one of Dry Creek's enforcers. That crew doesn't bother Jaantzen much, so they haven't spent much time on Starla's radar. Moses turns away from Angeliq and grins up at Veyda. "I'm here to talk to her."

"Fuck off," yells Veyda.

Moses laughs and signals to someone up in the booth; the harness barely holding Veyda jerks upwards and she screams, clinging to the railing while her toes scrabble for purchase on the platform. Starla grabs her sapling of an arm.

Her grip won't do a thing if the harness operator pulls Veyda all the way up, but that doesn't seem to be the plan — yet. This was just a scare, and at Moses's signal, the ropes slacken once more, giving Veyda a chance to settle onto the platform.

What is Dry Creek here for? Ransom is her first thought, but Dry Creek is a small crew that gets its revenue mostly from street drugs and minor extortion. Kidnapping a Bixian celebrity would be a stretch. Is it a random attack? Are they extorting Angeliq?

Do they just want tickets to the sold-out show?

From the way Veyda's looking at Moses, though, she knows exactly why they're here.

"You think you can cut us out?" Moses asks.

"What are you talking about?" Angeliq snaps. "We've paid our dues this month."

Moses grins at her, baring jagged teeth. "Oh, did our little princess here not fill you in on her own agreement with us? We had a deal, and she decided to go behind our backs." He lifts his chin to Veyda. "Go ahead, tell her."

"I *told* you to fuck off," Veyda says. Apparently she's not interested in sharing.

Moses shrugs. Gestures to the booth once more and the ropes holding Veyda's harness lurch. She screams as she's torn from her grip on the railing, fingers clawing at Starla's arm.

Starla can't hold on to her. If she's yanked off the platform, Starla's weight will snap her brittle bones like twigs even if the Dry Creek operator in the booth doesn't simply let them both plummet to the stage.

Before she can decide, Moses signals again and the ropes slacken once more.

"Tell her," Moses commands.

Veyda pants for breath, her knuckles white on the railing. "It's all part of the show," she finally says; she's not quite looking at Angeliq. "My fans want the full experience. Zero G. Weightlessness."

Starla frowns at her, not believing what the pop star is saying. You can't spend as much time at nightclubs as Starla does and not know your basic mind-altering designer drugs. She's never tried anything but the occasional tablet to add a pleasant hazy aura of feel-good sparkle, but she's seen plenty of other moods on the market. And heard plenty of talk of the more popular drugs on other planets — which means she's pretty sure what Veyda is referring to.

Angeliq must know, too, because the look she gives Veyda drips with disdain. "Silver mist?" she asks, incredulous. "Last thing I need in this club is a bunch of wasters throwing themselves off balconies."

Silver mist is one of those drugs developed for party kids in the black. Starla's heard it makes you feel like you're experiencing the faintest effect of gravity, drifting ever so gently in an infinite free fall while filling your mind with visions of ancient stars and alien planets. Drifting through galactic worlds, they say. One with the vast universe.

Though the effect isn't quite the same if you're already in gravity. Starla's heard that it can still be fun with the right dose, but take too much — or take it while drinking, or under the influence of something else — and it can give you a messy combination of delusion and the spins.

"We agreed that Dry Creek would handle distribution," Moses says to Veyda. "So what's this I hear about you keeping your shipment to sell yourself?"

Veyda scowls at him. "I said, f—"

This time when Moses signals to the person in the booth, Starla's ready. She grabs Veyda's harness rather than her fragile arm, and as the ropes tighten once more she launches them both off the platform. They swing in an arc towards the soft mats the backup dancers had earlier used to cushion their own falls, though this one won't be nearly so gentle.

Starla slashes through the rope tethering the harness as they hit the peak of the arc, then twists in the air to roll them both as they hit the mats. The roll and Starla's own body should help cushion Veyda's fall, and fortunately she weighs only as much as a child.

Starla springs into a crouch, signing for Veyda to stay down. The pop star seems too winded to do much else.

Starla charges into action.

Simca has already taken down one of Moses's minions, and seems to be holding her own while grappling with another. Luc seems fine in his fight against the third, and the fourth — typical Dry Creek — splits as soon as it becomes clear this isn't going to be easy pickings. Moses looks like he's about to do the same, until Angeliq steps into his way with a crowbar in her hands.

Moses pulls a gun from his waistband, pointing it directly at Angeliq's chest.

"We had an agreement with Dry Creek," Angeliq says again. "If this is how you do business, I might have to rethink it."

"Get out of my way and I won't tell my bosses you said that."

"Your bosses." Angeliq scoffs. "You all got so bold under Coeur, but you're just parasites on this city. I'm done letting you rule my business."

Goddammit, Angeliq. She's baiting him, and this isn't going to end well unless Starla can get that gun away from Moses before his wounded pride causes him to do something even more asinine. From behind a curtain, Luc catches her eye.

"I'm in his blind spot," he signs, indicating the heavy leg curtains masking the wing — and hiding his position from Moses. "I can get closer."

"Do it." Starla glances around for a plan, then smiles. "At my signal, grab Angeliq."

She blinks off her lens's transcription — the smattering of text from Moses and Angeliq's argument isn't helping her concentration — and creeps forward, trying to make as little noise as possible. Moses doesn't seem to notice her, though. Or Luc in the wings.

By their body language, the argument between the casino owner and the enforcer is coming to a head. Angeliq takes a menacing step towards Moses, crowbar raised like she doesn't believe he'll shoot her. If he's smart, he won't dare — Starla can't imagine the hammer that will come down on Dry Creek if one of theirs oversteps and kills someone like Angeliq Shaw. But that's a lot of risk riding on Moses being smart.

Starla shouts for Luc, betting on him understanding her signal, and slashes at one of the ropes tethered to the stage left pin rail. She spins back to Moses and Angeliq, hoping she followed the lines correctly. And — yes!

Luc tackles Angeliq out of the way just as a heavy border curtain drops from the fly loft. Moses goes down in a tangle of rich black velvet, pinned by a rail. Simca grabs the gun from Moses's outstretched hand and steps back to cover him while Luc helps Angeliq back to her feet.

Starla doesn't see any other Dry Creek trash around, and she doesn't expect to — not after they got their asses handed to them so spectacularly. Angeliq will need to watch her back after this, of course, but that's a problem for farther down the road.

She finds Veyda still slumped in the cushions and holds out a hand to help her to her feet. This time she's pretty sure Veyda does thank her, but by the time Starla's blinked her transcription back on, Veyda's attention has shifted past her to a very, very angry Angeliq.

"Who do you think you are?" Angeliq demands. "I don't care how famous you are on Bixia Yuanjin, you don't know the first thing about this city."

Veyda tries to speak, but Angeliq holds up a hand for silence.

"Are you injured?" Angeliq doesn't look like she really cares. "Can you perform?"

Veyda licks her lips and nods.

"Good. Because I'm going to have to triple my security after this disaster, and you're paying for it with your share of ticket sales." Angeliq turns and stalks away. "And you'd better not be selling that silver mist shit on my property," she calls over her shoulder.

Veyda turns to Starla, already with a demand, but Starla ignores the scribble of diva-speak on her lens. "You're welcome," she signs; Veyda stares at her blankly. "I hope you have a nice show."

It seems best to stay out of the way while the Bulari police collect Moses — and the Horus's theater staff descend to repair the damage — so Starla joins Simca, Leti, and Luc back in the wings.

"Guess that means no security gig for us," Simca signs as they watch the preparations.

"Now you're show security," Leti signs, then jabs a finger at Luc. "You're on, too. Since whoever Angeliq originally hired just let Dry Creek waltz right in."

Simca brightens. "Maybe they'll try again," she signs, and slaps an open palm against her fist. "Because that was fun!"

"Your definition of fun worries me," Leti signs with a laugh, then waves an arm at Angeliq as the casino owner stalks across the stage to join them. Angeliq is all business now, any trace of the gushing, simpering fan she'd shined on for Veyda before the Dry Creek fiasco washed away.

She holds out a hand for Starla to shake. "You're Jaantzen's girl, aren't you?"

Starla's lens transcribes it, but Simca's also stepped reflexively into Starla's view to act as interpreter. It's a role she's played for family and friends since she was a child.

"I am," Starla confirms. Of course Angeliq would know that; it's the one fact anyone knows about Starla.

"Your reputation precedes you," Angeliq says. "Glad to know you live up to it."

Starla blinks at her, startled. *Her* reputation? As herself, and not just "Jaantzen's girl"? But before she can ask, Angeliq's moved on to Simca.

"Simca Anahoy, right? I've seen your name at Herran's, haven't I. You get in the ring?"

"Yes, ma'am." Even answering for herself, she continues signing for Starla and Leti. "I've been fighting at the amateur nights."

"If you're as good in the ring as you were here, you'll move up quick."

"Just requires money," says Simca. And she straightens her shoulders, meeting Angeliq's gaze. "And a patron in show biz doesn't hurt."

Angeliq gives a surprised laugh, but her expression quickly becomes serious. She steps back to scrutinize Simca.

"I like your style," she finally says. "The way you comport yourself, and your look — it's a good package. Tell me next time you're scheduled to fight. If I like what I see, we'll talk."

Someone must have called for her, because she turns and shouts, "Coming!" over her shoulder. She gives everyone a nod, then turns to deal with more pressing matters.

Simca grabs Starla's hand, bouncing on her feet with an infectious grin.

"Did you see that?" she signs.

"She said you'll talk," Starla points out, but she's smiling, too. Partly because Simca's getting her break, partly because the gears in Starla's head are starting to turn, too. This had ended well, but it shouldn't have happened at all. So many places could be run better, more securely. They all need someone they can trust. Someone who can help them with custom setups that actually work, and keep watered-down crews like Dry Creek out of their doors.

The gears continue turning as she settles in to watch the rest of the preparations from the wings.

For all the excitement of the last few minutes, Veyda's a pro. She's got her chin held high, not letting slip for a minute just what an ordeal she's been through, or the feud she's currently having with Angeliq.

Though she's much less quick to snap at the stage-hands now.

Simca jostles Starla's shoulder for attention. "I bet I could score us a couple doses of that mist stuff," she signs. "Sounds fun."

Starla laughs. "Absolutely not."

"We'll make El babysit us. He can sit and read a book and make sure we remember to drink water and whatever." She elbows Luc. "Wanna join?"

"I tried it on Sapis once," he signs with a shrug. "Not worth the hype."

"How fancy." Simca rolls her eyes. "You've been to Sapis."

Starla smiles as Simca and Luc keep up their banter, though a bittersweet current pulls at her light mood. She never would have chosen Bulari, but she loves her family here — as much as Jaantzen seems to be trying to push her into something apart from him. And though she would love to travel the stars, she can't help but think of her cousin Mona, drifting through the Belt with no connections, forced to make a new life everywhere she lands. Or Absolon and Luc, constantly on the move to amazing new places but never settled enough to make friends.

She wants to see the stars, but she's spent enough

time untethered, not putting down roots of her own. The stars aren't going anywhere.

She opens a group message with Jaantzen, Manu, and Toshiyo.

*CAN YOU MEET TOMORROW MORNING? I HAVE A BUSINESS PROPOSITION.*

---

"It's called Admant Security," Starla signs. The logo she talked Simca's brother El into mocking up for her late last night floats gently in the center of the table.

Jaantzen, Manu, Toshiyo, Absolon, and Luc have all joined her in Jaantzen's penthouse, and each of them seems absorbed in the hologram presentation she whipped together last night while still buzzing with energy from the performance.

"We already have three clients," Starla continues, describing the bar she and Luc sold a new door scanner to, the lead she has on consulting for a restaurant's second location, and the security staffing contract she inked with Angeliq.

Angeliq had been eager to fire her old contractors. During Veyda's performance, Starla pinged Toshiyo to do some digging. Turns out the company was owned by one of Moses's cousins — so it was no wonder they let him walk right in. As soon as Starla passed that on to Angeliq, she'd hired Starla's yet-unnamed security company on the spot.

When she finishes, Starla lets her fingertips rest

lightly on the table, resisting the urge to fidget. For a long moment, no one else moves. The others are waiting for Jaantzen's cue; the way he's watching her, Starla can't tell if he's upset or impressed.

"You've sold services to three businesses without even having a company," he finally says. It's a sign of his concentration on the problem that he's not derailing his focus by attempting to speak USL. Manu has been interpreting Starla's presentation for him and Toshiyo.

"Sell it first, build it later," Starla signs. The corner of Jaantzen's mouth twitches in a smile; he's told her that more than once. "And it wasn't a hard sell. People like Angeliq need a company they can trust, and they know they can trust you. This could be a subsidiary of RKE."

"They can trust *you*," Jaantzen says. "Angeliq's the only one of your three sales who knew you're my goddaughter." He steeples his fingers in front of his lips, frowning at the logo in the center of the table. "If you do this, it should be a separate business, not affiliated with RKE." Not affiliated with *him*, she suspects he means, and a thrill twists in her stomach. If she does this, it will be a thing of her own. A chance to prove herself without his name. "You have people you can trust to do the work?"

"Simca and El," Starla signs. Simca will be thrilled to leave her desk job with the bank, and El's always free for the odd gig. Starla smiles at Luc and Absolon. "And I already have a supplier."

"Plus a stack of those shock batons I ordered last

month," says Toshiyo, and, at Jaantzen's look: "They were on sale. I was planning on taking them apart."

Jaantzen lifts an eyebrow. "And doing what with them."

"Experimenting." Toshiyo shrugs. "Don't worry about it, boss."

"Hmm." Jaantzen turns his attention back to Starla. "Then yes. Please start a business that includes secure storage for any of Toshiyo's pet projects that might turn Cobalt Tower into a crater."

Starla doesn't try to stop herself from grinning. "Of course." She's floating from success — though that may be exhaustion, since she was up all night preparing this presentation. But Jaantzen looks happy for the first time in ages. Manu and Absolon both look proud. Toshiyo looks excited. And . . . Luc's trying to smile at her, but she can tell it's pained.

As the others filter away to refill coffees in the penthouse's kitchen, he lingers; Starla does, too.

"They loved it," he signs. He glances over his shoulder, but no one is watching. "But when you said you were too tired after the show last night, I figured you were going to sleep. Not launching a business empire."

Guilt twinges through her. "It was kind of last-minute." Which is a stretch of the truth. After the show, he'd hinted they should go back to her place together, but she'd already called this meeting with Jaantzen. And, truth be told, she didn't want to tell him about it last night. Luc Chevalier is all travel and stardust and incredible adventures on other planets. She didn't trust herself to go to bed with him and still have the resolve to pitch Jaantzen on a plan that would keep her feet firmly on New Sarjunian soil for at least another few years.

But when the idea had hit her, it had felt solid. Right.

It had felt *hers* in a way few things ever have, and the more she'd poured herself into making the presentation, the more her excitement had grown. This was a way to use her skills and passions to make a name for herself. A way for people to know her as Starla Dusai — not Jaantzen's goddaughter or Raj and Lasadi's daughter.

Besides. Luc will be on-planet for the next few weeks. They can mix business and fun while she works out what she needs to order from Absolon, can't they? She's let lovers walk out of her life before, this isn't her first time around. And Luc's a professional drifter. He'll know better than to fall too hard.

A safe, uncomplicated romance that will be simple enough to walk away from when the inevitable comes, she thinks. Easy enough, she tells herself as she makes plans to meet him later. Not a problem.

But even she can tell she's lying.

# TROUBLE

*This story takes place during the events of* Double Edged, *in the blank space between Oriol's prologue adventure on the* Dorothy Queen *and when he finally meets back up with Manu.*

*Because of that, it doesn't quite stand on its own the way the other stories in this collection are meant to. I'd recommend at least reading the prologue of* Double Edged *if you haven't read anything else in the series.*

*My favorite thing about this story is that it introduces a couple of characters who show up later in the series: Nacea and Mel. What's not to love about a couple of badass women who are extremely fond of blowing bad guys up?*

BACK ON PLANET'S ALWAYS A NICE SPOT TO BE: real food, real gravity, real air.

Oriol Sina can take advantage of the second two, at least — they're free to all God's children on this rock.

Real food, on the other hand, requires the ability to access your bank accounts without alerting all the people who might be after you that you made it to the surface alive.

He's just about starving, though — adrenaline will do that to you. Coming back to New Sarjun was supposed to be his vacation: spend his hard-earned long-haul security cash on food with flavor, work his tan back up, see if Manu's found anyone new.

The usual.

Things aren't getting off to a good start.

He overrode the auto-return and instructed the casino's escape pod to an emergency soft landing just outside New Sarjun's capitol city of Bulari, and he's managed to extricate himself and hitchhike back into town without getting arrested.

Turns out casino magnate Aiax Demosga uses the same escape pod contractor everybody in New Sarjun orbit does, and since the pods are needed so rarely, the contractor's slow to react. Good thing there wasn't a real emergency or the desert would be filled with injured, crash-landed tourists and nobody home to help them out.

Oriol did the Demosgas a favor, didn't he, testing out the lifeboats to see if they're still operational.

He's shedding clothes: that suit's gotta go, because both Aiax Demosga and whoever killed Sister Kalia are going to be putting out alerts for a pale-skinned dude with an Arquellian accent wearing an off-the-rack suit. Plus, the camouflage that helped him blend into the *Dorothy Queen* crowd is definitely going to make him stand out in the places he's headed. He borrows a maintenance suit and work boots from a locker once he hits the terminal. Oriol rips off the corporate label, then runs a hand through his hair and heads to the one place he knows he's not going to catch flak.

Geordi Jimenez Space Terminal, Level B. A repair shop whose windows are stuffed with a selection of standard home electronics aimed at locals, and last-minute gifts for tourists doing a final wander-through before their shuttle back up to orbit and home. One-trick robots, personal media players, mini holoprojectors with slogans about loving Bulari.

The sign above the door reads Hallelujah, It's Fixed!

Oriol stops outside long enough to see that the store's namesake, Hallelujah Oni, is alone. He pushes through like nothing's going wrong, nothing at all.

"Louis!"

The other man's face lights up with a smile, and he carefully sets aside his tools, standing and wiping his dark hands down his apron before pulling Oriol into a hug. He lets go, then gives him a once-over. "What kind of trouble did you bring me, *mon ami?*"

That tone of voice, Louis is maybe just talking about Oriol's prosthetic, though Oriol's not a great actor, and he's got more than one scrape seeping blood.

"Can we talk in your back room?"

Louis sighs pointedly, then hits a button on his desk. A forcefield sizzles to life over the door and windows, and a pair of cartoon angels appear on the door holding a sign between them: *Back in five minutes.*

Louis holds back the heavy curtain and gestures Oriol through.

The back room of Louis's shop looks like a messier, more cluttered version of the front. It's also filled with more interesting things than those he displays to his browsing customers. Like his prosthetics collection, of course — Louis doesn't like to have them out front because they make the tourists nervous.

His examination chair is back here, too, something salvaged from a doctor's office years ago. Oriol hops onto the chair, but he's not ready to have Louis look at his leg. Not yet.

Louis cocks his head skeptically. "Tell me, *mon ami*. Where does it hurt."

"Everywhere, actually." Oriol launches into a short-of-it version, leaving out the most unsavory bits, but giving Louis enough of an idea to figure out what kind of trouble he's in.

He was contracted by a religious type named Sister

Kalia to steal a ring before the Demosgas could buy it. Only she'd been double-crossed by someone even scarier than Aiax Demosga, and Oriol had barely made it out alive.

With the ring.

Oriol describes the man with the wicked scar and the ice blue eyes. "You heard of this guy?" he asks. "He said something about the Dawn."

Louis doesn't hesitate. "Bennion Zacharia." He purses his lips, thinking. "You more worried about the Demosgas or the Dawn?"

"Who should I be?"

"The Dawn, I'm thinking."

"A bunch of religious creeps out in the desert."

Louis shrugs, then taps on Oriol's knee. "I'm looking at that, too?"

"Just the ankle's acting up." Oriol unlaces his stolen boot, kicks it off. "What do you know about the Dawn?"

Louis settles on a stool in front of the exam chair, hoisting Oriol's prosthetic foot in his lap. "More and more I'm hearing stories like the one you brought me. I know enough to stay away from them, and you should, too."

"Too late."

"I know they're buying firepower with all that drug money they've been earning. And a few mercs I thought better of have been tempted by the money they're flashing around." Louis sighs, though it might be at the state of Oriol's ankle joint. "Better off leaving it, I say."

"If they're after me — "

"You said yourself, maybe they think you're dead."

"Or maybe they're still after me."

"How long you been off planet?" Louis asks, and whether he's done talking about the Dawn or just making a sideways step in the conversation, Oriol isn't sure. Louis circles a finger around his own dark face. "You look like you haven't seen the sun for a good long while."

Oriol settles back into the chair. "Eight months. Too long. Any good gossip?"

That one-shouldered shrug — there's plenty going on. Just depends on what you think is the most interesting thing to hear about.

"You looking for employment? Or you heading back to your gunslinger's man?"

Oriol's worked for Willem Jaantzen, Manu's employer, off and on for the better part of two decades. It's always good work, the man pays fair and treats his people well, but Oriol's never been a regular of any place. Bartender learns his name and he starts heading somewhere else. Kebab stand boy learns his order and he won't ever go there again. Hallelujah Oni's workshop is just about the only place he's made himself a regular, and that's because the man does good work.

And because Manu trusts him. When in doubt, Oriol lets Manu's instinct for reading people stand in for his own natural distrust of others.

Manu trusts Jaantzen, too, but heading back there every time he gets home stinks of habit. Plus, most of the time when Oriol gets back from a trip he's set for at least half a year. He would be this time, too, if he'd actually gotten paid for the job on the *Dorothy Queen*. Instead, he ended up with a mysterious ring in his pocket and a price on his head.

Ah, well. Job's done and over and learned from. Wallowing in self-recrimination after a mistake never kept anybody alive for long.

"I'm keeping my options open," he says.

Louis nods sagely. "Dawn's purse is tempting, but I'm only telling you so you stay away."

"What do they need mercs for? Kidnapping kids to work in their shard factories?"

"I only know they're starting to collect soldiers. I'd suggest you don't let them collect you."

Wariness pricks the back of Oriol's neck.

"Noted."

But the way Louis is looking at him, he knows there's something more the man wants to say. "Avoiding them isn't simple as that," he says. "They're trapping people with religion. People in high places. People you might trust."

Oriol frowns at him. "What do you mean? Who are they working with?"

He expects Louis to shrug it off as he always does, letting the cryptic statement hang out in silence to keep everyone wondering. Manu's so much better at getting information out of Louis than Oriol is.

But Louis gives him a serious look. "I don't know exactly," he says, and Oriol can tell that's the truth. "But they have spies everywhere."

"You're not afraid that I'm one of their spies?"

Louis laughs, that spark of darkness vanished from his eyes. "No offense, soldier. But you don't have enough guile in you to be a spy."

"You don't know what I've done, Louis."

And Louis sobers. "I know that whatever you've done, you've spent too many years atoning for it." He snaps Oriol's shin plate into place, then lifts Oriol's foot back into his lap and begins to manipulate the ankle joint through its range of motion. "And you're too clever now to let someone like that pull you into their traps."

"You said they might have people I trust on their side. Who did you mean?"

Louis sets down Oriol's foot and pats his thigh. "You feel that?"

Oriol nods.

"Good. Everything's working fine."

"Louis. Who's working with them?"

Louis shakes his head. "I don't know specifics, *mon ami*."

"You don't have names? Or you don't want to tell me?"

Louis regards him a moment, serious. "Why do you come see me instead of some other tinker?"

"For the korris joint next door," Oriol jokes. But Louis isn't smiling. "Because you're discreet."

"This is a very important subject to be discreet around." Louis turns away, carefully arranging his tools back into place. "Any more questions before you hit the road, soldier?"

"Where can I find someone who's less discreet?"

Louis's laugh lights up the room.

"How are you at mystix?" he asks.

---

Oriol buses all the way across town to tap into an unmarked account he's ninety-nine percent sure no one knows about. He pulls out the daily limit — it should last him a couple days — and every nerve in his body is burning with anticipation. But no one jumps from the alleyway, no one grabs him from behind, poison darts don't fly from any open nearby windows.

If he'd touched any of his personal accounts, or the account Sister Kalia put his deposit into, he might trigger someone's tripwires. He'd like the Dawn to wonder if he's dead for as long as possible until he figures out what's going on.

Hopefully this mystix player Louis has sent him to is as loose with her information as Oriol'd like. Louis's warning that the Dawn is in tight with people Oriol wouldn't expect — people he might trust — has him worried about going home until he knows the lay of the land.

So he'll play a few hands of mystix, he'll chat with Louis's contact to learn who the Dawn works with, and then he'll know who he can trust to help him get this target off his back. After that, he'll be free and clear to tap into his accounts and head back to Manu without a tail of trouble.

Until then, this'll buy him dinner and entry to a mystix game, and he's got any dozen of friends who won't ask questions if he shows up and asks to sleep on their couch for a few nights. Perks of being the mercenary in town who doesn't ruffle feathers. Everybody knows him, most everybody likes him — even if they don't always like that he sometimes pulls jobs for Jaantzen and shares a bed with the man's lieutenant.

He takes the long way back to the bar Louis gave him an address for, pretending to doze but keeping an eye on his surroundings to make sure no one is following him. It's hard not to just let the bus rock him to oblivion, though. Blackout sleep isn't good sleep, and he probably wasn't blacked out for long in that escape capsule anyway. Given the deliberate confusion of night and day on the *Dorothy Queen*, he's not even sure how long he's been awake.

The bar doesn't have a sign, and Oriol walks past it twice before realizing it's his destination. Every face along the dingy stretch of barstools and gaming tables turns to look at him when he pushes open the door, and he immediately sees why. Where some bars have their cocktail menu or rows of liquor bottles, this one has a bank of monitors showing the outside of the building. Watching for police maybe, local crews, surly drunks who got kicked out and want back in, poor losers who are looking to get their money back the hard way.

Or folks who can't find the poorly-marked entrance.

The bartender grins at him. "Some guys walk past that door five or six times," she says. "What'll it be?"

People are still watching him, gauging his reaction to the ribbing. Oriol flashes her a grin. "Helping us get our exercise in, yeah? I'll have a scotch and soda." He claps the shoulder of the man next to him, who's still giving him an ugly glare. "And another one of whatever this fine gentleman is having."

He tips generously — he's really going to have to get access to his accounts soon — then turns to look down the game tables. There's a woman at one who matches the description Louis gave him. Brown skin, brilliant green eyes, hair streaked blue and purple and tied up in a ridgeline of messy buns. The table she's at is a player short, and Oriol slips into the chair and prepares to lose some more money.

Three hours later she wipes him and their remaining tablemate out with a killer marriage: bandit queen and loup-garou. The other guy swears and shoves back from the table, calling for another drink. Oriol leans back in his chair with a groan and tosses his cards down.

The woman with the neon buns frowns at them. "What even is that?" she asks. "Were you going for a run or a skate? For a while, I was wondering if you were a shark. But I'm starting to think you just suck at mystix."

Oriol laughs. "I'm better with a knife."

Her smile doesn't fade at that; it sharpens. "And what kind of work do you do?"

"The kind that pays. Been out of town for a bit and now it turns out I'm flat broke."

She laughs, sweeping the pile of marks in front of her into the winner's return slot on the table to be counted for credit. "What makes you think I have work?"

"Hallelujah."

The woman goes still, a quirk of her lips as she considers him. The mystix table on one side of them has cleared out, the one to the other side is playing so raucously they can't possibly make out this conversation.

"I'm looking for information on the Dawn," Oriol says. "Had a little run-in with them, and Louis thought you might be willing to chat. Help me figure out who in this town I can still trust."

"He told you that."

"He said you didn't have any love lost. That you'd been following threads."

"And what did he tell you I was planning?"

"To draw some Dawn blood."

She smiles, tight and fierce. "How do you know Louis?"

Oriol stretches out his left leg, raps his thigh. "The man's kept my leg working for twenty years. My name's Oriol Sina, I've worked with half the players in this town. You can ask around if you want."

But the woman just shakes her head. "I'll be calling Louis to check your story. But it turns out I could use some muscle for a job coming up. You want information, we can talk after the gig."

Oriol's expecting this after his conversation with Louis. Information doesn't come free — and anyway, he could use the cash. He nods.

"Good. Subtlety's gonna be key." She cocks her head, studying him. "You do subtle?"

"Alliance Special Ops," he says. "If that doesn't bother you."

"Not a problem."

"Good. Because I have versatile talents."

And she grins. "I believe it. Come grab a drink with me." She finds them a pair of open stools at the bar and waves at the bartender. "You like sugar vipers?"

Oh, hell no.

Oriol's shaking his head. "That's not on my agenda for this lifetime."

"C'mon. They're just like a shot."

"But they ain't."

She laughs and holds up two fingers to the bartender, who lifts the lid off a matte black canister with an opalescent hologram of snakes on the front. The bartender reaches in gingerly with tongs and pulls out a pair of writhing snakes, each about as long as Oriol's forearm and wide around as his pinky. One's glowing turquoise, the other's neon yellow.

The woman takes them from the bartender and hands him the yellow one. "Guava's best for your first time. Bottom's up."

She nips off the head of the turquoise snake and downs the body in one slurp. The bartender's watching him with a bemused smile.

"C'mon, tough guy," the woman says, and he sighs, giving up containing the writhing sugar viper in his hands, follows suit. It's sharply sweet and artificially fruity, and the venom hits his bloodstream faster than the cheapest vodxx. Or maybe that's just his long-empty stomach. He makes a face. He's too old for everybody's weird-ass mercenary hazing rituals.

"Better than any liquor," the woman says with gusto.

"Have you had a good whiskey?" Oriol asks. "Or a really shitty whiskey, even?" He wants to hate it — blood whines in his ears, but the colors behind the bar flicker brighter, like someone upgraded the video card for the whole world. Like *before* he was experiencing everything through a glitching, ancient holoprojector. He turns to look at the woman; her messy neon buns pulse in time with his heartbeat. Oh, shit.

The woman grins at him. "Let's go, soldier."

---

In the next rundown bar — private booths, better suited for business — Oriol learns that her name's Nacea and her story's this: she makes her money on cards and the occasional jewel theft, and the first time she heard about the Dawn was two years ago when her daughter told her she'd prefer the straight and narrow. The girl'd been living with her dad, and maybe Nacea didn't understand what it meant when her daughter said she got religion, maybe the girl's dad wasn't paying attention to her friends, but the Dawn got their claws in before either of them caught on.

Nacea's ex-husband had called her first, worried about the fasts.

Oriol shrugs at that — fasting is normal. "Just for holy days, sunup to sundown, that sort of thing?" He still keeps the new-year's fast every year, though if he's honest now it's his own private tribute to Tae rather than the spiritual reasons of his youth. She kept him faithful, kept him in the fold, and even though it's been a long, long time since he's felt close to God he'll still fast for her memory.

Memories have no place on a job, though. He acknowledges them, lets them continue on their path.

"They'd fast for weeks at a time," Nacea says. "Her dad couldn't get her to eat a bite, and she'd scream at him when he tried to force her. After that, she moved out. Said she couldn't make herself pure enough to pass through the fire while living with an unbeliever. They brainwashed her, they took her."

The pain on Nacea's face is sharp and bright, and Oriol watches her, wary. If the gig's recovering a potentially hostile asset, he's all right with that. That's always a good time. What he's not all right with is going in with the girl's mother. Doesn't matter if Nacea's the best jewel thief in the world — nobody's good enough to shove emotion like that aside well enough to make smart decisions. Not when it comes to rescuing their kid.

"She still there?" he asks, and Nacea's heist-planning game face cracks in grief.

Ah. Shit.

"I'm sorry," he says.

"She's dead. Nothing to do about it now."

Nacea pulls a minidesk from her shoulder bag and unrolls it between them; Oriol does a quick sweep, but no one's watching whatever she's about to show him.

"Since then, I've made it my business to learn everything I can about them." She looks up at him with cold fire in her eyes. "And to take them down."

So this is a revenge gig.

Good to know.

Revenge is as powerful an emotion as fear for one's child, but it's one Oriol's willing to work with. It's more stable, more predictable. He knows Nacea will have a shark-like focus on the target going in and he can rely on her not to second-guess her training. But he can also count on the fact that she'll make stupid, revenge-based decisions when it looks like their objective is close. He just needs to make sure he's playing his game, not hers.

She's watching him steadily. "That work for you?"

He nods. "Let's do this."

The pile of greasy appetizers she ordered shows up while she's powering up the minidesk, and Oriol helps himself to the least unhealthy-looking thing on the table: fried mushrooms in peanut sauce. He's chewing as the first image blooms between them.

Jackpot: Tanned complexion, shaved head, eyes blue as ice, an old scar running down one cheek.

The man from the hotel room on the *Dorothy Queen*. The man who killed Sister Kalia.

"Bennion Zacharia," Nacea says. "He's their head guy in Bulari."

"Spiritual leader, like?"

Nacea shakes her head. "They have a prophet living back in Redrock prison. Zacharia's that guy's brother, and he's the one in charge of all the shard operations and security here in town. From what I can tell, the shard operation and the religious side of things are linked, though it seems like it's different branches of the organization. I've seen guys like Zacharia swarming around the shard operations. But in their temples you have these priests."

She swipes, and here's a collection of people who look much more holy than Bennion Zacharia. White suits with stars pinned to their lapels, gray suits with no stars. He zooms in on the one woman he recognizes: olive skin and long black hair pinned tight in a bun.

Sister Kalia, may God show her mercy.

"Don't let the holier-than-thou suits confuse you," Nacea says. "These bastards are experts at brain-washing people into doing what they want."

"You think it's all mind games?" With Sister Kalia, he'd made a simple transaction: money for services. But he got a sense of how persuasive she could be if she put her mind to it.

"Not just," Nacea says. "They had my girl hooked on something, too. Not shard, but something equally addictive to make her do what they wanted." She clears memories out of her throat, her jaw clenched. "They're two sides of the same coin. Maybe Zacharia's trying to fulfill the prophecy while making a dime selling shard. But these priests are preying on children to do it."

"Prophecy?"

Nacea gives him a tight smile.

"'And God will transform this broken planet and its unfaithful people as one,'" she recites. "'After the fire burns away the impure, the pure will become devout. And when the pure become devout, we will see a new era unlike anything humanity has ever experienced.'"

A shiver touches the back of Oriol's neck; Sister Kalia's words echo in his memory:

*Your soul burns pure. We'll need all the bright ones when it comes time to pass the test.*

"They believe the world will be cleansed by this plague, something brought about this serum they're trying to manufacture, they call it the gift of the Fallen."

"Why not just go to the cops?"

"They have spies everywhere," Nacea says. "Converts at all levels of the government, people you wouldn't believe. You can't trust anyone, not when it comes to this."

"You trusted me."

"I trust Hallelujah Oni."

"Fair."

*Converts you wouldn't believe*; the phrase eats at him. "You have names?" he asks.

"I have rumors, no proof. But I've been putting together a list."

"Who?"

Nacea just smiles. "Ask me after the job." She pops a deep-fried mushroom in her mouth and turns back to the minidesk. The clutch of people in white suits are still smiling at them, but now the smiles seem secretive, sinister. Oriol studies Sister Kalia's face, wondering just what her role was in all of this. Was she working to stop Zacharia from getting his hands on something that would help him destroy the word? Or was she simply working toward that goal on her own, hiring Oriol to help bring about the destruction of humanity?

The ring Oriol stole from Bennion Zacharia on the *Dorothy Queen* hangs like an anchor around his neck. What the hell is on this thing that's so valuable?

"What's the job?" Oriol asks.

"Hitting them where it hurts," Nacea says with a grin. She swipes at the minidesk and an architectural hologram appears between them. "I have it on good authority their main manufacturing facility is in this building. It's just north of Dry Creek, out on Maraka Valley road — set back from the road and well guarded. Not much else around it. You know how shard is made?"

"Never bothered to find out."

"The ingredient list is insane. I don't know what idiot looked at this pile of toxic chemicals and said, that'll get me high, but somebody was putting their chemistry genius to bad use." She's zooming in on the basement of the diagram. "They have secure storage for the most volatile stuff, but they're storing barrels and barrels of anhydrous ammonia in the basement. We shut off the water main, break into the building, get those barrels leaking, break a couple of pipes? When we turn the water back on, the basement floods."

Oriol's eyebrows shoot up.

"Levels the whole building."

"Or more," he says. "Sounds sketchy."

"I'll do the dirty work. I just need someone to watch my back."

"Are there guards?"

"I've been watching it, seems like four overnight."

That's not many, especially to a woman who makes her money sneaking into places and a man who's good at neutralizing troublesome security teams. But now he's fought some of these Dawn guards, and going up against another fighter like that woman back on the *Dorothy Queen*? That makes him pause. There was something unnatural about her speed, her strength. Back when he was on payroll, the Alliance had plenty of drug regimens to boost your physique. They probably have even better stuff, now. But her? She was on something way more advanced than he's ever seen.

Nacea misreads his hesitation. "I'll double your

fee," she says, and Oriol nods slowly. That's not going to help.

"Use it to hire another gun," he says. "I know a gal."

———

Mel's in, even when Oriol tells her it's a revenge job. She's consistently unfazed by shit like this — it's why Oriol likes working with her. Nacea sets up a time for them all to meet, transfers a fifty percent deposit to Mel and hands Oriol his on an unlinked chit without questioning why. There's lots of reasons someone in his line of work might not want the deposit showing up in his account. Being afraid that the Dawn or Aiax Demosga is keeping tabs on him is only one of them.

Hands shook, demolitions plans made, Oriol finally finds himself a bed. It's a flophouse, the sort of place that doesn't ask for a name and accepts payments from unlinked chits. There's a nightclub thumping bass on one side and a burned-out husk of an old building on the other, protective elasteel webbing sagging around the perimeter.

It looks like a war zone. Specifically, it looks like a backwater town in New Manilla around twenty-four years, three months ago, when Oriol walked into an NMLF boobytrap and lost his leg. Right down to the retro *sambusao* beats coming out of the club.

He acknowledges the memory, lets it pass on.

The room's just big enough for luggage and a bed,

which is just big enough for Oriol. It's cramped, but at least it's not a crew bunk on a freighter, which means he might actually get some rest without breathing someone else's recycled snores and gas.

It's the first night in eight months Oriol hasn't had a roommate, first time he's really been alone.

He desperately wishes he wasn't.

This time of night, Manu's probably on his way home. He's probably stopped at Jade's to pick up dinner, if he's remembering to eat. He's probably lining up the toe points of his shoes beside the door, hanging up his suit jacket and flicking lint off the sleeve, pouring himself a precise finger's worth of whiskey, and sitting at the empty kitchen counter to finish up the day's work. He's probably eating straight out of the takeout container so he doesn't have to run the dish sanitizer.

Or maybe he's out with someone.

Oriol didn't expect Manu to wait that first time he hit the road, and he doesn't expect him to, now. The fact that he continues to is marginally baffling, and Oriol understands just how lucky he is to have found someone who will tolerate his wanderlust and still welcome him back every time.

Thing is, luck runs out eventually. He's got the fake leg to prove it.

Oriol hasn't powered up his own comm since he landed — doesn't need it helpfully trying to access the nets and giving away his location. But he's got a certain fifteen digits memorized, provided Manu hasn't changed those.

Oriol's exhausted, but he pulls his boots back on. He remembers seeing a market back on the corner, the sort of place still heating yesterday's roller sausages, selling everything from obscure InstaMeal flavors to throwaway comms.

The cashier's currently sharing a case of beer with a guy in a Bravitzi Delivery uniform, who doesn't break stride in bitching about his boss when Oriol pushes through the door. The cashier waves him quiet and lifts his chin to Oriol.

"What're you looking for, friend?"

"Just here for a shouter." He loves the Fingers slang for the disposable comms, perfectly named for their poor connection quality.

"What color?"

"Surprise me."

The cashier pulls one off the stack at random and tosses it over the counter. It's the exact shade of acid green Manu's manicure had been when they'd met; Oriol wonders what color his nails are today. He takes the shouter with a rueful smile, taps credits from the chit.

The Bravitzi Delivery guy pulls another beer out of the case cracked open at his elbow and pops the top off on the battered counter's edge. He lifts it to Oriol in invitation.

"I'm good." Oriol flashes him a smile of thanks;

getting drunk the night before a gig is a younger man's game.

Bravitzi takes a swig. "No beer? Man, I got something stronger," he says. The cashier gives him a look like, *You dealing in my store?*

Everybody's got something stronger these days, and Oriol almost shrugs him off before he remembers why the harder shit's so ubiquitous. The Dawn. Probably this guy's just the low man dealing, but there's a solid chance he knows something about the organization Oriol doesn't.

"What do you got?"

The cashier's shooing hands at them. "Outside, outside."

Oriol nods in thanks and pockets the shouter; the delivery guy follows him out.

"I got whatever you're looking for," the guy says, his foot barely outside the door.

"Where's it from?"

Bravitzi shrugs. "Same place it all comes from."

"The Dawn."

A look askance at the shadows. No one's around.

"Just asking." Oriol smiles. "Seems I hear their name around a lot lately. Lots of big names involved, yeah?"

"I just know enough not to talk about them. If you're not gonna buy, man. . . ."

"Who's up the chain from you?"

"No way. They listen to everything." Bravitzi turns, but Oriol's quicker, has him up against the wall, his karambit out and the tip pricked against the jugular. The delivery guy's bloodshot eyes go wide.

"Sorry," Oriol says. A single drop of blood traces the line of the delivery guy's throat. His breath is beer-sweet and shard-rot-rank. His heartbeat is thrashing against Oriol's forearm. "But I wasn't asking."

---

Oriol doesn't recognize every name on the list the guy gave him, but he recognizes enough to be nervous. Enough that he doesn't go back to the flophouse.

It's not worries about the delivery guy following for revenge that have him spooked, but what Bravitzi said about the Dawn chills him to the core: *They're everywhere. They own everyone.*

Oriol bins the shouter unused — *They listen to everything* — and thinks about binning his powered-down comm, too. But he's just being paranoid at that point.

Right?

He rents a body locker at the train depot and sleeps like the dead in a rusty bunk the size of a coffin. Wakes ravenous and buys a bowl of ramen from the first food cart he sees, then heads off to meet Nacea and Mel to do some demolitions.

Mel Nehrusitha shows up the same time he does, all muscle and scar tissue, with a snake tattoo wrapped around each golden forearm and the ovaries of steel to wear her sleeves rolled up like she doesn't care who knows she used to run with Zmiya. Twenty, thirty years ago that would have gotten you jumped. But maybe these days anyone who was stung by that mess is dead or has forgotten. Or maybe Mel just doesn't look like the kind of woman you jump.

Nacea notices the tattoos, but if she's got opinions about a long-dead group like Zmiya she keeps them to herself.

By the time they drive out to the desert they've been over the plan at least a dozen times: Get in position early. Watch the guard change and the worker shift end, then head in under cover of dark. Turn off the water, faucet on out back to drain the pipes. A distraction to draw out the guards, then Nacea slips in with Oriol to cover her and Mel at their backs. Break open a couple of dry water tubes, break open a couple of barrels, sneak back out. Turn on the water from a safe distance. Head back to town.

Bonus points for both Nacea and Oriol if they can pick up more intel about the Dawn — she wants to continue hitting them where it hurts, he wants to figure out how to get his hands on Bennion Zacharia before Zacharia comes back after him. Most likely that means swiping one of the guard's comms or, hell, asking questions about supply chain logistics the old fashioned way with an electric barb and a blade.

Nacea's lobbying for the former, Mel wants to see the latter — that old Zmiya love for blood, Oriol suspects. He's happy with whatever's fast and effective.

Oriol likes being in the desert, especially at this

time of the day when the sun's dropping low and the contrast is high, every red pebble edged in black shadow, every ripple in the rock face showing in high resolution. The colors are rich, the fragrances richer as flowers and shrubs unclench from the heat of the day. It's like the whole world is taking a breath, a collective sigh of relief and anticipation: *We made it through another day, what do you think the night will hold?*

It'll hold thrill, violence. A job whose outcome Oriol isn't attached to so long as he gets out of here alive and doesn't get Mel killed by inviting her on a job with an untested backer. And so long as it gets him one step closer to walking the streets of Bulari without a target painted on his back. One step closer to letting Manu know he's back in town and finding out what Manu wants to do about it.

"Hey, Sina."

Oriol's been meditating on the desert for the last twenty minutes, resting muscles and mind before he calls on them to work at full strength. Mel doesn't take to his philosophy, but at least she's not a talker. She's been checking her guns while they wait, each rhythmic snap of bullet into magazine her version of inbreath, outbreath.

Nacea, apparently, doesn't like the silence. Oriol lifts an eyebrow to her.

"You got someone waiting for you at home?" she asks.

"Could be." The phrasing is out before he means it — thinking about Manu has him talking like he's from the Fingers himself. He resists a glance at Mel to see if she's smiling at the slip.

Across from him, Mel snaps another bullet into place. "You're one lucky bastard if he's still waiting," she says. "How long you been out of town this time?"

"Eight months," Oriol says, and Nacea whistles low.

"Damn. So that's a no."

*Snap.* Mel tosses the full magazine to Oriol, starts filling a fresh one. "You'd be shocked," she tells Nacea. "He always has been before."

"'Before?' How many times?" And when Oriol's slow to answer — he honestly can't remember — Nacea shakes her head. "That's a hard ask to make of somebody."

"I don't ask him to do anything."

Nacea makes a face but doesn't push it. She turns to Mel. "How about you?"

But Mel Nehrusitha just lifts her chin to the factory. "Right on time." She snaps the last bullet into place and holds out the magazine to Nacea.

"I'm good," Nacea says.

Mel shakes her head and pockets it. "Thieves," she complains to Oriol.

Right on the hour, a bus is pulling up outside the factory and an unruly column of bedraggled, shard-stoned workers is dripping out. There's about a dozen of them, a wide range of ages from gaunt old men who look like they were swept out of an alleyway to pierced and tattooed kids who probably ran away from home. The security guards are herding them roughly, shouting commands and insults at the workers as they get them onto the bus. One of the kids falls in a stoned daze, struggles to get to his feet again as a security guard's boot connects with his ribs.

Oriol spares Nacea a glance and sees only hard fury in her eyes. That's good.

They wait in silence until the bus pulls away, until an ORV crunches gravel up the road and the guards change shifts. They wait another half hour to let them fall into their pattern. Then Nacea straightens.

"Ready?" she murmurs.

Mel racks a bullet into the chamber of her pistol. Grins.

So far, so good on the plan. Nacea is wearing a fancy thief's night vision kit, lenses in both eyes flickering the faintest blue when you catch them at the right angle, feedback gauntlet on her left arm, high-grip biosilk gloves drinking up the light. Oriol declined her offer to get him an ops lens — he's thoroughly spooked off them after the gig on the *Dorothy Queen*. He'd rather rely on the light of the moon and his trusty firefly swarm as a last resort to give him visibility if he needs it.

Nacea handles shutting down the water main and turning on the drain faucet while Oriol and Mel create a distraction to draw out the guards. Two of them come to see what's up — excellent — and Mel snaps the first one's neck while Oriol grabs the second, hand over his mouth to keep him from crying out. He presses his gun to the man's temple.

"In a few seconds, I'm going to lower my hand," Oriol says in his ear. "Then you're gonna call back to the others that it was just wild dogs. No need for them to come check. You do that, you can go." The man nods against Oriol's palm.

When Oriol lowers his hand, the man's breath comes panting in hot, rancid bursts. "I'm opening a channel," he says as he slowly, unthreateningly reaches for his comms belt. Oriol can't see his hand at this angle, but Mel can, and she gives Oriol a faint nod.

"This is Rael," the security guard says. His voice is carefully calm. "We checked on that disturbance, just a couple of wild dogs got into some garbage. We'll get rid of them. Out."

"Great," says Oriol. He reaches for the electric barb at the security guard's belt, sets it to stun and discharges it into the base of the man's skull. The guard slumps to his knees.

Oriol opens a line to Nacea. "We're good."

While they wait for her to join them, Oriol and Mel drag the stunned security guard to a nearby cement pillar and cuff his arms behind it. Oriol searches his pockets, finds his comm — hopefully jackpot — then powers it down and pockets it.

"If he wakes up, feel free to ask him your way where the other factories are," Oriol says to Mel. "Just keep it quiet."

He sees Nacea coming far before he hears the near-silent scuff of her boots. "Timer's set," she murmurs. She checks the time on her gauntlet. "We've got thirteen minutes, forty-three seconds until the water main turns back on. Let's do this."

Nacea and Oriol don't go in the same way the guards came out. There's another window, she says, it leads straight into the basement and they won't have to worry about running into someone in the hallways. She takes what appears to be a deck of mystix cards from her belt and folds it out into something like a giant spider with bread knives for feet and a suction cup for a body. She positions it over the window, and, with a professional *press-twist-flick* the window is silently out of its frame. She hands the window to Oriol, who leans it against the wall.

They could've just smashed the glass, really. But he supposes in her normal jobs the goal is to get in without causing any damage she can't repair. Jewel thieves are notoriously braggy about being able to pull a baffling locked-room heist.

Here, of course, any evidence of their entry will be blown to dust by the end of the night.

Nacea pulls a state-of-the-art biosilk breathing mask up over the bottom half of her face, gives him a faint nod, then drops effortlessly from the window to the basement floor while Oriol stands guard above. If her intel is right, the guards don't patrol constantly. Instead, they sit around playing cards to keep themselves awake on the night shift, only heading out if there's a disturbance. Or at set times for a routine patrol. They should have at least a few more minutes before somebody wonders why it's taking so long to get rid of wild dogs and comes looking for the pair of guards they took out earlier. Mel is listening in on the downed guards's comms, she'll let them know if the others start making moves.

Oriol's listening at the window, but he doesn't hear much inside. Nothing that would catch his attention — whatever Nacea is doing sounds like the normal clicking and whirring of pipes and machines. If he didn't know she was in there, he might think there was a rat loose in the basement.

Either she's incredibly impressive, or she's been lying to them about why they're here.

"The other guards are trying to check in," Mel says. "How are you guys doing down there?"

"Almost done," Nacea says, her voice sounding muffled through the breathing mask. "One more minute."

Oriol checks the time. That gives them less than five minutes before the water main automatically turns back on and liquid $H_2O$ rushes back to flood the basement and dance an explosive tango with the gaseous anhydrous ammonia Nacea is currently setting free.

"Fall back to cover position Alpha and keep monitoring that channel," Oriol says to Mel. "Nacea, let's move."

"Almost done."

He checks the time again. It's dropped below four minutes, still within a comfortable timeframe. But as soon as it hits two minutes thirty, he's out of here whether Nacea is with him or not; they've already agreed. He's listening intently, but now even the faint rat-in-the-basement sounds he could hear earlier are silent. He counts breaths, scans the horizon.

"Secure in cover position Alpha," Mel says a moment later. "They sent somebody to check on the guards. I don't see you guys."

The clock hits 2:58.

"Nacea," Oriol says. "We're off the timeline. Get your ass up here or we're gone."

For a minute there's no reply, then Nacea's voice comes muffled through the line.

"Coming."

Five seconds later Oriol can see movement in the gloom inside the basement. He recognizes Nacea's neon buns and reaches to help hoist her out. Her thief's black is dusty and smeared with grease, and she's grinning. "Let's go."

Around the corner, someone starts shouting.

"They found the bodies," Mel says unnecessarily. "Where are you guys?"

"Heading to rendezvous Delta," Oriol says, the rendezvous point they've already chosen to go with this particular guards-on-the-move scenario. "Cover us."

It's a balancing act, moving as carefully and stealthily as possible while also knowing that a blast of unknown size is coming less than two minutes from now. And as many times as Nacea has tried to reassure him it won't blow until the water main turns back on,

Oriol knows this isn't an exact science. Every fiber of his being is screaming to get away from this building as quickly as possible before something goes wrong.

Into the night of the desert, and it's not just a matter of not being noticed by the guards. Put your foot in a hole and twist an ankle? Surprise a snake and get a shot of venom into your calf? It's not sugar vipers that are lurking in these shadows, the snakes that live around here don't just make bar neon dance. Oriol reassures himself that at least if he startles something nasty, it's got a fifty-fifty chance of chipping its fangs on the wrong leg.

A shot rings out, spraying sand and grit to Oriol's left.

"Split up," he calls to Nacea, and she darts off to the right, caution forgotten. Another spread of bullets chews up the ground where they were just standing, but it cuts off early with the telltale crack of Mel's rifle. Oriol doesn't bother wasting time looking over his shoulder to see if the guard is down. Mel doesn't shoot to miss.

"Fall back out of the zone," Oriol says to Mel. Nacea has calculated how big the explosion is likely to be, and Oriol added on another fifty percent to the area for good measure. That's the Dead Zone, the area in which they are likely to be flattened just like the building.

"Copy get the fuck out," Mel says. "I'm — hold on. There's more guard chatter coming in."

Oriol can make out the cottonwood snag they

designated as the "beyond the Dead Zone" line for rendezvous Delta. It's less than 100 meters away; they're going to make it easily. He slows a fraction, listening. "What is it, Mel?"

But he sees it before she can tell him, and his stomach drops out.

Shit.

"Guess there's a night shift," Mel says. He can almost hear the shrug in her voice. "Bus is due to arrive right now."

And sure enough, the same bus that just took the last load of workers away from their shift is returning, Oriol can see silhouettes in the windows. A few more seconds and they will drive right into the Dead Zone.

Timing the explosion with the water main isn't like setting a charge. Oriol assumes it'll take a minute for the water to rush back through those pipes and start flooding the basement, but when it does the bus and all the people in it are going to be blown to bits. The security guards took on this job knowing exactly what they were doing, and Oriol doesn't spare a thought for them. Maybe some of the workers did, too. But a lot of them are just going to be stupid kids, who met the wrong friend and took the wrong drug, got into debt to the wrong person. Any one of them could have been Nacea's kid.

"Can you stop it?" he asks Mel.

"Turn around and head back into the zone? Not a chance."

Mel's apparently decided her life is worth more

than a bus full of shard workers, and Oriol doesn't blame her. Maybe there's a distraction, something he can do from a distance to keep them out of the Dead Zone, but still —

Dammit.

To his right, Nacea's sprinting for the bus, unarmed, alone, like she's going to stop it barehanded. Oriol had expected her stupid revenge-brain decision to be something more along the lines of being too vicious in taking out a guard and giving away their position. Not sacrificing herself for a busload of stoned shard factory workers.

"Get to safety, both of you," he says.

With his prosthetic leg, he's going to be way faster than Nacea. He races back the other direction, catches up with her easily and shouts for her to get out. Vaults a low wall and lands close enough to throw his firefly drone pod at the bus with all his might. It shatters against the windshield and the bus lurches to the side as the tiny glow lights swarm out. They won't hurt anyone, but the distraction gets the driver to slow. Oriol takes aim — one shot, two — and the driver slumps halfway out of his chair as he's reaching for his own rifle. The bus slows to a crawl, the weight of the driver's body pulling the controls to the right so it veers slowly, excruciatingly into a ditch to tip over.

"Get out and run," Nacea yells to the workers — she's just behind him, having ignored his order to head for cover. She pushes past him to help.

Oriol's grip on her arm is steel.

"We're in the buffer," he says; she's trying to pull away. "They might still be protected by the bus this far out, but you and me? Out in the open?"

Her eyes are wide.

"You can't avenge your daughter if you're dead."

A heartbeat more, and Nacea nods.

They run.

Another spray of bullets chews up the hillside along the road, pelting them with debris, and this time Oriol does look back to see the last security guard sprinting after them. Oriol returns fire; the man stumbles, then raises his assault rifle again.

The explosion is so deafening it's almost silent, the concussion of pressure taking the breath from Oriol's lungs — even this far past the edge of the Dead Zone. The bus rocks violently, tilting with a shriek of metal as though it's going to roll before settling back onto its side once more.

Nacea has her hands over her ears and a look of wonder on her face.

"Holy shit, it worked," she whispers.

"It definitely worked." Oriol coughs to get his lungs working once more. "Mel, come in."

She's on the channel in a breath. "I'm all good. What's your twenty?"

"We're on the road out."

"Perfect. I'll be right there."

The sun's rising well over the desert by the time they get back into town.

Nacea slumps in the passenger seat, hands draped

over her knees, blood running down her cheek and grinning like a goddess. "I think we got it," she says. "Did you guys get any intel?"

"I snagged one of the comms," Oriol says. "But I haven't had a chance to take a look." He pulls it out now, but either the battery is dead or it was triggered to go dark at the destruction of the security network, because now it won't turn back on.

"We'll get it some juice and see if we can get anything out of it," Nacea says.

"Guy woke up after a minute," Mel says with a satisfied smile. "I got addresses of three other places he guards."

"That's great," Nacea says. She's got that post-gig manic exhaustion stretching a grin across her face. "That's really fucking great. Let's get back to my place, I'll get you guys the rest of your fee, and we can talk about doing something like this again. That is, if you two are up for it."

"I'm in," says Mel. She swerves them around a pothole, shifts down to take a run at a steep hill. "That was good times."

Nacea rolls her head to look over at Oriol. "How about you, Sina?"

For Oriol, it depends. Will the intel on this security guard's comm help him shake the Dawn target painted on his back so he can head home without dragging trouble to Manu? Will he even have a place to stay once he does make contact?

Oriol quirks his lips to the side, thinking. "Gotta get some stuff figured first."

"No problem. Where'd you sleep last night? Flophouse?"

"Bodylocker at the train depot."

"God. You smell like it. You can use my shower while we get this comm repaired and charged up. And if you want we can start planning the next gig. Or head on to the next thing." Nacea shrugs. "All the same to me."

"I'll take that shower and let's get that comm powered on. Then we can talk."

---

The comm is blinking on the kitchen counter when Oriol gets out of the shower. Mel and Nacea are hunched over the coffee table, looking excited and putting pins on a map of Bulari.

Oriol's clean, but he doesn't have anything to wear but the stained fatigues and old T-shirt he stole from the maintenance locker. They still reek, but not much he can do about that until he gets back to his old closet or buys some new ones. And since he'd rather wear these than go through the hell of shopping, this is what he's got.

He helps himself to one of the chewy freeze-dried calzones Nacea's run through the rehydrator and settles in to boot up the comm.

It starts chiming insistently with a red alert, but

that seems to be an incoming message, not a security thing.

"Shut that thing up," Nacea says.

"Working on it."

The comm's a mass security model, locked but with an easy soft reset sequence Oriol figures out quickly enough. He gnaws on another calzone while he waits for the dead guard's messages to load. He opens the most recent one — the one that keeps chiming like crazy.

"Thank you," Nacea says. "Anything good?"

The message is a note about an attack on a Dawn facility last night, with instructions to bring in the perpetrators.

"Looks like they're caught on to us. There's a . . ." Oriol trails off as he scrolls through the message, frowning at first in confusion, then with a chill. The calzone tastes like ash.

Nacea frowns at him; she peels herself from the couch to perch on one of the stools beside him. "What's wrong?"

And her eyes widen.

Couched in all the religious language is the level of punishment that will be meted out on the perpetrators. Break their bones, rend their flesh, debase them, use them, bring them to their knees. But bring them in alive to face the test of purity — this is the order of your prophet.

"Huh," says Nacea, but she doesn't look worried — her eyebrows are drawing together in confusion.

Because it's not her and him and Mel that Bennion Zacharia's so pissed about. They may have leveled one of the Dawn's most prolific shard manufacturing centers a few hours back, but apparently theirs wasn't the worst attack against the Dawn last night.

No.

The names and images on this all-unit bulletin of torture and mayhem are some of the only people in this world Oriol cares about. Manu Juric. Toshiyo Ravi. Starla Dusai. Willem Jaantzen.

"Who the fuck are they?" Nacea asks.

Oriol powers down the comm and shoves it into his pocket. "Friends," he says. "I'll send you everything I find on this that'll help you, and give me a call if you're doing this again. But I gotta go."

# HOLIDAY

*"Holiday" is a short story set just after the events of* Kill Shot. *I wrote it in part because after the emotional roller coaster of the Bulari Saga, I figured my characters needed a break — and so did I.*

*This story also answers the question I ask in* Negative Return *when Manu and Oriol first meet: will they ever go on that vacation?*

*The answer is yes.*

*And, to the shock of no one, Manu is extremely bad at vacations.*

*Enjoy!*

*One note: I grew up in the heart of hop country in Washington State. My dad didn't farm hops, but we had neighbors who did, and I was fascinated by the hop kilns and the whole process — so unlike the hay and wheat I grew up helping my dad harvest.*

*When I moved to the city and started working at the Elysian Brewing Company, I laughed to hear Dick Cantwell and the other brewers talking reverently about trips to the Lower Yakima Valley to meet with hop farmers. And as the region's wine tourism blossomed, I kept meeting people who gushed about their vacations there.*

*I grew up wanting to get away from the valley, but suddenly I was surrounded by people who thought my hometown was some kind of paradise.*

*I may live in and write about the city now, but I couldn't resist writing a fantasy version of my home soil into this story.*

*Complete with a hop kiln.*

---

"You're going to gouge out one of my eyes, and I get to choose which one," Manu Juric says. "That's what you're telling me."

"Not what I said at all." Oriol Sina doesn't look up from swiping through options on the hotel room's desk. "What I said was, 'I'm going to book a river cruise, would you prefer tomorrow or the day after.'"

"But you're telling me the river cruise is non-negotiable."

"Yes."

Manu twitches the hotel room's curtain back into place, satisfied with the sight lines and the inactivity in the garden below. "The day after."

Oriol leans back in his chair, legs stretched out and comfortable, watching as Manu tugs out the cushion from the other armchair to check for . . . weapons, surveillance devices, whatever passes for danger in an Alusinian hotel.

"You're hedging your bets," Oriol says.

"Am not."

"Hoping there will be some catastrophe between now and two days from now and we'll have to go back to Bulari."

Manu drops the cushion back in place, having found nothing but lint. "I'm not hoping for a catastrophe."

"Liar. You've been crawling up the walls since we checked in."

"Catastrophe's a strong word."

"Time to resign yourself to your fate." Oriol turns his attention back to the local entertainment options, ignoring Manu's glare. "Your man's not going to call you back. I overheard him talking to a certain someone about how he'd sent you here to relax, and he expected you to stay here at least a week."

"Talking to Phaera?"

"Talking to you, babe. I was standing right next to

you when he said — and I quote — 'Go take care of this thing, then take a week or two and unwind. I hear Alusina is gorgeous this time of year.' Do you want to tour a sheep farm?"

"No. Do you?"

"Nah." Oriol runs a hand through his shaggy bronze hair. "They've got everything taken care of back there. Say a prayer of thanks the most pressing thing the man needs from you these days is to meet with a hops supplier in a beautiful place with a river."

"I'm sure it's lovely."

"And I am going to find every one of the local swimming holes. Stop pacing, you're making me crazy."

Manu sighs and throws himself down on the hotel bed, staring up at the unfamiliar ceiling texture. It's pristine, spotless, like everything else in the rather nice hotel room Oriol chose for them. The bed surprises him with its comfort; last time he slept away from his own bed in years was in the Maraka Valley deathtrap, and those cots were hardly designed with proper spinal support in mind.

"You ever swam in a river?" Oriol asks, like the answer could possibly be yes. Manu lifts his head enough to give him an incredulous look. "Seriously no?"

"You don't know what's in there."

"Fish, Manu. There's fish in the river." Oriol tilts his head, realizing. "You can't swim, can you."

"Where would I find a river to learn in?" It's case

closed to Manu, but Oriol seems to expect an explanation. "What, were they supposed to teach us in school?
Maybe I skipped that day."

"Skipped that year, more like."

"Learned everything I needed to."

"Then tell me this. Why the hell did they build the
capital of New Sarjun in the middle of a wasteland,
when there's a perfectly good river valley right down
here?"

"Mining." Manu may not have sat through a
history class, but he's read enough plaques on monu-
ments during the inevitable downtime waiting around
on jobs. "Richest mineral veins were around the Bulari
area, made the most sense to build the spaceport there.
Early settlers were shipping goods in, not trying to
grow their own food. And eventually the government
structures all got built there."

"And now the population of the entire city is as
ornery as a dust storm."

"I'm not ornery."

"Here's my idea. We go read by the pool for a
couple of hours, then walk through the neighborhood.
Visit some galleries. Have dinner. That sort of thing."

Manu rolls his head to stare at his husband in
disbelief. "Reading by the pool? I thought the point
was to get away from work."

"I find reading relaxing." Oriol says it like he's
explaining it to a child; his patience is obviously
wearing thin. "What would you find relaxing?"

Manu has no goddamned idea. But twenty plus

years with Oriol has taught him that tone — it means he's running the risk of pushing one too many of Oriol's buttons. He forces himself to breathe deep, tries to imagine the breath reaching his toes or whatever it's supposed to do. Pretends it makes him feel less tense.

"I would watch you read by the pool," Manu finally says. "Will you be working on your tan, too?"

Oriol's smile tugs to the side. "If it helps you unwind."

"I think it would."

"Then I'll work on my tan." Oriol flicks to a different page on the desk. "For the galleries — don't make that sound, I know you like art."

"Yeah, but they'll make you put your shirt on if we go to a gallery."

Oriol scrolls down, ignoring him. "There's a Davica Siobhani exhibit. All new work."

Manu pushes himself up on his elbows. "Really?"

"There we go. I knew my Fingers boy had at least one sophisticated bone in his body." Oriol stands and grabs his book. "Ready?"

"I was told this was a shirts-off activity."

Oriol's fingers catch the hem of his shirt, peel it over his head in one fluid motion to reveal sculpted golden abs and a wicked, bone-white scar scrawled low along his hipbone. "Shirt's off. And I have my own request: No comms."

"What if he needs — "

"Your man don't need anything, Manu. And if he does, it can wait."

Manu hesitates, then finally drops his comm on the bedside table. And snatches it back up when it chimes a split second later. He frowns at the screen, not understanding.

"What is it?"

"The deal is off," Manu says. "Deal. Is. Off. No explanation. The seller knows we came all the way from Bulari. Knows who their buyer is. And they're cutting off the deal without giving me a reason?"

He cracks his neck; Oriol takes a deep, calming breath, probably imagining the breath reaching his toes.

Manu grins. "Let's go see what the trouble is."

---

Manu's been in a lot of warehouses in his day, but opening the door to this one greets him with a hot, damp blast of some verdant aroma that makes him choke. It feels like he's drowning. For all he hears people raving about the good humidity does for your skin, turns out Manu is not a fan.

"What the fuck is that smell?" Manu yells over the sound of engines.

Oriol inhales deeply, content. "Hops," he yells back. "It smells green."

"It's suffocating."

"Someday I'm going to get you off this rock and take you to the forests around where I grew up."

"I'll hate it."

"And I'll enjoy watching you hate it. We can go for a hike."

"Sounds claustrophobic."

"It's incredible."

The warehouse is divided into two long halves; the half they entered is open to the roof, the cement floor obscured by a drift of leaf debris. To their left, a cement wall rises halfway up the height of the warehouse, forming a lofted area where giant mechanical arms are pouring and spreading a cascade of brilliant green hops. A series of doors in the wall are labeled Danger: Furnace. Do Not Enter.

Between the drone of the furnace fans, the grinding of the mechanical arms, and the paper rustling of the hops laid out to dry with air forced through them, Manu can't hear his own thoughts.

He leads, knowing Oriol's got his back and keeping up the banter even as they scan the building. Manu wants the buyer to know they're coming, but he's not about to walk into a trap.

Unless someone's hiding in the furnaces or buried in the hops, though, only two people are in the entire building — both in dusty navy jumpsuits and monitoring a flow of what must be dried hops into a massive bin at the far end. One of them breaks off their conversation when she sees Manu and Oriol approaching. Manu waves a friendly arm and she lifts a hand to tell them to wait.

A moment later, she switches off the stream of dried hops, checks something on a monitor, then gives the other person a thumbs-up. As she climbs down from the platform, the other person hits a switch. A plunger screeches down into the measure of hops.

Oriol yells something over the noise.

"What?"

"Maybe we can get a tour," he yells again. "Be good intel for you, now that you're getting into the farming business."

Manu shakes his head. "The boss and Tosh are getting into the farming business," he corrects. "I'm staying in the enforcing business."

Speaking of, it's showtime. Vacation is a nice idea, but give him a problem to solve any day. The woman approaching them is wary, but not afraid. She pulls down her ear protectors when the screeching stops, then pushes her safety glasses up onto her unruly black bun, leaving dusty streaks on her brown skin. "Can I help you?" she shouts over the rush of air, engines, machinery.

"We're here to see Lex Amalfi about the shipment."

Her jaw tenses. "I told your people three days. Hops only dry so fast."

"If it were just a delay, I wouldn't be worried," Manu says. "But I'm hearing we flew all the way from Bulari only to have Lex cancel our deal."

At the mention of Bulari, the woman's eyes widen; she thought she was talking to someone else. Manu slips his hands into his pockets, easy, and her gaze flickers to the flash of his shoulder holster.

"So I'd like to talk to Lex."

She takes a deep breath. "I'm Lex," she finally says. "Which means you're . . . "

"Manu Juric, I work for Willem Jaantzen. My husband, Oriol."

"A pleasure, ma'am," Oriol says.

The worry in her dark eyes lessens when Oriol speaks; he's exuding friendly charm, perfectly disarming and sweet, like he couldn't have her on the ground faster than she — or Manu — could react. But it's not just Oriol putting her at ease. The body language Manu sensed before she realized he was with the Bulari buyer has changed. She's steeling herself for a hard conversation, sure, but she's no longer afraid.

Seems like Manu's the tip of the iceberg of Lex Amalfi's problems today.

She shouts something at the person up on the platform before ushering Manu and Oriol out of the warehouse. The air in the adjacent building is a cool and comfortable relief after the fury of the hop kiln. It appears to be an office, the unruly mess of paperwork and charts all covered in a thin layer of grit — and not from disuse. Manu can feel the farm's dust caking his skin, coating his teeth.

Lex crosses behind the desk like she's glad to have it between her and the two men. "I'm sorry, gentlemen," she says. "I hoped you'd get my message early enough that you wouldn't have to come all the way out here."

Manu brushes dust off a chair and lounges into it,

Oriol leans against the doorframe. Lex looks between them once more, then sits gingerly in her own desk chair.

Something's wrong.

Manu's making her nervous, but he's not what's terrifying her, which means either she has no idea who he is, or something much worse is waiting in the wings.

"I'm so sorry you came all the way out here," Lex is saying. "The refund should have gone through."

"You approached us with the deal," Manu says. "Why?"

Lex swallows. "We've done a good local business, but we can't scale in Alusina. We need a strong buyer in Bulari, and when I read Phaera D's partner was opening a brewery, I saw opportunity."

"And then you realized who your buyer was and backed out?"

The look on her face says she has no clue. "I don't really follow Bulari gossip." She clears her throat. "But this season's harvest has been spoken for. I'm sorry for all the trouble. I can make some connections with other growers, but it might be — I'll make some connections."

"It might be what."

"It might be hard to find anyone with product that hasn't been sold yet." It's an obvious lie; Lex stands and takes a step towards the door, obviously meaning to dismiss them. She hesitates when neither man moves.

"You don't know who I am?" Manu leans forward, elbows on knees. Lex's gaze rakes over the scars on his left hand and she shakes her head. "And you don't know who my boss is."

"I know he's well-known." Her pulse is rapid in the hollow of her throat. "He seems to be respected, and he was prompt in his payment. Look, I'm sorry this didn't work out."

"If you'd looked into my boss, you'd know he's not the kind of person who goes back on his word. But you're telling me you are."

"You can't predict the harvest."

"Seems like your harvest is fine."

"It's already spoken for. I'm sorry. I want you to go."

Manu leans back in the chair, crosses one ankle over his knee. Settling in. "Sit back down, Lex."

She sinks back into her chair.

"Figure you'd know your harvest was spoken for before I flew all the way out here. So I want to know. What happened this morning to change your mind?"

"They were right," Lex says through clenched teeth. "You Bulari types are all the same. Coming out in an expensive suit to intimidate us into selling out at starvation rates." Anger flares through the fear. "This is my livelihood. My business."

"We can renegotiate the deal. The man will pay fair rates."

"It's not about the money. I need you to go."

"Lex." Manu keeps his tone soft. Leans forward once more; her gaze is filled with fury, but he's the witness, not the target. "What'll they do to you if you tell me?"

"They'll burn my farm to the ground." A single crystal tear glistens on her dark lashes. She scrapes it away with an unvarnished nail, glares at Manu like she's daring him to comment.

"Not if we burn through them first," Oriol says from the doorway.

And there it is: that first tentative spark of hope. Lex turns to Oriol like a drowning woman to a raft.

"You said we'd have a hard time making connections with another grower," Manu says. "Because they've all been told the same thing as you? Don't do business with anyone from Bulari?" He guesses wrong to see if she'll correct him and confirm his suspicion.

"Not Bulari," she says. "They said not to sell to your boss, specifically."

"You do business with Willem Jaantzen, he doesn't hang you out to dry," Manu says. "They gave you an ultimatum, but I'm giving you options. Call off this deal and we walk away, no hard feelings — though you'll never do business in Bulari again. Or? You tell us who out here has it in for my boss and we take care of them. Let you run things your own way."

"It's not that simple. And it's my business on the line if things go wrong."

"You gonna go to the cops?"

Lex shakes her head slowly.

"You gonna live with their ultimatum?"

Lex breathes deep. Lifts her chin.

"Then tell me what happened."

———

"Your man got any local enemies in Alusina?"

They're docking back at the hotel in their hired spinner, a flashy silver Tifani Blade that definitely helped Manu relax as he carved up the country roads on their way back from Lex Amalfi's farm. Manu pats the dash fondly when he cuts the engine.

"Not that I know of." He's been racking his brain, but he can't think of a single bit of trouble Jaantzen's gotten into down here. And Lex hadn't been all that helpful once he finally got her to talk. She didn't know the men who came to bully her into dropping her deal with Jaantzen, and she had no clue what the local crew scene might be. "Could be someone with a grudge retired here, though."

He pulls himself out of the driver's seat, grins at Oriol over the roof of the Blade.

"At least you seem more relaxed," Oriol says.

"Sorry the pool reading got interrupted."

Oriol sighs. "But you'll get a chance to have a dust-up with the local color. What would a vacation be without that?"

"No idea." Manu gives the Blade one final affectionate look before stepping into the bright afternoon light. The spinner docks are on the other side of the gardens from the hotel rooms, and the place between Manu's shoulder blades itches as they make their way through. Oriol's strolling, his deliberately casual pace catching Manu up short like a rope around his throat.

"That is literally true," Oriol says. "You have no idea what a vacation is. This is the first time I've managed to get you away from work."

"Maybe it's a practice," Manu says. "Like you say about meditation — it's not about are you meditating correctly, it's about the practice of sitting with your thoughts."

"How nice, he listens."

"I am practicing vacation."

"There *is* a wrong way to vacation."

"And I'm choosing the fun way." Manu pulls out his comm. "Gotta make a call to someone who might know the lay of the land."

Oriol settles on a bench framed by an enormous flowering wisteria while the connection request makes its attempt; Manu paces the meandering brick path in front of him. Twinkling hologram birds flitter around them — Manu can't decide if they're charming or obnoxious. After a long moment, a voice he hasn't heard in a decade comes over the line.

"Who is this?"

"Gabi? You got a sec? It's Manu Juric. I'm in town and I have a couple questions."

A sharp breath in, and for a minute he thinks Gabi Durham, the city of Bulari's long-retired chief medical examiner, will hang up.

She finally clears her throat. "You here on business or pleasure?"

"A bit of both. Can you meet up?" Oriol makes an irritated noise; Manu tosses him a wink. "Doesn't need to be a big thing. How about at the Davica Siobhani exhibit? Twenty minutes?"

"Fine."

Manu cuts the connection and slips his comm back in his pocket with a grin at Oriol. "See? Galleries. It's vacation."

It's a short walk from the hotel to the gallery through Alusina's charming downtown grid. Every block is perfectly measured and square, every sidewalk swept free of debris, the paint jobs all bright and clean and not scoured by sand and sun. It could be the set of every syrupy romantic comedy, and Manu has to stop himself from kicking walls to see if there's anything behind them.

They find the gallery easily; Durham's already there, studying a painting with one eye on the door. She doesn't make a sign when she sees Manu enter.

Manu has a piece from Siobhani's early career hanging in his office, an etching he bought on a whim because it appealed to him in some primal way he still can't put his finger on. The etching's composition is weighted at the bottom, giving it a heavy feel, the lines brambled there, clawing and dark. Things get more serene as the lines climb, the brambles falling away. Hope in a tangled world, it seems to say.

Siobhani's newer work is cleaner, but Manu's glad to see the artist's honed her skill without dulling the edges of her tempestuous subject matter. The colors are less tentative — maybe verging on the border of garish, but really Siobhani just seems more confident in what she's able to get away with.

And more confident in her ability to sell — Manu glances at the price tag of the painting Durham is looking at and lets out a low whistle. "Good for her," he says.

"Siobhani is an acquired taste, I think," Durham says.

"Isn't all art?"

"I suppose so."

Durham turns to study him. She hasn't changed much since her retirement. A few more lines in her face and she's let her hair go steel, but she's keeping herself fit, and her no-nonsense glare is as formidable as ever.

"Are you still living a life of crime?" she asks Manu.

He shrugs. "I don't think so? You might have heard the man saved the world a few months back, so I think I'm one of the good guys now. Oriol, this is Gabi Durham, she was medical examiner in Bulari until she retired a few years ago. Gabi, my husband Oriol."

Durham shakes Oriol's hand. "It's a pleasure to meet you," she says. "I've read so much about you in your partner's file."

"I don't have my own file?" Oriol asks.

Durham tilts her head. "Do you need your own file?"

"No, ma'am."

"Glad to hear it." She turns back to the painting, frowning at the thick, stylized strokes. "Now tell me. To what do I owe this pleasure?"

"The man's starting a brewery."

"Sounds very normal."

"Totally clean. A very respectable business."

"I'm sure."

"Thing is, we're looking to secure a hops connect with one of your local farmers, but she pulled the deal at the last minute. Went to pay her a visit" — he holds up his hands at Durham's sharp glance — "a cordial visit to see what the problem is. Turns out you've got a group of toughs playing at being in a turf war with the man and they shut down the deal. Said they'd burn down her farm if she sold to my boss."

"And you can't go to another supplier because the toughs will target them, too."

"Exactly."

"And you think I can do what, exactly? I'm retired."

"I bet you keep your ear to the ground."

"If it's information you want, I have no problem giving you that. There are a few pockets of corrupted youth with too much time on their hands here, but Alusina didn't have an organized crime problem. At least until a Bulari boy named Traval rolled into town last year."

Manu glances at Oriol; Durham catches it.

"You know him." It's a statement, not a question.

"He may have tangled with the man a while back,"

Manu says. "I kept an eye on him for a bit, lost track of him eventually. So he ended up here — very sorry to hear it."

"He seems to fancy himself a little warlord. I moved here to get away from that sort."

Manu gives her a faux-wounded look. "To get away from me? I thought we were friends."

"You left your fair share of bodies in my morgue, Mr. Juric."

"You don't have any proof of that." It's true, even if she hadn't had financial incentive to say otherwise.

"No, I don't. Though I'm honestly amazed I retired before finding you on my slab. I would've bet my savings on it."

Oriol laughs. "I've learned to never bet against Manu, ma'am."

"Traval," Manu says. "Local authorities haven't done anything about him?"

"He's going by an alias, and so far he hasn't done anything illegal they can prove."

"I got all the proof I need to deal with him."

Durham holds up a hand. "You can't talk like that in front of me."

"You're retired, Gabi. You got an obligation to report me if I make your little town a bit more livable by taking out the trash?" When she doesn't answer, Manu smiles. "Where do I find him?"

"I don't know that. I try not to pay much attention to these things."

"Losing your edge in retirement," Manu teases.

"I'm relaxing. It's nice." Durham smiles wryly. "Though I did notice you're being followed."

"I saw them," Oriol says; Manu did, too. A pair of young toughs in Bulari street fashion are loitering in the doorway to the gallery. "Those our guys?"

"I don't know." Durham turns to admire another painting. "But it's probably time for you to go. Give my regards to your employer."

"Will do."

The toughs melt out of the doorway when they see Manu and Oriol coming, fall into step a non-discreet distance behind them as they stroll the pedestrian street.

"Just the two of them, yeah?" Manu asks Oriol, who nods. "Good. Hold on."

He pulls out his comm and puts through a connection. "Hey, Tosh?" He can make out the throb of a heavy beat behind her.

"You know what time it is here?" Toshiyo Ravi asks.

"Two in the morning." Manu studies the window display for a cheese shop; in the reflection the toughs are still behind him. "Why. Were you sleeping?"

"No. How's your vacation?"

"It's getting fun."

"You're in trouble, you mean." Toshiyo yawns. "What do you need?"

"You remember Traval? I need everything you can get on him. Turns out he ended up in Alusina, and he's getting in the way of our deal."

"Yeah, okay. I'll see what I can do."

"Thanks, Tosh."

"Remember to have fun," Toshiyo says, and cuts the connection.

Oriol lifts an eyebrow at him.

"I am having fun," Manu says defensively. "Aren't you having fun?"

"You're taking me out to a very nice night on the town when this is all done."

"I swear."

"And hiking the Calata Canyon trail."

"Fine."

"And swimming in that river."

Manu frowns. "We'll see."

"You and I are getting in that river," Oriol says. He stops, leaning one shoulder against an ornate streetlight. "You want backup for your shoot-out shenanigans or not?"

"You wouldn't dare."

Oriol shrugs.

"You'd leave the love of your life to the mercy of local hoodlums all because he refuses to get in a river?"

"Yes."

"That's cold, babe."

Oriol waits. Over his shoulder, the toughs are pretending to be interested in a restaurant menu.

Finally, Manu sighs. "I will swim. Or wade, or whatever. But if I drown I'm haunting you for the rest of your life."

"I won't let you drown."

"Or get eaten."

"Or get eaten."

"Deal," Manu says. He leans in for a kiss. "I'll see you back at the hotel," he says, too loud; the toughs clock it.

"Be back for dinner," Oriol calls, and heads down a side alley.

The toughs are bolder with Oriol out of the picture, whether they know to be afraid of him or just prefer their new odds of two to one. Manu leads them another couple of blocks to be sure they're alone, then hangs a left beside a candy shop swarming with tourist children and psychedelic-colored drifts of sugar.

He gets a comfortable way down the alley before stopping to check a message on his comm. Footsteps, deliberately approaching. Manu glances over his shoulder; the toughs are grinning at him like they won the lottery. The closer one's tall and blond, with a nose like a hatchet though he's still got that youthful chubbiness in his cheeks. The other's wearing bold paisley and too much gold, though none of it's the real thing.

"Can I help you gentlemen?" Manu asks.

"Here to give you a message," Nose says. Behind him, Paisley grins. "Time to get out of Alusina."

Manu laughs. "You know who I am?"

Paisley's shrug is exaggerated, nonchalant. "Def, man." The affected Fingers accent ghosts over his soft Alusinian lilt, fake as his gold necklace.

Manu matches the kid's faux-casual pose, sees

uncertainty creep into his expression. "Not sure you do. I need to talk to Traval."

"Don't think you get it," Nose says. "He talks to you. And he says it's time for you to go home, man. Or else."

"Or else?"

Paisley reaches for him, but he's on his back before even Manu catches what's happening; Nose is on his knees with one arm behind his back, groaning in agony as Oriol puts pressure on his wrist.

"Tell me," Manu says, pistol in his scarred left hand aimed at Paisley's head. Paisley's eyes widen at the whine as it warms to Manu's hand.

"We know you went to see her, man," Nose gasps. "Traval told us to take care of you."

"Really?" Manu shakes his head. "What'd you do to piss him off, he sends you on a suicide mission."

"Wasn't supposed to be suicide," Paisley wheezes. He's frozen on his back, shaking hands shielding his face like they'll stop a bullet. "We were just supposed to watch."

"Watch and report back?"

Paisley nods fervently. "Keep you busy."

Manu doesn't miss the warning look Nose shoots him. "Keep us busy why?" Manu can guess the answer; cold realization is seeping through his chest.

Oriol barely moves when neither boy answers, but Nose's scream of agony echoes through the alley. "To teach that bitch a lesson," he sobs.

Shouting, footsteps running to the mouth of the

alley; the coast has been clear until now, but Manu holsters his gun and Oriol releases Nose's wrist as the security guards appear around the corner. Both of the young toughs stay cowering in place.

"You got a tourist-mugging problem in Alusina?" Manu calls to the guards. "These kids tried to rob my husband and me."

He's braced for suspicion, but the first security guard ignores him. Jabs a finger at Paisley. "Your grandma's going to be furious when she finds out," he says, then turns to Nose. "And you're not going to be able to talk your way out of this one and keep your job at the bank. You two gentlemen all right?"

Manu buttons his suit jacket over his holster. "We're fine." He cocks a thumb at Oriol. "Didn't know they'd be running into a veteran."

"Idiot kids." The guard shakes his head.

"Do you need a statement?" Manu's desperate to get going. If what they said is true, Lex is in trouble.

"Tried to mug you," the guard says, like it's all the proof he needs. Manu might be starting to like Alusina. "And we got a couple calls earlier from shop owners who said these two have been a nuisance to other customers all day."

"We're staying at the Meloda Hotel if you have any questions for us."

"Enjoy the rest of your stay," the guard says. "And I apologize for the trouble."

"No problem at all."

Manu manages to keep his gait casual until they're

out of view of the guards, then breaks into a jog, Oriol at his side. He opens a connection to Lex, curses when it doesn't go through. Tries again.

When she answers, she sounds breathless. "Sorry, I was on the other end of the kiln," she says. "What is it?"

So they're not there yet. Still, Manu picks up the pace. "Call the police," he says. "We caught wind they're coming back to see you. You're in danger."

"I can't call the police. They'll find out."

"They already know you talked to us, Lex. Call for help. We're on our way."

He skids to a halt beside the Tifani Blade and has the engine revving even before Oriol's in the passenger seat.

———

A dark plume of smoke is threading its way into the horizon, and Manu's got the Blade pinned as fast as these country roads will let him go. He drums his fingers on the controls, leans into a corner; Oriol's swearing beside him, but it's not at his driving. He's been trying to raise Lex for the past ten minutes with no response.

Manu's comm chimes and he patches it through the Blade's system.

"Tosh?"

"You busy?"

"Will be soon. What's up?"

"Tracked down Traval. He's been using an assumed name in Alusina, which is maybe why the local authorities didn't connect him with Bulari's wanted lists. But his security is sloppy — didn't take me long to compile a whole avalanche of evidence on what he's been up to."

"Can you get into the Alusina police's comms?"

"Um, yeah? Why?" He can hear the faint clicking of her fingernails as she types. "Are you in trouble?"

"Our seller is. Told her to call them, but I don't know if she did. Can't get ahold of her now."

He skids the Blade onto the turnoff from the main road, dust roiling up behind him as he leaves the pavement behind. Any hope the smoke is unrelated to today's troubles evaporates. The plume is coming from behind the hop kiln, near the office.

"I'm in," Toshiyo says. "Police are on their way, which means you should get out of there."

"Copy that," Manu says, and cuts the connection. He slides the Blade around the corner of the hop kiln to find a trio of ORVs and a half-dozen toughs standing back and watching the blaze, which is indeed licking up the side of Lex's office. A few others are away from the main group, adhering what are unmistakably detonation charges to the side of the fuel tank.

Normally Manu'd appreciate some fireworks, but not when he *just* promised Lex they'd stop these assholes from burning her livelihood to the ground. Manu swears under his breath and slams on the brakes, wrenches the controls, takes the Blade into a sliding arc that barely misses the fuel tank — the toughs climbing on its side scream as they jump for cover, detonators in hand. Manu lets out a whoop as the Blade comes to a stomach-churning stop, spares a grin to meet Oriol's look of resignation, then pushes open the spinner door into a cloud of dust.

As the dust blows past it reveals the pair of pyro-maniacs duck-and-covering on the far end of the fuel tank. Their eyes widen in fear when they realize they're staring down the barrel of Manu's gun.

"Drop the detonators and run," he orders.

They do.

Oriol's sprinting towards the main crew at the office fire; Manu can barely make out screams above the crackling of the flames and the shouts of the toughs taking shelter behind their ORVs. As he sprints through the dust and smoke, though, he can see Lex Amalfi struggling in the grip of two young men.

Manu wings the first one, and Lex rips her arm free of the second in his surprise. And runs straight into the flaming doorway of her office.

Manu charges after her, pulling out his comm as he does.

"Tosh!" he yells over the sound of crashing timber. "I need — "

"I know," Toshiyo says. "I'm in. They switched off the fire suppression, but I can remote override. She's in the control room, first left."

She cuts the line.

Manu crouches low to avoid the smoke, trying to

get his bearings. Earlier today, they'd come in through the door to the hop kiln, which means the office must be at the far end of this hall. First left is the control room, Toshiyo had said, and sure enough, the door is open. It seems to be the source of the fire: thick, toxic black smoke pours through the door.

"Lex!" Manu calls. He can't see anything through the deadly haze; someone's coughing, but it could be coming from anywhere. He pulls his shirt up to cover his mouth and nose. Fiery heat radiates from beyond the black smoke, and he crouches and tries to breathe shallow, eyes watering against the fumes, nostrils and throat burning.

He flings out an arm and singes his hand against hot metal. Tries again — swipes air.

*"Lex!"*

Another sweep of his arm, and now he's coughing too hard — he can't stay here. He grits his teeth, furious, and takes one more step.

His foot hits something soft.

Manu drops to his knees and his hands bury themselves in rough fabric, a jumpsuited body, thick mess of a bun. He grabs Lex under the arms and pulls with all his might, dragging her out of the control room and into the relative cool of the hallway. She's alive, half helping him, half fighting him. She breaks free once they're in the hallway, doubling over and coughing weakly.

"Lex. Get up." Manu crouches beside her as she manages to get to her hands and knees, pulls her arm over his shoulder.

"The system," she rasps. "Have to turn it on. Stop — "

"We've got it." Manu hauls her to her feet, and as he says it, Toshiyo is good for her word. A warning siren sounds above the roar of the fire, and soft, cool foam begins to spray from above. Manu keeps Lex tight to his side even as her feet slip in the foam. Propels them both forward through the door and into the sweet, fresh air.

The person who takes her from him is wearing protective gear. New lights are flashing from official-looking vehicles. Someone in a face shield is yelling is there anyone else in there, and Manu shakes his head. "Don't think so," he says. They're trying to get him to sit down, trying to press something over his nose and mouth — oxygen, he thinks — but he waves them away, searching the scene for Oriol.

A pair of police vehicles and a fire response truck have surrounded the three ORVs Traval's crew arrived in; in the truck, a tech is directing a swarm of drones over the fire. It already seems more contained than when he went charging in after Lex, the thick black smoke turning to white steam. As far as he can tell, the fire didn't spread beyond the office. A half-dozen bodies in various stages of groaning or being arrested are spread on the ground, and at their center, Oriol's lounging against the side of one of the ORVs, talking to a police officer. Arms folded across his chest, hair perfectly mussed.

Relief spreads through Manu's chest.

"You all right?" he signs.

Oriol nods. "You?"

Manu holds a thumbs-up, then turns to check on Lex.

The medic who took her from Manu has sat her on the ground a ways back from the fire and is checking her over with a scanner while she continues to cough. Manu crouches beside her and Lex breathes deep, tilts her head back to meet his gaze. Her eyes are bloodshot.

"Hey," Manu says. "You all right?"

"You saved me." She sounds surprised.

Manu shrugs one shoulder. "Course. Shouldn't've run back in there, though."

"How did you get the fire suppression system started?"

He hesitates, then opts for the truth. "I got a friend who's good at hacking. She figured it out."

"Oh." Lex seems torn about what she thinks of having her system hacked, decides it's all right. "Thank her for me. And thank you."

"Least we could do. Sorry for bringing on trouble."

"You didn't bring the trouble."

Manu's not so sure, but he's not about to disabuse her of the notion. And anyway, the police officer who was talking with Oriol is approaching. Hasn't arrested Oriol, so maybe their holiday isn't a bust just yet. Still, that itch on the back of his neck is telling him to get the hell out of here.

"Mr. Juric, I'm Officer Pine." The officer holds out a hand and Manu rises to his feet to meet it, wincing at the pop in his hip. "I understand you know why these lads were trying to burn down Lex's hop kiln?"

"I told him about Traval," Oriol says from over Officer Pine's shoulder. "Said we'd been warned by the Bulari police he was out here under an alias."

"That's about it," Manu says. "Traval got run out of Bulari, but I guess he thinks he can run your town. He here?"

Oriol shakes his head.

"That's all right." Manu pulls out his comm to scan through the packet of information Toshiyo sent over. "We've got his address in town, his alias, everything you'd need to make a case against him and put him away. I can send this to you. And obviously you've got Lex's testimony about what happened."

Officer Pine frowns at him. If this was Bulari and the cops had waltzed into this scene, he and Oriol would already be in cuffs or shooting their way out — assume all parties are guilty until proven otherwise is the rule of thumb. Officer Pine, though, seems suspicious yet too polite to accuse them outright of being part of the problem.

"You two are . . . law enforcement?"

"Nah." Manu smiles brightly. "Private security."

"They work for one of my brewery partners in Bulari," Lex says. She winces and tries to stand — the medic is telling her to stay put, but she ignores them, holds out a hand to Manu. He helps her to her feet. "I was lucky they were here."

"Happy to help," Manu says. "And glad to be working with you."

"Same." Lex takes a deep breath. "Doesn't look like the damage spread beyond the office. I'm going to see what I can salvage, but let's meet in the next few days to shore up the paperwork for real. How long are you two in town?"

"Two weeks," Oriol says before Manu can answer. "You owe me," Oriol signs.

"Fine," Manu signs back. He smiles at Lex. "Two weeks."

"And it's your first time in Alusina?" Lex smiles. "You're going to love it here."

"Already enjoying ourselves." Manu winks at Oriol. "Aren't we, babe?"

"Sure thing," Oriol says. "Though I do believe it's my turn to pick the activity."

"Have you taken the river cruise yet?" Lex asks. "It's truly lovely."

"Not sure we're — " Manu cuts himself off; over Lex's shoulder, Oriol's fixed him with a steely glare. "Not sure we have our reservations yet," he finishes. "But I can't wait."

# PART 3

---

# DELETED SCENES AND ALTERNATE POINTS OF VIEW

## ALTERNATE GLIMPSES

This section contains deleted scenes and alternate point of view scenes, which I've arranged to be roughly chronological.

What is all this?

The deleted scenes are ones that I originally wrote to include in the books, but ended up on the cutting room floor for whatever reason.

The alternate point of view scenes were written specifically for *The Bulari Saga Travel Guide*, to provide an alternate glimpse into the mind of a minor character during a pivotal moment.

What exactly is an alternate POV scene? It retells the actions and dialogue exactly as the original scene, but puts the reader in the head of a different character.

Each of these scenes provides a bit more context, lore, and depth to the world and characters — and they were all super fun to write.

Enjoy!

# MEETING TOSHIYO

## A FEW WEEKS BEFORE NEGATIVE RETURN
## [DELETED SCENE]

---

*Toshiyo has been one of my favorite characters since she first showed up in* Negative Return. *In that novella (which is all Manu's point of view), Manu wonders how in the world someone like Toshiyo — who clearly isn't part of the Bulari underworld — ended up working with Jaantzen. Her presence, and her ease with Jaantzen, is part of the puzzle that helps Manu decide to trust Jaantzen over Coeur at the end of that book.*

*I, too, wondered how Toshiyo ended up with this motley crew.*

*Part of her story was revealed to me at the end of* Crossfire *when I finally dipped into her point of view during the attack on Cobalt Tower. By that point, I was finally curious enough to start pulling threads and find the following story.*

*I never found the right place to include it in the books, though. Part of the story made it into Jaantzen's musings in* Heat Death, *when he and Toshiyo are talking in the deathtrap safehouse in the desert.*

*But I wanted to include the whole thing for you here — particularly since it's one of the only times we get to meet Tae.*

---

GIA'D SAID DRIVING ALL THE WAY OUT TO RUBY Basin to hire an ops tech was absurd. He could have gotten someone competent back in Bulari, even with his limited budget, but he wants to bring in new blood for this job Coeur's hired him for — someone he can trust isn't in Coeur's pocket. Companies like Blacklode sometimes loan out indentures for cheap, and there's one in particular whose name has reached Jaantzen's ears.

But it's not until Toshiyo Ravi enters the interview room that Jaantzen starts to think that Gia is right, and this trip was an extravagant waste of time.

*This* is the star ops tech Jaantzen's been hearing about?

Toshiyo stalls in the doorway with a nervous glance at

the Blacklode CEO and the head manager, who are sitting beside Jaantzen. She's barely out of her teens, with sallow skin and nervous eyes, her gaunt frame swallowed in an oversized sweater despite the heat. Jaantzen shares a look with Gia. He needs someone who can hold an entire job in her head, talk a crew full of rowdy mercenaries through hitting their marks, and pivot calmly under pressure.

This girl can barely introduce herself.

The interview goes smoothly, though, and once he starts asking technical questions, it's clear Toshiyo knows what she's talking about. But that's not what Jaantzen notices the most. He notices how she clams up anytime one of her employers says a word, that she winces as she shifts in her chair, and — when she finally looks up at him — the faint hint of a yellow bruise on her cheek, which she's been trying to hide with her long black hair. Two of her fingernails are torn to the quick and raggedly bloody.

He can't picture this skittish young woman running a heist, but the stutter, the hesitation all vanish the moment she sits in front of a terminal to run through the technical test. It's meant to be a disaster scenario, with cascading problems that simulate both the intellectual complications required to run a complex operation as well as the mental stress loads the operator must manage.

Toshiyo runs it with grace, pivoting with ease and averting disaster with an eerie calm, getting twice as far into the program before succumbing to cataclysm than anyone else Jaantzen has watched run this particular scenario.

When the screen flashes her score — profits saved (99 percent), equipment saved (96 percent), lives saved (100 percent) — Toshiyo sits back in her seat. Her gaze flicks to Jaantzen to check his reaction to near-perfect scores on this impossible test, but she still doesn't make eye contact with her bosses.

"We'll need to discuss," Jaantzen says.

Blacklode's CEO grins at him. "We'll give you a minute," he says, standing.

But Jaantzen stands himself. "I need to grab something from our vehicle anyway." He turns to Toshiyo, offering a handshake, but she gives him only a quick nod. Her lively eyes go carefully blank once more as her manager ushers her back to wait with the other candidates.

The sun bakes the shoulders of his black suit as Jaantzen walks back out to the spinner he and Gia drove all the way from Bulari in. He longs for the coolness of the office — but he doesn't trust Blacklode not to listen in to what he needs to say to Gia.

He leans his back against the spinner door, scanning the horizon, a sheen of sweat breaking out on his scalp.

"Fuck." Gia leans beside him. "That poor girl."

"She has the skills we need," Jaantzen says.

Gia takes a sharp breath. "She's good at her job. But will she be up for what *we* need?"

"You saw her. We need someone who can handle

anything that comes her way with calm and focus. She passed the test with almost perfect scores."

"A theoretical test." Gia cocks an eyebrow. "Do you want my opinion?"

"Of course."

"You don't care about the test results. You're looking for a reason to ride to her rescue."

Ever since he saw the bruise on her cheek, he's been itching to give someone else a bruise to match. "And you don't want to?"

Gia's expression darkens. "Of course I do. I've seen plenty of women with her look. She's still got soul now, but in another few years that'll be gone. Or she'll be dead." Gia shifts her back against the hot spinner. "But you didn't bring me here to be a hero. You brought me to ask you questions. So tell me, boss. You think hiring her is the right choice? The right *business* choice?"

When he doesn't answer, Gia sighs.

"You're going to put her in a room with a bunch of mercenaries. Killers. You think she'll keep her focus then?"

"She's clearly terrified of her employers, but when she got in front of that terminal, it was like they weren't even in the room with her." His heartbeat throbs in his jaw. "She's very good at compartmentalizing."

"So she knows how to shut out danger and work. But what happens after, boss. You hire her for this job, then bring her back and drop her off with Blacklode when it's done?"

There was the crux of the issue. Hiring her out was

well within his budget. Blacklode was downsizing, he knew that. The mine was drying up, and they needed the hiring-out money more than the extra mouths to feed. They'd let him borrow Toshiyo for cheap.

But then Jaantzen would be obligated to bring her back after. And from what he's seen today, that's going to be a problem.

"Would you let me?" he asks Gia, who shakes her head.

"Fuck no," she says. "And neither will Tae."

"Then it's settled."

"Good."

Jaantzen's getting a proper payday with this job. It's a risk, spending so much of that ahead of time, but it's a risk he wants to take. A risk he *has* to take.

He starts walking back to the office. Gia falls into step beside him.

Back into the blessed air conditioning, and when the CEO and manager offer to bring in more candidates, he asks to speak with Toshiyo Ravi in private. He ignores the warning glance from Gia; he doesn't need it. This place is certainly bugged, but he wants Blacklode to hear this conversation.

While he waits for Toshiyo to be brought back in, he studies the small office. There's the terminal with its seat. A pair of armchairs. A small desk with a chair in front of it. He dismisses the terminal — there's no place for him to sit, which means he'd be looming over her shoulder — and ignores the armchairs. Someone else might feel more relaxed in the armchairs, like they're on equal footing. But Jaantzen's a big man, and Toshiyo needs to feel safe if they're going to have a real conversation. The armchairs will seem too familiar.

He sits behind the desk, putting it between her and him, and leaving her the seat closest to the exit. Gia settles into an armchair, propping ankle on knee.

When the door closes behind Toshiyo, her expression shifts from carefully blank to cautiously wary. She doesn't lower her gaze, now that her managers aren't in the room, but she certainly doesn't trust Jaantzen. She sits carefully in the chair across from him with a straight spine, hands clasped in her lap, cascade of black hair still attempting to obscure the bruise on her cheek.

"Ms. Ravi. I'd like to hire you. Is that something you're interested in?"

Her brows draw together. "Yeah? I mean." She glances at Gia, then back at him. "You already talked to Blacklode?"

Ah. She doesn't think she gets a choice.

Jaantzen shakes his head. "I'm asking you before I make my offer to Blacklode. Because I'm not interested in hiring you out or transferring your indenture." Disappointment wars with confusion on her face. "I'll pay off what you owe to Blacklode, and then I'd like to offer you a job with me."

Toshiyo's gaze snaps to his.

"The job will be in Bulari. If you like the work, there will be more of it. If you don't, I'm sure your skills will be in high demand in the city. It shouldn't be difficult to find something more suited to you than what I do."

"What . . . kind of work?"

"I can explain the details on the way. But it's all what you're used to. Surveillance, monitoring. Coordination for an event with a few moving parts. Are you interested?"

Her shoulders have straightened, her eyes brightening as she begins to understand he's offering her something more than just another gig with a shitty mining corp.

"Just you two?"

"No," says Jaantzen, and that wariness clicks back into place. "But you'll be working very closely with myself and Gia." He knows he's not the most reassuring person, so he adds quickly, "It's one event, a week at most. After that I'll have ongoing work, but I'll also be happy to introduce you to someone else if you prefer."

She finally nods. He can see it in her eyes that she understands what he's offering her, she's just looking for a catch.

"Why me?"

"Your scores were highest," he says. "And you remained the calmest. I need someone with a cool head." And he could feel Tae's heart breaking for her from here.

But the last thing he wants her to think is that he's hiring her out of pity. A year ago, he probably wouldn't have. Falling in love with Tae might turn out to be extremely bad for business. "Will you take my offer?"

A tiny nod. "Okay." She glances from him to Gia. "Yeah."

Jaantzen leans forward and holds out his hand to shake, and at first he thinks she'll refuse again. But finally Toshiyo reaches for his hand, shifting forward awkwardly as she does so. For a minute he doesn't understand why, but then he realizes the movement has kept her oversized sweater from riding up on her arm.

He gently tightens his grip so she can't pull away — she tenses, but doesn't try — and pushes back her sleeve with his other hand. Her forearm is a tapestry of fresh, livid bruises layered over faded older ones, color blotched under pale skin.

"I got my arm caught in one of the carts," she lies.

Jaantzen lets her hand go; her arm disappears under her sleeve, under the table. He touches a finger to his cheek to mirror where hers is bruised. "And this?"

"It was dark, and I walked into — "

"Was it any of the men who were in this room?" Jaantzen asks, cutting off whatever lie she was about to offer. Gia clears her throat, but he ignores her sense of caution.

Toshiyo's answer is a quick shake of her head.

"But they know about it."

She doesn't answer, but her jerky shrug and terrified glance at the door say yes. She takes a sharp breath. "Mr. Jaantzen. It's not what you think, I promise you. I keep my mouth shut, I keep my head down. I'm not a troublemaker."

Jaantzen's chest tightens with simmering rage; he'll let it simmer until it's useful. For now, he smiles faintly. "I am."

A furrow appears between her brows.

"I make trouble, Ms. Ravi," he clarifies. "Professionally. Especially if someone under my protection is threatened. I don't know what you've been through here, but I swear that while you work for me, no one will dare touch you."

Toshiyo nods slowly, and for the first time that dark wariness in her eyes is replaced by a spark of hope.

"My offer of employment starts immediately," Jaantzen says, standing. It wasn't what he'd talked to Blacklode about, but if they want to keep him from burning this entire operation to the ground, they've forfeited the right to dictate any terms. They'll understand that shortly. "We'll leave as soon as you've had a chance to gather your things and say your goodbyes. Gia can help you while I see to the rest of the details on your contract."

"Thank you, Mr. Jaantzen."

"It's just Jaantzen," he says, and she nods.

Gia's giving him a *Don't do anything rash* look as she ushers Toshiyo out the door, but it's resigned.

Jaantzen is definitely about to do some damage.

Toshiyo has slept in some strange hiding places over the course of her young life, but she's never tried sleeping in a moving vehicle. She's barely been in one — not much call for it since she's never left the Blacklode property before. She was born there, with technically only a few years to pay off the indenture her parents left with their early death, but Toshiyo had never expected to make it long enough to see freedom.

She opens her eyes again and the spinner is still jostling its way through the desert. Across the cabin, Jaantzen hasn't bothered to fit his massive frame onto the bench meant for sleeping. He's sitting up and reading something on his comm.

Toshiyo watches with half-lidded eyes, wary of him catching her, but not wary of him. She's never felt so instantly at ease with a stranger as she had with these two. It's like he's emitting some kind of electrical field that disrupts the buzzing, predatory energy of the world around him, allowing her nervous system to settle down a notch for the first time in years.

She doesn't understand what she's doing here, but she trusts this man when he says she's safe.

He catches her watching him, though, on and off for maybe a half hour. He doesn't acknowledge it, but he does have Gia pull over so he can drive, even though it's his turn to rest. "She's not comfortable enough to sleep around me," she hears him say to Gia outside the spinner as they trade places. It's not true. But Toshiyo does eventually fall asleep.

She's asleep when they slide into Bulari, so she misses the transition from the empty starlit desert to the city bright. She sits up blearily, gazing out the window. It's dark, well after sundown, and glaring streetlamps shine in her eyes. She's aware she's staring out the window like a spectacle-starved country kid who's never seen the city, but, hey. That's exactly what she is.

Gia's driving again, and Jaantzen notices her awake. "My wife and I have a guest bedroom," he says in that deep, soothing voice. "If you like, you can stay with us until we get you settled. Or we can set you up at a hotel for now."

A hotel? Like she's some sort of heiress. Like she's a queen.

Toshiyo tries to decide which Jaantzen would prefer her to choose, but his mild expression gives her no clues. She's never stayed in a hotel, of course. And she's never stayed in someone's guest bedroom — but the thought of being dropped off to navigate a host of new social mores and dangers among strangers spikes panic in her chest.

"Staying with you would be fine," she says. He nods and returns his attention to his reading.

They dock at a townhouse. Inside, it's colorful and bright, warm after the nip of chill in the night air, and it smells amazing. Stewing tomatoes and garlic and fresh bread and rosemary, and other scents Toshiyo can't place.

A woman with a black ponytail, light brown skin, and a wide, smiling face greets them at the door. "My wife, Tae," Jaantzen says in introduction. The woman holds out a hand to Toshiyo, hugs Gia, kisses Jaantzen on the lips, and something in her body language says the kiss is cut short by company. Toshiyo looks away.

"Come in," says Tae. "Dinner's almost ready — I'm sure these two didn't stop anywhere worth eating at. They're all business on the road."

"Nowhere worth eating at between here and Ruby Basin," says Gia, following Tae in.

"Still," Tae tosses over her shoulder. "You need to feed the girl."

"We brought rations," Gia protests, and Tae laughs in response.

Toshiyo follows that laughter up into the house, into the bright kitchen, where Tae rushes back to pots and the oven, chatting the whole time. She offers Toshiyo a glass of water — or something stronger, she says; Toshiyo accepts water — and Toshiyo hovers awkwardly, not sure what to do next.

"Guest room's set up," Tae tells Jaantzen, and he nods at the subtle command. Toshiyo doesn't always understand people, but she gets a sudden flash that Jaantzen doesn't know what to do in Tae's warm and cheery household much more than she does. It makes her like him even more.

"Right," he says awkwardly. "I can get you settled." He picks up her bag — there wasn't much to pack — and leads her up a set of stairs. At his nod, Gia follows them. The guest bedroom feels crowded with the three of them, and there was no reason for Gia to come, but Toshiyo thinks she understands the consideration in the gesture. Jaantzen was trying to remove any worry she might have of being alone with him. Not that she has any.

The bedroom is comfortably furnished, with an attached bathroom and shower, and though he apologizes for the size, it looks like heaven.

"It's been a long trip," he says. "Take a shower if you like. We'll have dinner when you're ready."

A shower, scalding hot and scouring her clean. Toiletries that smell like flowers and indulgence. A mirror she avoids looking in, but which isn't cracked and graffitied. A bed she can sink into, she can sprawl over, that's all hers. A door that locks.

Toshiyo lies back on the bed, staring at the ceiling and trying to figure out what happened.

There's been some sort of mistake, she thinks. Jaantzen picked the wrong person, or she misheard, back at the office, and she's only on loan to him before she'll have to go back to Blacklode again. She hadn't asked for more details about the job in the spinner because she hadn't really cared. She'd been made to understand that whatever Jaantzen did, it was illegal, but she wouldn't be in any danger, and she'd be free to go afterward.

The legality doesn't bother her — what does "legal"

mean, anyway? Blacklode had done whatever they wanted, regardless of laws, and their people had, too. There'd been rules, of course — written and unwritten — and consequences for breaking those. For example, if the men who left her bruised and broken had incapacitated her so she couldn't do her job, they'd probably be reprimanded. If she ratted them out, she'd probably be attached to a deep mining detail and never see the light of day again.

But out here? The rules have changed, and so have the consequences.

And she has no idea what any of it means.

She doesn't know how long she lay thinking before a soft knock sounded at the door. She sits up, stiff and starving; her long, thick hair is almost completely dry. She swings her legs off the bed, a stab of panic over unknown rules and unimaginable consequences. "Come in?"

The door opens. It's Tae. "You're not sleeping?"

"No, sorry, I'm — "

"That's fine, that's fine." Tae smiles at her and pushes the door open the rest of the way. She's carrying two plates balanced on one arm. "I thought you'd be hungry."

Another stab of horror. "You were waiting for me to eat," Toshiyo says. "I'm so sorry."

"It's all right." Tae sets the plates down on the small table near the bedroom window. "Giaconda and Willem are eating already, but I wanted to come eat with you. If that's all right?"

She's not used to so many people caring about her preferences. "Yes?"

"Willem thought I should leave you alone and you'd come down when you were ready. But he's the king of avoiding uncomfortable personal problems, so what does he know."

Tae sits, smiling, radiating warm energy and practical charm. After a moment's hesitation, Toshiyo sits across from her. The food smells incredible and tastes just as good, but Toshiyo restrains herself as she eats, knowing from experience just what a bad idea it is to stuff yourself on an empty stomach.

They eat in companionable quiet for a moment, Tae making random, benign small talk, when finally the other woman puts down her fork.

"Look," Tae says. "Willem went to Ruby Basin looking for you. You specifically, not just any ops tech."

Toshiyo blinks at her, her fork halfway raised from her plate. "What do you mean?"

"He didn't tell you because he thought it would alarm you, but I told him you're probably sitting in here wondering what the hell's going on." She sighs. "He's been looking for someone with your skill set for a while, asking around, and he heard about some prodigy ops tech at Blacklode. He interviewed other candidates because he wanted to make sure he was making the right call, and because he didn't want Blacklode to jack up the price if they found out how interested he was in you."

Tae's expression softens. "When you came into the

interview room and he could see how badly you'd been treated, he lost it. He's worried you thought his anger was directed at you."

Toshiyo shakes her head. "No. He was . . . kind." The gentle way he pushed back her sleeve, the softness in his voice as he asked who gave her the bruises, the way he gave her space — he'd been attuned to her needs the entire time.

"He is. But right now he's beating himself up for frightening you."

"No," Toshiyo says quickly. "He didn't. He made me feel safe."

Tae's smiling softly. "That's what I told him. Toshiyo. I want you to know that you are safe here. Our home is secure. You can stay here as long as you want — and I think you should, until you get used to the city. But we can also start looking at apartments tomorrow if you'd rather have your own place."

Toshiyo just nods; she can't imagine living on her own just yet. Let alone how one affords an apartment or where food comes from. The last thing she needs right now is to be cast adrift in a sea of strangers.

Tae's expression shifts to concern. "There's one more thing," she says. "And I promise this isn't some bullshit corporation medical test thing. But Gia — she's a doctor, even though she doesn't always seem like it. She wants to take a look at you. Make sure you're okay."

Toshiyo flinches, and Tae pats the air in front of her, soothing. "Love," she says. "We can take you to a clinic if you prefer. But you're clearly malnourished. You've been hurt. You need help."

Toshiyo takes a sharp breath. "Now?"

"It can be tomorrow, when you're rested. Unless there's something you want to talk to her about tonight."

"I think I'm fine," Toshiyo says. "I mean . . ."

What is fine? She's covered in years of bruises left where no one will see them, her body marked with someone else's ownership, layered like a painting so she doesn't even look at herself in the mirror anymore. The stress and malnutrition have wrought havoc on her monthly cycle so she never knows when it will come — at least, she hopes it's only the stress. Her hair's been falling out in handfuls lately. She lifts her hand to her mouth and she's aware a split second too late that her loose sleeve has fallen down to reveal the bruises on her wrist to Tae.

But then, Jaantzen and Gia have already seen them. She has no one else to keep it a secret from, and it's that relief more than anything that causes her to start crying.

Tae doesn't hesitate to gather her into her arms, and the kindness and proximity of this woman, the warmth of her skin, the flowery, earthy scent of her hair, the soft gentleness of her curves saps any remaining stoicism from Toshiyo's body. She lets Tae guide her to her feet, sinks with her on the end of the bed, buries her face in her shoulder and sobs. The other woman combs her fingers gently through

Toshiyo's hair, absently teasing apart damp tangles, and Toshiyo can feel the rhythm of Tae's heartbeat like a guide. Slow and steady and soothing. Eventually her own rabbit pulse slows to match.

Finally her sobs become sniffling hiccoughs, and Tae kisses her on the forehead and hands her a handkerchief. Toshiyo mops her face, blows her nose. She feels drained, feverish from the release, a headache tightening around her temples and an unfamiliar lightness in her chest. Tae's warm hand strokes her back.

"I'm sorry," Toshiyo says.

"Friends let each other cry on their shoulders," Tae says, and Toshiyo gives her a confused look. "Forgive me if that's presumptuous," Tae says. "But I have a feeling you and I are going to be friends."

# PHAERA AT LEONE'S PARTY

## ALTERNATE POINT OF VIEW FROM DOUBLE EDGED

---

*When I first wrote* Double Edged, *I added Phaera D to the mix of characters as a potential ally. She first appears in the scene where Jaantzen attends a dinner party at Justice Geum-ja Leone's house.*

*Phaera doesn't show up again until* Crossfire, *when she comes to ask Jaantzen to help her deal with Levi Acheta and his attempts to run a protection racket in the Casino District. She's flirty and confident, which I expected her to be. But she also ends that scene by basically asking him out to dinner.*

*That caught both me and Jaantzen off guard. But from that moment, Phaera took the reins and barged into the story.*

*And, of course, when I looked back at the original scene in* Double Edged, *her intentions and the chemistry between them are extremely clear. It's just that Jaantzen and I were both too obtuse to notice.*

*Julieta Yang noticed, though.*

*Part of the reason I was caught off guard by Phaera because I'd vowed I would never write a love story.*

*I made this vow in high school, when I didn't understand the point of them. All these heroines, making choices based on the heart and not their brains, compromising on their dreams and making decisions that seems out of character because some boy had a pretty smile.*

*I was a kid from a small town who wanted to leave and see the world. And in fiction — and around me — it seemed like one of the surest ways to fail in that dream was to fall in love early with the wrong person.*

*I definitely wasn't going to let my heroines make the same mistake.*

*There are probably a lot of things that High School Jessie would find surprising about the Jessie of today, most notably how much I enjoy talking to strangers, and how much I enjoy wearing bright colors.*

*(Though I also still wear a lot of black and gray.)*

*But one of the most surprising might be that a love story is so integral to the Bulari Saga. And that my second series, the Nanshe*

*Chronicles, is essentially one long romance plot line wrapped up in a spare pirate adventure.*

*I knew the Nanshe Chronicles had to have a romance plot, because it's the backstory of Starla's parents meeting each other and getting married. But I was completely blindsided by the love story in the Bulari Saga.*

*Willem Jaantzen is a man who guards himself carefully. He's got a family to protect and an ever increasing number of problems on his plate. Neither he nor I thought he had any time for romance.*

*When Phaera D walked on stage, she was just an intriguing character who I thought might play a bigger role later. But when my husband read that scene the first time, he pointed out that Phaera was hitting on Jaantzen. When I reread the scene, I knew he was right. There's a hint of flirtation underneath her swagger — and Jaantzen and I had both missed it.*

*I thought her flirtation might provide an interesting bit of tension, so I revised the scene to make it more noticeable. Of course, Jaantzen still misses it.*

*Phaera makes sure Jaantzen understands her flirtations clearly when she reappears in Crossfire, and what follows escalates more quickly than either of them anticipated.*

*What fascinated me about writing their story was that they weren't youngsters figuring out what they need out of a partner. They were adults with their own lives, ambitions, businesses, and people to protect. They had to navigate their growing affection and reliance on one another within the context of their own established identities and obligations.*

*Jaantzen definitely falls in the category of an alpha hero: the strong, guarded, protector type. A widower who already blames himself for his wife's death, and isn't about to let Phaera get in harm's way. In a lot of alpha hero romances I've come across, the moral seems to be that sometimes in order to be strong, a woman has to learn how to ask for help from an even stronger man. That always rubbed me the wrong way.*

*Phaera called bullshit on that right from the start.*

*Refusing to be "kept safe" made Phaera more of a liability than she would have otherwise been — and she easily could have devolved into the action genre caricature of a woman who's stubbornness causes the male lead to lose ground or get sidetracked having to save her ass.*

*And maybe that would have happened, if Jaantzen had been the sort of alpha male lead who refused to trust his partner.*

*Yes, life gets more complicated for both Jaantzen and Phaera as a result of the mutual attraction. Yes, she becomes a liability once he realizes how deeply in love with her he's fallen. But when I look at the end of the series, I honestly don't think Jaantzen would have been able to defeat the Big Bad if it weren't for Phaera. Neither was strong enough on their own.*

*I think High School Jessie would appreciate a romance plot line about a relationship that has its challenges, but avoids the shallow, artificial drama of miscommunications and trust issues.*

*In the end, Jaantzen and Phaera do change for each other. They make space for each other in their lives. But Phaera isn't required to give up her independence and ambition. Jaantzen isn't required to give up his strength or his pride. Together, they usher in a new era in Bulari, side by side.*

*I think I was able to write this kind of nuanced romance plot in part because I'm married to my own alpha male partner who has never asked me to compromise my own independence or ambition. We've grown together, we strengthened each other, and I'm grateful we haven't had to go through half of the challenges Phaera and Jaantzen do in the span of five books.*

*So when I was thinking of alternate point of view scenes I wanted to write, this one seemed a natural choice.*

*I wanted to know exactly what was going through Phaera's head when she first sees Jaantzen at Leone's dinner party.*

*Enjoy!*

---

PHAERA D WOULDN'T NORMALLY ANSWER A CALL while in the middle of the most important social engagement of her calendar, but her head of security would interrupt her for only one thing.

Unease knots in the pit of her stomach: Acheta's back.

Phaera tosses a smile to banker Teo Lordeur and trade commissioner Youssef Tabari and excuses herself from the card table where the three of them have been sitting. "The work of the wicked doesn't pause even for dinner," she says with a wink and levity she doesn't feel. Levity she won't feel again until this mess with Acheta has been taken care of.

In secret, she's relieved to have left the conversation. She loves Teo. He was critical to financing her second casino, and his mind is still sharp even as his body melts into his new wheelchair. But. He's her grandfather's age, and he's never quite grasped that she's no longer a cocktail waitress. He and Youssef were about to ask her for a coffee refill, she could tell.

She touches her ear, accepting the call. "Yes?"

"I'm sorry to bother you, ma'am. But you told me to tell you the minute his people came by again."

"Thank you, Hiro." Phaera casts around the sitting room for a place with relative privacy, then settles on the window seat. It looks out over Chief Justice Geumja Leone's lovely back garden, and gives her a nice view of the rest of the room and its occupants, too. The room is becoming crowded; dinner will be served as soon as a few more of Leone's regular guests arrive. "Tell me what happened."

Phaera listens as her head of security explains Acheta's most recent extortion attempt. Phaera's worked in the Casino District most of her career, and while it's always been an adventure, she never used to consider it dangerous. But something shifted recently. Since Thala Coeur — Blackheart — was murdered, the power vacuum she left has ratcheted up tensions between the local street crews. Last week Dry Creek shot up the corner store on Veritas and Third; the next day, two of that crew were found dead in the park on Fourth and Huaihai.

It's bad for the neighborhood, and it's bad for business. A Ganesh-class transport is currently docked in orbit, and Phaera's casinos should be flooded with tourists and the transport's crew on shore leave. Instead, they're too afraid to venture outside downtown Bulari, and she's having one of the slowest months on record. To add insult to injury, a captain in Blackheart's crew, Levi Acheta, has started asking the casino owners on the drag for protection money — as though his people aren't the ones causing the troubles.

Paying Acheta for protection is absolutely *not* going to happen. Not on Phaera's watch.

She has some experience keeping outsiders from edging in on her turf. Last year, she organized the other casino owners to shut down an Arquellian chain that had tried to force their way in — and she won. But she knows how to fight on the fields of public relations. She doesn't have the tools to fight someone like Acheta.

Fortunately, she's acquainted with someone who does.

And, speak of the devil and he shall appear — Willem Jaantzen has arrived. He's tipping his cocktail glass against Leone's in the entry to the sitting room, but his dark, cold gaze roams the room, taking in the guests who arrived before him. When it lands on Phaera, she shoots him a smile of greeting and taps her earpiece apologetically: *I'll be with you in a minute.* He spares her no more friendliness than he does any of the others.

"When did they say they'd come back?" Phaera asks Hiro.

"They didn't." On the other end of the line, Hiro sounds troubled. "Ma'am. I suggest we consider paying — at least for now."

Phaera's not paying them a goddamned cent.

"We'll talk about it tomorrow," she says, and cuts the call.

By the time she's ready to rejoin the party, Jaantzen has drifted further into the room, drawn to the grand settee where Julieta Yang is flanked like a duchess by Mizal Seti and Lhasa Demosga. Mizal stands to greet him.

"Willem," Mizal says with a handshake. "Just the man I wanted to see. I was just telling Julieta and Lhasa about the developments in Jet Park."

Phaera laughs from the window seat. "You've got to come up with a better name for the neighborhood," she calls; she and Mizal were discussing it earlier. Jaantzen's gaze lands on her once more — is that a hint of a smile? — before he turns back to Mizal.

She has both Mizal and Jaantzen in her sights tonight, for nearly the same reason. Acheta's crew is trying to cut the business owners in the Casino District apart from one another, picking them off one by one. If they can band together they'll be stronger. And stronger yet if they can expand to the business owners in Jet Park, where Mizal Seti already owns a gentech therapy center and Willem Jaantzen is looking to open a business. A brewery, of all things. It's a good sign for the neighborhood, and a better sign for Phaera, who desperately needs allies.

Allies like Jaantzen.

She pretends to check a message on her cuff and watches as he interacts with the others.

They've spoken many times, of course, and he's always been deferential. Polite. A perfect gentleman, despite the torrid rumors about his rough-and-tumble past. Some of his older friends call him Willem, but she's never heard him introduce himself that way. He's always simply Jaantzen.

And as someone who also styles herself by a single name, she approves.

They're both misfits in this crowd, though in different ways. And if she understands the whispered rumors right, they're also both former service industry workers who are having trouble shaking their pasts while rubbing elbows with this new posh crowd.

Only, Phaera had served cocktails to high rollers; Jaantzen had served bodies to the morgue. He'd cleared the city of Blackheart as a favor to Leone and the rest of her circle, and though the war left scars throughout this room, he and his people took the brunt of the losses.

He's a widower, say the rumors. His family lost in the crossfire. No wonder he's surrounded by a dark shroud now.

It makes him unapproachable. And, like any unap-proachable man, irresistibly intriguing.

Jaantzen isn't conventionally handsome, but he is striking. Physically imposing, though he holds himself with a reserve that makes a girl wonder just what he's keeping back.

Phaera's seen a lot of powerful men in the course of her career, and they fall into two types. Most are like

Aiax Demosga: peacocks who can't stop talking about themselves, who gather power like an overripe mango gathers flies. Others simply *are*. Centers of gravity in whatever room they occupy, whether or not they say a word.

Phaera may not be able to stop being intrigued by Jaantzen, but she can read the signs. The man's all business, completely unavailable — which is a good thing, because she's looking for a business arrangement. She owns two of the most popular casinos in Bulari. She's influential. She's powerful. And she's not yet met a man who didn't want to put her in a box. She's definitely not interested in working with a man who wants a woman to put on his arm and tame.

Jaantzen seems like the kind of man who can manage a business partnership without assuming she belongs to him. He might even be the kind of man who can manage a fling with no hearts involved.

Just like she likes it.

Now he's in polite conversation with Lhasa Demosga, who's droning on about triticale futures; Phaera rises from the window seat, ready to save him from Lhasa's dreariness.

"Jaantzen, Lhasa, good to see you both."

Lhasa's smile is polite yet icy, even as she leans in for a perfunctory kiss of greeting. "Phaera, how lovely."

Lhasa never wanted Phaera in this room, that's been clear from the start. Not many did, at first — in the early days, Phaera knew, she'd been here by Geum-ja Leone's grace alone. But everyone in this room knows Bulari isn't a town of old money, it's a town of hard-won money. Even those like Aiax and Lhasa Demosga who come from rich parents can't afford to turn their noses up; this isn't Arquelle, after all.

Hasn't stopped Lhasa from snubbing her, though. And good riddance. Phaera's not sad when Lhasa excuses herself after the briefest of niceties.

Phaera turns to Jaantzen, holds out her hand in greeting. She catches him looking, of course — the body-skimming raw silk jumpsuit is meant to turn heads — but his expression now is pure business.

He's still holding the cocktail Leone gave him, some project of one of Leone's pet distillers. Phaera wonders what favors the woman owes the judge now. She spares a moment's pity for her, knowing intimately what comes once you've cast yourself on Leone's grace. Leone thinks Phaera owes her the world for inviting her to these soirees, and with every favor, Leone's attention tightens like a noose — but that's a problem for another day.

"Are you biting?" Phaera asks, tilting her chin at the cocktail in Jaantzen's hand. "Leone already talked me into a hundred cases for the casino."

"It is good."

"Help out a friend, et cetera." Phaera gives Jaantzen a secret smile. "So. I hear you didn't do Blackheart in."

Those cold eyes fix on her; she can't read much in his expression, but it's clear he didn't expect questions about Thala Coeur's murder here. "Word gets around."

"It was Hinoja, then? I suppose I can ask her when she arrives." She leans in conspiratorially. "Unless you've already worked your coup on Blackheart's gang." Gods but if that were true, how many of her problems with Acheta would be solved?

"Not quite," he says. He frowns, considering his words carefully, and when he speaks again his voice is pitched a touch louder. "There's been an upset in Blackheart's crew, but that may lead to opportunity for like-minded businesspeople."

Phaera tries not to let surprise show; a hush has fallen on those nearest to them. Geum-ja Leone, who had been heading out of the room to check on dinner, pauses in the doorway.

"What happened?" Phaera asks.

"Naali won't be making it tonight," Jaantzen says. "She's dead."

Anyone who hadn't heard Jaantzen's initial pronouncement certainly heard this; shock reverberates through the room. For a moment, the only sound is a quiet clanging of pots from the kitchen.

Phaera clears her throat in the silence. "Did you do her? Or are you two-for-oh?"

Jaantzen takes another sip of his cocktail; is that amusement in his eyes? "No, I did not."

"Levi?" Leone asks from the doorway. It's Phaera's guess, too, and she turns to agree with Leone. Then freezes, her blood running cold.

Because Levi Acheta is here.

He cleans up well, and has donned a trim suit and a god-awful real leather coat with gold trim that screams *Impostor*. He grins, clearly amused by the stir he's caused.

"Sorry I didn't let you know ahead of time, Madame Justice," Acheta says. "But I'm here in Naali's place. For good." His gaze skims the room; he gives Phaera a leer, locks eyes with Jaantzen, then turns back to Leone. "I did what I had to do, Madame Justice. Thank you for hosting."

He's holding out a slim package in elegant wrapping paper, a hostess gift that Leone takes warily.

"You're welcome, honey, of course." Her tone turns sharp. "But I won't have any trouble in my home."

"With Blackheart gone, Naali didn't have what it takes to keep things together," Acheta says. The speech is clearly rehearsed for this crowd. "Things would have gotten out of control, under her. I did this city a favor, and I'll be bringing true prosperity back to Blackheart's crew." Acheta glances at Jaantzen. "You know how it is."

"I'm not sure what you mean," Jaantzen says.

Leone clears her throat, spearing Jaantzen with a look. "We've lost some good people these past few days, son," she says, turning back to Acheta. "This isn't how regimes are changed. Not these days."

Acheta lifts his chin, defiant. "It's how they *changed*. Whether it's by the rules or not, it's the new reality."

Electric energy sizzles through the room. The rarefied crowd who attend Geum-ja Leone's soirees have indulged a glorified cocktail waitress. They've warily tolerated a crime lord who once did them an enormous favor. And they did business with Naali Hinoja out of a healthy respect for and fear of Thala Coeur — despite Blackheart running her business from exile.

Asking them to accept the man who murdered Naali in cold blood is a step too far.

Isn't it?

Leone straightens to her full height. "We do business with Coeur's crew, no matter who runs it," she announces. If Phaera wasn't standing so close to Jaantzen, she might not have noticed the muscle jump in his jaw.

"You're welcome to join us for dinner tonight," Leone says to Acheta. "May I offer you a drink?"

It's clear no one else wants Acheta here, but after Leone's pronouncement, none will question it. Still, there's a subtle parting of the crowd as Leone takes his arm and leads him through the sitting room.

No one wants to be in his way. No one but Jaantzen, who doesn't flinch as Acheta's shoulder hits his, doesn't shrink from the other man's cold smile.

"You got my message?" Acheta murmurs.

"I see you made your move before Hinoja could make hers," Jaantzen says. "Who'd you find to hold your hand?"

A wave of fury floods Acheta's face at the question,

and Phaera takes an involuntary step back. Every nerve is screaming at her to get out of the way of whatever violence is about to pass between these two men — but leaving the room won't solve anything. She's already caught up in whatever comes next.

"Naali would have given up our crew to you," Acheta growls. "I'm making alliances to make us stronger. Watch out, old man." His pushes past. Jaantzen watches him go with mild calculation in his gaze.

No one else seems eager to follow Leone and Acheta into the dining room. From beside Phaera, Mizal Seti takes a sharp breath.

"The nerve of that child," he murmurs.

"Nerve is a good trait," says Julieta from the grand settee. "Anger is not."

"I'm not sure I like his direction." Mizal's looking directly at Jaantzen as he says it. A challenge? A command? Around the room, others — but not all — murmur assent.

"Dinner is ready," Leone calls from the doorway. Slowly, the room begins to empty.

Phaera lifts her glass to Jaantzen as the others begin to follow Leone in. "I always appreciate an opportunity to work with like-minded businesspeople," she says, echoing his phrasing from earlier; he inclines his head in acknowledgement. "Let me know what you need."

There's that evaluating look again, but this time he seems to be seeing her as more than just a polite colleague.

"I'll be in touch," he finally says.

"I look forward to it." Phaera clinks her glass against his, then leaves him standing beside Julieta. She finds a seat as far from Acheta as possible, but nowhere is far enough to keep her skin from crawling.

Jaantzen doesn't join them for dinner.

# BETO MAKES THE CALL
## DURING DOUBLE EDGED [DELETED SCENE]

---

*Benedicto Kulikutan and his co-pilot Arund-hati Singh barely show up in the Bulari Saga. But they were much more pivotal characters in the first draft of* Double Edged — *before Jaantzen and his crew became the protagonists.*

*I couldn't pass by an opportunity to include one of my favorite old Beto scenes in this collection. Maybe someday I'll return to this world and give Beto and Ari and Lourdes and Paulo the spotlight story they deserve.*

---

BETO KULIKUTAN TOSSES SLICES OF CHORIZO soy into the wok.

The sizzle in the oil is satisfying, and the spices aromatic, but there's something beneath the surface, something flat and listless about the soy sausage they don't quite manage to mask. Something that screams, *This will be palatable, just add some sauce, you may not even notice it's fake.*

Beto scrapes at the wok, the spatula catching in places where the cheap chorizo soy is already burning to the sides.

He's rewarded by an overdramatic round of coughing from the other room. "Are you burning dinner?" Paulo calls.

"Just your portion," Beto calls back to his nephew.

He can't even count the number of years it's been since he's had proper chorizo, made with proper pork. Ari brought some into the office once as a treat from some mythical pancit truck she'd found outside the Geordi Jimenez Terminal, which never showed up again. Before that, it was in his mother's kitchen, back in New Manila. Twenty years ago or more.

Poor Paulo doesn't know better than chorizo soy. Thirteen years old and he's never even smelled the good stuff.

It's not that you can't get actual pork or actual spices or actual New Manilans here on New Sarjun — it's just far beyond Beto's ability to afford.

But someday, once his entire savings isn't going towards Lourdes's indenture, he's gonna splurge for them all. Or for him and Lourdes, at least. Paulo can stick with soy until he's old enough to appreciate the real thing.

When Manu Juric first started throwing him odd jobs, Beto had let himself imagine that someday might come sooner than he'd hoped. He'd known instinctively he shouldn't look too closely at the gigs, and he'd been right. Maybe the money'd been good, maybe the jobs had been relatively sure bets.

But Ari's right. Lourdes, Paulo — they can't afford for him to get caught up in a net like what Willem Jaantzen's got tangled up around him. Sooner or later it's going to catch little fish like him along with the shark himself.

As a parting gift to his brief prosperity, though, he did at least stop by the New Manilan bakery on Level A of the terminal to get a few packs of those lemon coconut cookies that Lourdes likes so much.

She'll ask him why.

He'll tell her just because.

She'll be pissed at him for spending the money.

He'll pretend not to care but secretly feel like shit, because those three packets of cookies represent an hour of her indenture, and he hates that his mind makes that calculation every time he spends a single mark.

Fistfuls of chopped onions go into the wok next; even beneath the sizzle he can hear a game's electronic beeps from the next room.

"Oy, Paulo. You working or you playing?" Beto calls. The beeps stop abruptly.

"I'm doing homework."

"Good." Beto slices open a head of cabbage with a knife kept razor sharp. "Because if you're bored, I got something for you."

Paulo appears in the doorway, his comm dangling in his hand. The screen flashes gold-purple-gold with a game pause screen. "Like, actual work?"

"Yeah, actual work." In goes the cabbage. "I need a trajectory calculated for a job next week."

Paulo rolls his eyes. "Why don't you do it yourself?"

"Because you need to practice your math."

"What do I get for it? Do I get a cut?"

Beto laughs. "When you're old enough for a work permit. But I'll give you one of those packs of cookies before your mom gets home and counts them."

Paulo narrows his eyes. "Two packs."

"Not likely."

"We're talking about hours of work here."

"One pack is enough sugar to get you through that. Besides, I only bought three." Beto drains rice noodles into the sink, turning his face away from the clouds of steam. "Plus, you still owe me for that time I fed and raised you and taught you how to do math in the first place."

Paulo sighs. "That's not going to work for much longer." But he settles down in front of Beto's tablet at the kitchen table anyway, thumbnail caught between his teeth as he buries himself in the problem.

From outside the kitchen window comes the stutter-and-stall of a moped's engine, the dragging clink of a metal chain, the click-and-hiss as a keycard passes over the door. Beto slides a pack of cookies across the counter just before Lourdes walks in. Paulo slips them into his pocket.

Beto's sister looks exhausted, her curly black hair gray with dust, her angular jaw smudged. For a moment she looks skeletal, a ghost of the laughing, loving big sister he had always looked up to, all her soft edges scoured away by New Sarjun's sand and mines.

But then, "Cookies?" Lourdes's face lights up and she reaches for one of the packs, her fingernails black with grime. Beto swats the back of her hand.

"Dinner first," he says. "And you're filthy, you're gonna get grease all over them. Go wash up, yeah?" He elbows her out of the way to dump noodles into the wok. "And make it quick, we're almost ready here."

"You're worse than Dad." Lourdes leans a hip against the counter, crossing her arms in a fake pout. "What are you up to, P?"

"Uncle Beto's trying to get me to do his work for him."

"Will it make you better at math?"

"Yes," says Beto.

"No," says Paulo.

"Then you should do it. We all know there's no more hope for your uncle's career prospects. What's he bribing you with?"

Paulo sighs. "A lifetime's worth of feeding and

raising me," he says, the lemon coconut cookies tucked deep in his pocket.

Beto winks at him. "Go get cleaned up, Lolli. Dinner's done in a minute." He adds the sauce before turning back to grab bowls out of the cabinet. A second packet of cookies is gone from the kitchen counter when he turns back; he hears the crinkle of the wrap from down the hall.

"Am I the only one who can save cookies for after dinner?" he calls, but the shower hisses on full blast in the bedroom, and Paulo doesn't answer at the kitchen table. He's absorbed in the calculations now, tongue caught in his teeth while he types strings of numbers into his comm.

Beto can't help but be proud. With any luck, after Paulo's years at the local Hypatia school, the kid will score an indenture with one of the big corporations, a good job crunching numbers and mining data rather than working down in the mines themselves. Though maybe the better option would be to have him drop out of school now so Beto can bring him on at Twin Star Salvage. Paulo's only a second-level, which means it wouldn't cost more than a month or two of Beto's salary in fees and fines to take him out of school, and Hypatia offers a reasonable payment plan on that. Paulo wouldn't have the long-term potential to earn like he would with a good indenture, but, hey. At least he'd get to pick where he wanted to spend his good years.

Unlike Lourdes.

Beto had been too young to legally take an indenture when they were forced to leave Indira by the wars with the Alliance. So he found work at Geordi Jimenez Terminal, whatever jobs anyone would hand him. He was drawn there first because of the international atmosphere, the smells and accents that reminded him of home. Eventually he met Ari, and together they scraped up enough to start Twin Star Salvage.

The ability to set his own schedule is a luxury. But it's more than that. He likes Ari, and mostly the rest of their crew, and the pay's been decent enough that he can siphon some off to pay down Lourdes's indenture more quickly — especially when they bring down a bonus haul or two.

He's dishing pancit onto plates when Paulo pumps his fist in victory. "I got it!"

Paulo grins. He points at the screen, where strings of code glow under a screen sticky with a dusting of powdered sugar.

"Hey, careful with that!" Beto dashes the dish towel tucked in his belt across it. "Lolli, dinner!"

Even at a glance Beto can see the numbers laid out in perfect simplicity on Paulo's comm. The kid's brilliant, Beto has to give him that. Beto ruffles his hair. "That was fast. I owe you another packet of cookies. Later."

"I'm open to profit-sharing options, too."

"Thirteen-year-olds get cookies. And a free place to stay, and meals cooked for them."

"This is child labor."

"This is you getting an education that'll help you get ahead in life. Help me set the table."

The race Benedicto Kulikutan runs every evening isn't just will he beat Paulo home. It's will he beat Lourdes to the table? By the time she sinks starving into her seat, will he have set something reasonably edible in front of her?

Most days, he wins.

Today, he wins with shining colors.

"Oh my god, this tastes just like Dad used to make it," Lourdes says through mouthfuls, like she's forgotten what real chorizo tastes like, and maybe she has. Beto accepts the compliment anyway.

"And how many cookies did you eat first?"

"Three," she says, and she's probably lying, but it doesn't matter. Lourdes starts to reach for the hot sauce bottle with her right arm, winces, then reaches again with her left.

"Lo?"

She's ignoring him, focused on the hot sauce. Deep red splatters hit her pancit. "Tell me about school today," she says to Paulo.

And the conversation derails into that, Lourdes avoiding his gaze for a few moments, Paulo regaling them with something from school. They eat hungrily in comfort, then — the ritual — try to stay up for a few minutes with each other before drifting to bed.

Tonight they make it about half an hour before Lourdes is yawning so wide it seems like her jaw will break.

Beto stands and stretches. "I gotta go to bed. You got school in the morning, P?"

"Yep."

"Good night, kid."

Paulo's bed is a pullout in the living room. He'd slept with his mom a bit after his dad died in the accident, but he'd been five then, going on six, going on ten, going on old enough to not need his mother's presence at night. They could afford a place with more than one bedroom if Beto was willing to spend his surplus on housing rather than on Lourdes's indenture. But it's not like Paulo is being put out by sleeping in the living room. And Beto will live.

Beto switches on the light in his bunk cubby, a space off the hall just big enough for a bed and a reading lamp and definitely not a girlfriend. God, that'll be a conversation someday, when he finds someone worth more than one date: Hi, I'm Benedicto and I live with my sister and her kid; how do you like spaceships, mine's pretty sweet for a salvage craft; I'll bring a blanket.

He pulls back the covers, but his hands still at the hiss of pain coming from the bathroom. The door's cracked, and he doesn't hesitate to nudge it open with his toe. Lourdes is standing in a tank top, strong brown arms bare, unpeeling a bandage from her right forearm with finicky tugs and muffled profanity. When she meets Beto's eyes she at least has the decency to look embarrassed.

He slips inside and shuts the door behind him so

Paulo won't hear, careful not to brush against Lolli's injured arm in the tiny bathroom. "Here," he says. She sits on the lid of the toilet and holds out her arm, and he sets to work peeling off the rest of the bandage. She's looking away, jaw clenched tight, her face gaunt.

Beto pulls back the last layer to reveal a steam burn covering most of her forearm. It's a blistered raw pink, but it doesn't look too deep. He lets out a low whistle.

"I didn't want to upset Paulo," she finally says.

"I'm totally with you on that, sis." The kid doesn't need to know about this. "But you were trying to keep it from me, too. And you were, what, just going to wear long sleeves for the next year? I was gonna find out." He drops the bandages in the bin. "Did you at least see the doctor?"

"Yes. He told me to change the bandage tonight and come back tomorrow morning."

"Did he give you anything for it?"

"I thought we still had some ointment left. But I couldn't find anything."

Translation: She didn't want to pay for it.

"I think Ari has some of the good stuff from when Karis had that engine blow up on her," Beto says. "I'll ask her for it tomorrow." Because there's no way Lourdes will buy it from the company doctor, he knows. She'd rather go without than go even another few marks in debt to the company.

"Stay here," he says. They may not have any medicine right now, but an aloe plant's managed to root itself in the baked clay outside the front door. It's the same kind their mother used on nearly every skin problem when they were kids, its fat sword leaves as scarred and pitted as Lourdes's own arms. Paulo's are still smooth, still young. Beto'll do whatever he can to keep them that way.

Outside, night is quickly sapping the last of the evening's heat from the air, and Beto takes a deep breath. He doesn't know how long he's been holding it, but his chest feels as though it's being squeezed in an over-pressurized environment suit, and for a moment the world feels as black and enormous as when he steps outside the salvage vessel and into the void.

He's been making payments, whenever he can spare the extra cash. Two hundred marks here, a thousand once, when they'd had a particularly good haul.

He's never told Lourdes, but he's probably shortened her indenture by nearly a year since he started at Twin Star — and with the few odd jobs from Juric in the past few weeks, he's managed to bring that down another full month. Even with that, she has eight left before she'll have paid off the debt that brought her, her husband, and her kid brother to New Sarjun.

"A job like this could buy you freedom."

When Juric had said it yesterday, Beto was ashamed that his immediate thought was for himself. Freedom to do whatever he wants, to take the gigs he wants. Freedom from the constant pressure of finances.

But the windfall Juric's offering him could take six months off Lourdes's indenture.

Someone calls his name, and he tumbles out of the

void, comes crashing back to gravity. He puts on a smile, raises a hand automatically to greet Marsia across the street, hunched on a chair on her front porch with a bottle in her clawed hand. A few houses down, a baby is crying and a dog is barking. Two teens on bicycles are laughing and swerving around the potholes in the dirt street. He recognizes the girl as Paulo's friend Samhita and waves.

He breaks off a leaf of the aloe plant and returns to find Lourdes in the bathroom. Her hiss tightens his throat as he squeezes a dollop of gel onto her arm. She swats his hand away to smooth it in herself.

"I have some pain pills in my cubby," he says once he's helped her cover the burn with a new bandage. "At least take those."

Lourdes nods.

"Good. Lolli, we're a team, remember? We're getting through this as a team."

"Go get me drugs," she says, but she's attempting a smile. "And get your ass to bed."

He has a sudden, boyish urge to throw his arms around her neck like they're kids again, but he doesn't want to jar her arm. He squeezes her shoulder instead; the muscles there are solid as stone. "On it, sis," he says.

He rummages through the drawers below his cubby, and as he crouches down he feels the bulk of his comm in his hip pocket. All he has to do is take it out. Open up a message to the number Juric gave him.

Say yes.

He hands Lourdes the pills, then kisses her cheek, levers himself into bed, and pulls out his comm, telling himself that it won't matter, that Juric will already have found someone else. He wants to feel relieved by that, instead he's beating himself up for waiting so long.

And he opens up a message to Juric.

*I'M IN. WHATEVER YOU NEED.*

# COEUR AT THE GREENHOUSE
## ALTERNATE POINT OF VIEW FROM DOUBLE EDGED

*When I ran a Kickstarter to fund the production of this odd little collection, I asked backers to vote on a handful of alternate point of view scenes they'd like to see.*

*Overwhelmingly, they wanted me to write the climax of* Double Edged *from Thala Coeur's point of view.*

*I'd weirdly enjoyed being in her head when I wrote the short story "Bad Intentions," and so I was looking forward to hearing her take on the events that happen in Julieta's greenhouse.*

*I don't know what I expected to find when I dove into this piece. And I don't know if understanding what's going on in Coeur's head here makes her any more redeemable (see my essay on villains in the next section).*

*But Blackheart's gonna Blackheart. And she delivers as strongly as ever in this scene.*

---

"Give me a knife."

Coeur's got her eyes closed when she says it, so she doesn't catch Manu's reaction. She assumes it's skepticism at best, maybe closer to disbelief. Probably not pity, though, no matter how bad she looks. None of Jaantzen's crew owe her pity.

"No," Manu says. Predictable.

"Wrap it up in my hands." Coeur lifts the bandaged ruins off her lap a moment, still doesn't open her eyes. The gentle movement of the spinner rocks her; Manu's been driving long enough that they must be nearing Julieta's home in the country. "They won't check there."

"I'm not giving you a knife and letting you loose. Especially not near my crew."

Coeur lets herself laugh; it hurts her ribs. "You have issues with delegation and trust."

"Doesn't mean I'm not right." A pause from the driver's seat before Manu takes a sharp breath. "You know, if you hadn't double-crossed the Dawn, none of us would be here. Not double-crossing people is actually pretty easy."

Is it, pup?

Those scars still shining on Manu's left hand, that look of pure fear he gave her when the elevator doors opened between them back at Cobalt Tower, despite the fact she was in a wheelchair, her hands shattered? Manu didn't have to double-cross *her* all those years ago, either. And he learned his lesson: Don't fuck with Blackheart.

Coeur's learned hers, too: that she was right, the religious freaks were goddamned easy to play.

She rolls her head to face him, finally opening her eyes. "It was a lot of money to leave on the table. Plus, they brought me back here, didn't they? If I'm gonna die anyway, it's gonna be in my city."

"You . . ." She can see him working out her plan with the Dawn in his mind. "You thought if you double-crossed them, they'd capture you and bring you back here."

"Plan worked."

"They just about killed you."

"Nobody gets a free ride, Juric."

His jaw opens. Closes again without speaking

"One knife," Coeur says. "That's it."

"I'm supposed to bring you back out of here alive." The way Manu says it, Coeur knows she's won.

"Giving you a knife seems like it'd put you in harm's way."

"Then what do you call sending me in unarmed? Fucking like this?" She lifts her bandaged hands. Pain throbs through every nerve.

"How will you even use it?"

How indeed, Thala.

But she's been punched down plenty throughout her life. She's ended up on the floor, choking on her own blood, more times than she cares to count. It's not always physical strength that cows an opponent. It's the fear of your crazy. And a wild animal is the most dangerous when it's nearest to death.

Coeur gives Manu a feral grin. "Bitch, who do you think you're talking to?"

Manu turns his attention back to the road, scarred knuckles shining as his hands grip the controls. She's rattled him. She should feel guilty about rattling him right before they both head into battle, but she doesn't — she needs a weapon, and sweet-talking Manu doesn't work.

And guilt never made things better anyway. There are only three lives in this world Thala Coeur feels guilty about, and she can't do shit now to make that fuckup right.

Manu slows the spinner to a crawl as they approach Julieta's long driveway, scanning for Dawn guards. Before he makes the turn, he reaches down to pull a knife from his boot, drops it in her lap. It's small but well-built, sturdy. Coeur grins.

She tears at the bandage on her left hand with her teeth, unraveling the fabric and gauze to reveal mottled purple and yellow and black, a sickly tapestry beneath her normal earthen-red skin. Her splinted fingers sing in pain as blood rushes in, so she moves quickly, pressing Manu's knife along the back of her wrist and wrapping it tight as she can. She finishes rebandaging her left hand as they pull up into the center of Julieta's driveway, her injured right throbbing with the effort.

Jaantzen's Dulciana JX is in front of the green-house, which is the only building with its lights on. Must be where the Dawn are hoping to make their ambush, then. Coeur does a quick scan of the other buildings — the low house, the gardens, all perfectly placed around the circular driveway. So this is how Julieta Yang lives. How sickeningly elegant.

"They must be in the greenhouse," Manu says. "Let's go."

Ah, yes. The part of the plan she's going to hate the most: asking for help. Coeur takes in a sharp breath.

"Don't tell me you're scared." Manu gives her an impatient look, which she returns with fury.

"Of course not. But I can't — " Fuck. "I don't think I can walk." Each word feels like a hot coal.

For a moment she's afraid he'll look at her with pity, but Manu's gaze holds only contempt. And maybe a touch of satisfaction.

Fair.

"That's fine," he says coolly. "I've been there."

Coeur bites back an acid response — who says you

can't teach old dogs new tricks? — then closes her eyes, taking a deep breath and gathering her strength. Manu exits; a moment later he's opening the passenger door, hand gripping her elbow, arm around her waist to haul her to her feet. She can't help the hiss of pain.

"We're going in," he murmurs to whoever's listening in on the comms, then he pulls his pistol from its holster. Jams it against Coeur's jaw.

"Grab the case," he orders. "Let's go."

"Ah. Smart." The gun will add an air of realism, make it look like she's not here of her own accord. But that's probably not the only reason Manu's pulled it on her.

"Shut up." Manu half carries, half drags her towards the greenhouse, stopping about ten meters back. Every nerve in Coeur's body screams. She drags her left foot — maybe a touch more than she needs, but her knee can barely hold her weight. "I brought you Blackheart," he shouts.

Silence.

City silence is a warning: Something bad just happened, something dangerous is about to go down. But desert silence? It's fucking eerie.

Coeur grew up where the city spilled into the desert — it was less than a five-minute hike from her mother's shack in the slums of Altamira to the empty desert in the bluffs above the ravine. They'd climb up there in the heat of the day — her and Ximena — and spend hours contemplating the city laid out like a gift below them. They'd go at night, too, with nothing but their heartbeats and the wind to keep them company, the occasional police siren drifting up from the city below.

Even the police sirens can't reach this far out in the desert.

A wolf howls, somewhere not too far away.

"C'mon," Manu whispers. She can feel his heart beating slow and steady against her shoulder blade.

Finally the door to the greenhouse opens, and a single figure appears in the doorway: a woman with a silver braid and a plasma carbine slung casually across her chest. T.J. Meijer, who Coeur's come to think of as the Dawn's silver fox.

Too bad about her, Coeur's always thought. Those chiseled arms and pretty eyes, she could have been fun if she wasn't such a freak for her cause.

Meijer beckons them forward, then nods to someone behind her. Coeur grits her teeth against the pain as Manu hauls her forward a step.

Just stay conscious.

She may not be all that useful now, but she won't be able to do shit if she passes out.

Movement in the doorway behind Meijer, and Coeur blinks away stars to see Starla and Julieta. Neither look injured, though Starla's helping the old woman walk.

Starla nods at some sign Manu's given her, then helps Julieta across the driveway. She ignores Coeur entirely, has barely given her a second glance since Coeur ended up under Jaantzen's roof, like Coeur's less nuisance than a fly. Coeur likes that for her — she'll take the girl down a notch later if she needs to, but right now her lack of giving a shit about Coeur is refreshing.

Julieta locks eyes with her, though. Her face is a mask of grief. Finally swam in too deep, eh, Julieta?

Two hostages brought to safety, Manu turns his attention to Meijer as the spinner doors close behind them.

"Where's Jaantzen?" Manu says. "I need to see him before she goes anywhere."

Meijer shakes her head. "Give me Coeur and the case, and you'll get your boss back."

Manu digs the pistol harder into Coeur's jaw. Coeur sucks in a breath despite herself. "I'd be very happy to kill her," Manu says. Coeur has no doubt he means it, too. "Just give me a reason."

He drags her another step forward; Meijer's plasma carbine swings towards them.

"You're not going anywhere, Juric."

"We had a deal," Manu says. "Bring me Jaantzen, you can do whatever the hell you want with Coeur."

Meijer gives him a long look, then finally turns to bark an order at someone behind her.

And Manu stiffens. The air around them turns electric, and Coeur can tell from Manu's kicked-up heart rate that something's gone wrong even before she hears the sniper's shot crack the night.

Someone screams, falling. Another shot and Manu grunts in pain, his steady presence beside her faltering;

Coeur tries to support herself but her bad knee gives out. She hits the gravel in a tangle of limbs and pain and fury.

She can't see what's going on but she hears Manu fire at Meijer, feels him dig something out of his pocket and fling it at the greenhouse, tastes iron as glass walls explode. Of course he's blowing shit up; the thought comes almost fondly, though whatever he threw at the greenhouse packed far more of a punch than the hornet tags he'd used back when they first met. A fine spray of glass shards and gravel pepper the arms she flings up to cover her head.

She opens her eyes just in time to see a bolt sear into Manu's chest. Not in time to do a goddamned thing about it.

He crumples, hand twitching, eyes rolled back in his head. Coeur reaches for him, but there's nothing she can do. New hands catch her under the arms and haul her to her feet, dragging her backwards to the greenhouse.

Manu doesn't move.

I'll fuck 'em up for you, pup, she catches herself thinking, then thinks it again for real. A glow of feral rage kindles in her chest, washing away the pain. Whatever comes next, these fuckers deserve it. Whatever comes next is for Naali. For Chase. For Manu.

Coeur grins through bloody teeth.

Willem Jaantzen looks like hell; gray pallor under his rich brown skin, sheen of sweat on his brow, eyes threaded red and nose rimmed with blood. He's doubled over in a chair, and the soldier in front of him is clipping an electric barb back on his belt.

When Jaantzen lifts his head to meet her gaze, she sees a look she knows all too well. Calm, calculated fury, and for once it's not aimed at her.

Whatever payoff Bennion Zacharia promised that soldier, Coeur hopes it's worth the hellish payback he'll get from lifting a hand to Jaantzen.

Meijer has Coeur under a beefy arm, and not in the good way — she feels like a doll being towed by a careening toddler as Meijer plows her way through the debris-strewn greenhouse. The woman's shoulder is streaming blood from the bullet Manu managed to put in her, but if she feels the pain she's not showing it.

Fucking supersoldiers.

Bennion Zacharia doesn't give Coeur a second look, or give her a chance to say something to piss him off, not that she trusts her vocal cords. Her entire body feels like it's made of crunched glass and lava. Bennion motions for Meijer to lead the way and the big woman stomps on, Coeur under one arm, the silver case under another.

"This isn't the first date I imagined," Coeur says to Meijer once she's caught her breath; the other woman blinks down at her in surprise, looks back at their path through the greenhouse just in time to get slapped in the face by one of Julieta's jungly vines. Meijer grunts at it, annoyed. Pushes on.

Coeur probably would have been searched before bullets started flying and Manu detonated the place, but now no one's going to bother. She's taken advantage of the chaos to work the thin blade beneath the bandages of her left hand so that the tip is exposed beyond her fingers. If she balls her hand into a fist, she's got a good five centimeters of steel to work with.

She's close enough to Meijer that she could distract her again, slash the woman's throat easy. But who knows if she can even be killed. Coeur will only get one shot at this surprise, best save it for the one who really matters.

"This is a fantastic deal, though," Coeur says; Meijer doesn't look down at her this time, though a muscle jumps in her jaw. "You wouldn't believe how much I paid the last time I got well and truly fucked like this."

"Will you sh—"

The ceiling explodes above them, and Coeur ducks her head to protect her face from the rain of broken glass. Something lands on the path in front of them: a figure covered head to toe in black combat gear. Shock of blond hair under his helmet, flash of pale eyes: Manu's soldier, isn't he. Oriol.

Meijer drops Coeur; she crumples to the ground with one leg twisted painfully beneath her. Meijer sets the case down — much more carefully, thank hell —

and as she launches herself at Oriol, Coeur tries to roll to pick it up. Something crunches in her knee.

One of Bennion's soldiers snatches up the silver case before she can reach it, and continues down the path. Coeur snarls after him.

"Take her," Bennion shouts, and yet another pair of hands are on her. Coeur blinks away burning tears of impotent rage, forces herself to breathe. Let it go, Thala. Bide your time.

These new hands are gentler than Meijer's or Manu's, though. A touch more cautious about hurting her, surprisingly careful as they manipulate her arm over broad shoulders.

Jaantzen's arm is sturdy around her waist. She can feel the warmth of his cheek near hers, smell his cologne and sweat, feel the effort of his breath in his lungs.

"Get me close to that asshole," she whispers into the glinting diamond stud in his ear.

She can't tell if he nods.

They're heading out the back, which Coeur gathers was meant to be an easy getaway before Jaantzen's people turned the place into a war zone. And her own people, she supposes, if Manu was able to get through to Castor Nikahr in time. Life and death was a good enough reason to burn that favor owed.

Bennion keeps close to Jaantzen, like Jaantzen's bulk will shield him from stray fire, but he's on the wrong side. Coeur could lunge for him. Normally she's got a killer jab that tends to catch opponents unaware.

But her hands aren't normally in a dozen pieces. She can't trust that jab today.

Bennion prods Jaantzen with the muzzle of his gun towards a waiting spinner. "Your people won't shoot if they know you're in here with me."

"Leave us and I'll be sure they don't," Jaantzen says, and Bennion transfers the muzzle of the gun from Jaantzen's side to the base of his skull.

"Of course, they'll assume you're alive," Bennion says.

Coeur doesn't need Jaantzen, honestly. Having him around makes her plan a thousand percent harder. But she's not gonna let Bennion kill him. And it's not that Jaantzen saved her life a few days ago. A blood debt should trump everything else — but she's never let that keep her from doing what needed done before.

Just, if anyone's going to put a bullet in Willem Jaantzen's skull, it's going to be her. A lightweight piece of trash like Bennion Zacharia hasn't earned the right.

"Willem."

Bennion's too close, she can't repeat what she said earlier, but she thinks it with every ounce of might she has left: *Get me close to him.*

Slowly, Jaantzen bends to put Coeur into the spinner. It's perfect, designed more for transport than comfort, with two bench seats facing each other across a cramped aisle. In such a small space, she can't help but be close to Bennion.

A shot rings out as Jaantzen settles Coeur on the bench. The soldier closest to Bennion falls.

"Thala!"

No. *No* — Coeur lunges past Jaantzen, lunges towards her sister's voice as more shots ring out. The back window of the spinner spiderwebs and Ximena grunts in pain.

Coeur reaches the door to the spinner, screaming her sister's name. Just as Bennion shoots her in the head.

Ximena slumps to the ground, a mantle of black spreading beneath her shoulders, eyes wide-open to the night sky. Coeur can't tell if she's still screaming through the ringing in her ears, she can't breathe, can't react as Bennion's remaining soldier shoves her brutally back into the spinner. Bennion dives in after, pulling the door closed behind him. He yells something at the driver, but Coeur can't hear him. Can't hear, can't feel anything as they careen through a gate, as bullets spark and fade against the shell of the spinner, as the soldier beside her braces his arm across her to keep her from smashing against the door in a sharp turn. That white-hot throb through her body could be her injuries, could be her heart exploding in grief. She's aware of nothing but a gnawing black rage spreading like oil through the fire of her pain.

Did someone say her name?

Coeur blinks, letting the image in front of her slowly resolve until she's staring straight into Bennion Zacharia's eyes.

He's sitting on the cramped bench seat across from her, his back to the driver, Jaantzen beside him. He checks the ammo in his gun, lays it in his lap so the barrel points at Jaantzen. Smiles at her like she's some broken bird to be pitied.

"That was your sister, wasn't it?"

Wasn't it.

Coeur's learned better than to let the black rage show. She stays glassy-eyed and expressionless, letting herself sway with the shifting of the spinner, the jostling of potholes on rough desert road.

Bennion Zacharia will die. He will die screaming in fire, and Blackheart will be the one who lights the match. If it's the last thing she does.

She knows the boobytrap she put on this case, and everyone else seems to know it, too, the way they've been handling it with such care. Her original plan was to leave here with the case in hand, ditching Jaantzen somehow, her own future secured. There's another way to end this, though. And it's starting to seem a lot more appealing.

She glances at Jaantzen, who's watching her with an odd expression. She doubts anyone but his closest friends and longest-running enemies could read that stony expression, but he's worried. About her.

The fuck does this glorified old street boss have to live for, anyway? That fierce goddaughter of his can more than take care of herself, and Manu . . . she could tell him. *Should* tell him, that Manu's probably dead, that she watched him die. He's chosen vengeance over life before, he might just do it again now.

Grab that gun from Bennion's hand. Fire it at the case.

Boom.

A fitting end to her and Jaantzen both.

"Yes?"

Coeur flicks her attention back to Bennion, keeping her lids hooded and head bobbing. He's taking a call, but he lifts his weapon pointedly to Jaantzen as if to reassure him that he's paying attention. He doesn't spare a glance at Coeur, though.

Almost like he lives in a world where he doesn't need to pay attention to Blackheart.

A world where Blackheart is gone and dusted while she can still spit blood.

Wrong, bitch.

She lets the motion of the spinner shift her gaze back to Jaantzen. Raises an eyebrow in question when their eyes meet.

Jaantzen cuts his gaze to the soldier sitting beside her, then back. Raises his own eyebrows.

Coeur's response is a bitter quirk of her mouth: *Who do you think you're asking?*

Jaantzen gives her the faintest of nods.

Showtime.

Coeur drives her teeth through the tip of her tongue and breaks into a hacking cough, doubling over in her seat with hands hanging limply over her knees, the fingers of her shattered left hand straightened to hide the tip of the blade. The soldier looks over in alarm as she continues to cough blood; Bennion pauses in his conversation, studying her with disdain.

She ignores him like the speck of spittle he is.

"And just like that, Willem," she says when she's caught her breath. She wipes blood from her lips onto the back of her bandaged right hand; the soldier beside her flinches back. "A little gun to your head is all it takes for you to give me up. I thought we were friends."

"Quiet, please," Bennion says, finger touching his ear like a goddamned secretary. He's still trying to follow the conversation on the call.

Jaantzen ignores him. "I'm not sure where you got that impression."

"You think you can sell me like this and take my crew? Like you could try — you're not half the man you'd need to be for that." Coeur laughs, flashing the gap where the Dawn knocked out an eyetooth. "You'll be bored without me."

"Quiet," says Bennion.

"I have plenty of other enemies," Jaantzen says.

"Religious fanatics?" Coeur rolls her eyes. "Brain-washed idiots who got themselves an arsenal."

"We seem to have bested you," Bennion says irritably. "Now please be quiet."

"Strong man's snatched an invalid. Very impressive, I'm swooning."

Bennion sighs sharply and gestures to the soldier. "Shut her up."

The soldier snatches his electric barb from his belt

and reaches for Coeur, but she twists in her seat. Deflects his clumsy cross with her right hand, a howling fast jab with her bandaged left straight at the base of his throat.

A throat punch is dirty play in the ring, even dirtier when there's steel beneath your wraps, dirtier yet when that steel's a blade stabbing through flesh — but Coeur's not fighting for glory here, she's fighting for Naali and Chase and Manu and Ximena.

The soldier falls back, his hot blood pouring over her hands.

Jaantzen reacted the second she moved, well before Bennion, grabbing the dead soldier's pistol and jamming the barrel into Bennion's temple. Coeur grabs the soldier's electric barb, holding it awkwardly with her thumb on the button. Bennion slowly raises his hands, but doesn't move to set down his own pistol.

"Ben?" yells the driver.

"Keep driving!" Bennion calls. The spinner lurches as the driver punches the gas. Bennion's gaze doesn't waver. Neither does Jaantzen's aim.

"I am not your enemy here," Bennion says calmly.

"You're the one holding me hostage."

"Ignorance is the enemy. Kill me, and you won't do anything to stop the inevitable. Join me, and at least you'll go to your fate with your eyes open. Maybe your sacrifice will even help save some of your crew, your daughter."

Coeur laughs, spits blood. "'Ignorance is the enemy.'"

But Jaantzen is watching Bennion, serious. "Tell me what's coming."

"Now he wants answers," Bennion says with a faint smile. "I'll tell you. After we get Coeur and the case delivered safely."

"You're not listening to this," Coeur tells Jaantzen. He can't be.

"You and me, we have no chance to save ourselves," Bennion says. "But if the work I do saves others, I consider my life well lived. And your daughter? She still has a chance. So long as you don't throw it away."

Coeur reaches for Bennion's gun, taking it in her bandaged hands and tucking it out of reach. Jaantzen cuts his gaze to her, then back to Bennion.

"Tell me what you know."

The spinner's wheel drops into a pothole and Bennion lunges for Jaantzen, using the momentum of the vehicle to knock his weapon out of the way. A bullet slams into the body of the spinner beside Jaantzen's head — the driver firing back over his shoulder — and then the two men across from her are grappling, for control of the gun in Jaantzen's hand.

Coeur grabs the silver case into her lap and hauls the safety harness over her skeletal chest to secure both her and it, then takes aim with the electric barb.

"Hold on," she yells, and Jaantzen grabs for his own safety harness as she hits the button. The interior of the spinner crackles with energy as the barbs hit the driver in the neck and shoulder, then everything blurs in a cocktail shaker of pain as the spinner tumbles off the road.

———

Coeur doesn't remember passing out, but when she opens her eyes next the spinner is on fire, the reeking smoke of charred metal and scorched flesh filling the cab. The driver is dead — can't not be with the side of his face smashed in like that — and Coeur's pinned beneath the body of the soldier. Bennion Zacharia is gone. So is the case

And Jaantzen . . . Coeur shoves the big man with her elbow. Blood's streaming from a cut on his forehead, but he's breathing, eyes fluttering.

She takes stock of their situation. It's a quick inventory: fucked. Even if she wasn't trapped, she can't move fast enough to get out of the spinner. But Jaantzen could still get out.

And he's not the one who deserves to die in the fiery carcass of a destroyed spinner.

Coeur shoves him again. Shoves him harder and he gasps for breath, eyes flying open.

"About fucking time," she yells.

Jaantzen comes to in a snap — a small mercy — and wrenches himself free of the safety harness. The door beside him is partway open, which must be how Bennion took off, but Jaantzen doesn't follow suit. He reaches for Coeur, trying to move the dead soldier off her legs.

No common sense, this one.

"Go," Coeur yells. She grins at him, trying to get him to understand. Breathing has become hard; between the heat and the smoke the edges of her vision have blurred. "Right way for me to end, yeah?" Darkness is washing in. She welcomes it. "Always figured I'd deserve this," she murmurs. It doesn't make her mistake right, doesn't bring anyone back from the dead. But it fits. Poetic, even.

Her eyes close.

The next bit comes in flashes. The rush of fresh air as Jaantzen shoves the door open. The roar of the inferno sucking in new oxygen. The stench of her braids catching fire, tongues of flame licking her face. The tearing, wrenching pain of Jaantzen's hands under her armpits, hauling her bodily out from under the dead soldier and into the desert, away from the charred remains of the spinner.

Coeur's eyes flutter back open.

Jaantzen's not looking at her, his attention caught by something in the distance. She blinks, trying to see what he does, and realizes that flash of silver is Bennion Zacharia and the case just as Jaantzen lifts a rifle and fires.

The case will withstand the impact of being dropped when Jaantzen hits Bennion, thinks Coeur, but that's not what happens.

The bullet tears through the case, and a chemical fireball consumes the road, a complicated, multipetaled bloom of retina-burning oranges and bloody reds. A wave of heat washes over them both and flakes of grit drift gently down to coat their faces.

Coeur gapes at him in shock. "You missed," she hisses.

"I didn't," he replies.

# DEATHTRAP
## DURING PRESSURE POINT [DELETED SCENE]

---

I wrote this scene in Pressure Point, but decided to cut it because the book was getting long and I didn't feel this scene was moving the plot forward.

But I still love it, and am delighted to be able to share it with you here!

This scene is lovingly dedicated to my father, who would 100% build a boobytrapped underground bunker in the middle of nowhere if given half a chance. Love you, dad.

The murdercopters came from a newsletter poll I did after discovering a similar terrifying-looking contraption at an aviation museum.

You'll find more murdercopter action in Heat Death. And I promise Starla will get to ride that Trespass once she gets it fixed back up.

*You can find my original murdercopter post here: jessiekwak.com/murdercopter*

---

So this is going to be their refuge.

Starla Dusai puts up a hand to shade her eyes, turning to survey the property. It's at the far west end of the Maraka Valley, a few hours north of Bulari after a bumpy, featureless drive through desert scrub. It was a haul to get out here, and so far the prize at the end of the journey is pretty lackluster.

"It doesn't look like much from the outside," says the woman who's selling them the property. Luli Ocampo is a drama vid stereotype of a Maraka Valley resident: dry, graying hair cut short and spiky to frame her brown, sunworn face; wide nose and narrow, suspicious eyes; clothes the same drab taupe as the dust around them. She's missing two fingers.

Ocampo's laugh bares perfect teeth. "Doesn't look like much on the inside, either," she says with a shrug. "But it's a good piece of land, once you get all of Dad's traps cleared out." El Anahoy is interpreting, since Starla didn't trust the network out here to be strong enough for her lens's transcription to work. He finishes, then raises a skeptical eyebrow at Starla.

She knows. She *knows*. But they need a safehouse far from the city, away from prying eyes. Somewhere

Lucky — their new alien friend — will be safe from the Alliance's clutching claws and they all will be safe from the wrath of Chief Justice Geum-ja Leone.

The property's unimpressive exterior consists of a large, rusted hangar with sliding doors, and a one-room shack with a small front porch about twenty yards away. It's textbook homesteader, more focus on a place to keep transport and machinery than somewhere to live.

"Looks rustic," Starla signs.

"Dad wasn't much for frills," Luli Ocampo says. "But there's a ton of space once you get downstairs." Ocampo takes a look around the group, obviously aware that she's got her work cut out for her if she's going to nail this chance of finally offloading her father's estate. Besides Starla and El, Toshiyo Ravi has come along to help make the decision as to whether they can keep the alien here. And Giaconda Áte is lounging back against her spinner with arms crossed, expression neutral. She's the one who brought the idea of this property to Jaantzen's attention. Starla wonders if she'd seen it first, or just knew Ocampo was discreet and would sell for cheap.

"Shall we?" says Ocampo. "Stay on the path and don't touch anything."

She unlocks the front door of the shack with a physical key; there's no biolock, just a mechanical deadbolt. For a guy who was so paranoid about security, thinks Starla, he's not off to a good start. The shack's windows are wrapped in yellowing film, and in the gloom Starla can make out a narrow cot, a counter, a cookstove. A rickety wooden chair matches the pair sitting out on the front porch.

"I came by this morning and fired up the generator," says Ocampo, hitting the lights and crossing to where a faded family photo is mounted on the wall; Starla recognizes Luli Ocampo as a little girl. Ocampo slides the photo aside to reveal a switch. "All this is set dressing."

When she hits the switch, the bed — and the floor it's on — slides aside on grooves Starla can't even see. It reveals a set of stairs leading down into a dimly lit basement.

Toshiyo is grinning.

"Clever," Starla signs.

"Paranoid," counters Ocampo. "C'mon."

Ocampo leads them down a surprisingly long set of stairs and into a narrow hallway with doors on both sides. Because Starla's looking, she's starting to notice the seams of sliding panels. When activated, all of these panels slide open to turn the stairway into a kill chute from top to bottom, Ocampo tells them.

She also tells them she'd disabled most of her father's deadly traps over the year and a half since he'd passed away. "Should be safe now," she says with what Starla is starting to think of as a typical Maraka Valley practicality. Doesn't mean there aren't more in this deathtrap she missed.

Whereas the shack on the ground level was dusty

and broken down, the stairwell, hallway, and bunkers buried below are airtight. Stuffy with disuse, sure, but not nearly as trashed as Starla was expecting given the exterior. That's a good sign. If critters haven't been able break into the bunkers, Lucky probably won't be able to break out.

"Kitchen," says Ocampo, waving a hand at the room to their left once they reach the hallway. It looks more like a shard lab than a place to feed people; El gives it a look of contempt.

"We'll sterilize it and bring in some new equipment," Starla tells him.

"Probably want to nuke it outright," he signs back.

"Bedroom." Ocampo is ignoring their side banter; she doesn't seem to be able to follow even the most basic USL. She pushes open a door to reveal a narrow cot that makes Starla's back hurt just looking at it, along with a rail for hanging clothes. She pushes open another door to reveal drifts of electronics, coils of wires, and broken machinery. "I've cleaned out all of Dad's personal stuff, but there was a lot of . . . junk. I don't know how valuable any of it is, but it comes with the property."

"Is this an autotiller?" Toshiyo asks, peeling back the tarp covering something that looks like a dish sanitizer had an affair with a swarm of shuriken. Her grin is pure joy.

"I think we found Toshiyo's office," Starla signs to El; a little dimple appears in his warm brown cheek and he tucks a strand of electric blue hair out of his eyes. Now that she knows to look for it, his shy infatuation with Toshiyo is obvious. How did she miss it for so long?

"What did your dad do with all these rooms?" Starla asks Ocampo.

She shrugs. "He was prospecting out here, but he also wanted my sisters and I to move our families in with him. He thought — " Her lips press together.

"He thought what?"

"I don't like to talk politics."

"The Alliance," Gia says. Ocampo shoots her a glare.

"Why was he so worried about the Alliance?" Starla asks. She doesn't expect a straight answer — if he was a criminal or wanted by them, Ocampo's not going to tell her. Just like Starla wouldn't be straight with her if she asked the same question.

But Ocampo just shrugs. "Shouldn't we all be?"

"He was building a place to get his family off the grid if New Sarjun joined the Alliance," says Gia. "It's okay, Luli. There's no love lost for the Alliance with this group."

Ocampo relaxes. "Not if," she says. "When. He thought it was inevitable." At Starla's skeptical look she raises her hands. "He followed politics, not me. But I don't think he was wrong. Down here's the bathroom. Recycler unit, shower. It doesn't look like much but you should have seen version one-point-oh."

The rest of the tour reveals even more bunker

rooms. Some furnished, some cluttered with junk, some completely empty.

"I'd be lying if I said I thought this was all there is," Ocampo says once they've reached the second set of stairs at the other end of the hall. "I have a map, and like I said, I diffused all the boobytraps that were on it. But knowing Dad, there are probably a dozen more rooms down here he didn't bother to map. That's half the reason I haven't tried hard to sell this place — I don't want to be responsible for anybody blowing themselves up. But Gia told me you run a security company, or something like that? Just, if you want the place, be careful. That's all I'm saying."

"Strong sell, Luli," Gia jokes.

Ocampo shrugs and starts up the stairs. "I wouldn't wish this place on anyone. Wanna see the hangar?"

The hangar is a treasure trove of tetanus and broken bones and blood poisoning, and Toshiyo is in *heaven*. Starla can't help but smile as Toshiyo turns in glee to take in the haphazard — and hazardous — contents of the large outbuilding. After all, she's pretty excited herself at the potential held here. There's an ancient ORV cargo hauler that can probably handle the roughest road without problem, Starla can fix that up and use it for some of their remote clients at Admant Security. And here's — holy shit, it's a vintage al-Jurjani moto, a GS3 from their now-banned Trespass line. You can't even buy these anymore. Simca is going to be over the moon at a chance to ride it.

And over there — what the hell?

Toshiyo's eyes go wide. "Ooh! Look at the murdercopter!"

The contraption in the far corner looks like a personal helicopter that's designed to be folded up for easy storage and transportation. Fold out the blades and lock each section into place, then telescope up the harness and controls. The standing platform spirals outward above the blades — and it looks flimsy as hell. There's no way Starla would ever get on one of these, you're only one loose bolt from becoming a finely julienned ramen topping. The whole mess sits atop a set of self-inflating runners that elevate the blades and make it possible to land on soft sand or rocks. Maybe even water, if you can find a body of water large enough around here and aren't afraid of probably drowning.

Starla raises an eyebrow at Ocampo, who looks somehow both resigned and proud.

"My dad invented them," she says. "This is one of the early unigiro prototypes, but they actually did get better." She pulls away a tarp to reveal murdecopters, plural. The later models do look slightly less like a tornado crashed a wind turbine into a side table, and more like something Starla would actually attempt to ride. "He made them and sold them. There are a couple of people out here that own one of dad's unigiros."

"I've seen a few of those people at the clinic," says Gia. "One with a fractured tibia, one with a dislocated shoulder and multiple lacerations on her leg. Those would be best scrapped for parts."

Gia's probably right, but Starla's far too intrigued by the murdercopters to make any rash decisions yet.

Luli Ocampo waves an arm around the hangar. "There's probably some valuable stuff in here if you take the time to sort through it. I haven't — it's all part of the property if you want it."

Gia's already given them what she suspects is Luli's ballpark price. It's so reasonable that Starla would pay it just to get her hands on that al-Jurjani GS3 Trespass. But she needs to be sure it will meet their needs, too.

"Give us a second," Starla signs, and Gia and Ocampo wander off, talking about something Starla doesn't catch with her lens off. She tilts her head to Toshiyo. "Well?"

"We can turn one of those bunkers into a home for Lucky," Toshiyo responds in her usual rapidfire mishmash of USL and fingerspelling. "It would be easy enough to secure, right?"

El nods and pulls out his comm. "We have some leftover titanium fencing from that project at the governor's house." He finds what he's looking for and hands his comm to Starla so she can see Admant Security's current inventory list. "And plenty of that ballistic-grade mesh. The network out here is terrible."

"I can boost it," signs Toshiyo. "And as for our defense, I can get some of Luli's dad's boobytraps working again."

Starla makes a face at that. "Come up with a list and we'll talk about them." There might be some legitimately useful ones, but others — like the kill chute in the stairwell — seem like a tragedy waiting to happen. "El, can you help her?"

"Of course." His sharp cheekbones flush red; Starla pretends not to notice.

She turns slowly, taking in the hangar. Thinking about the bunkers downstairs. They were cramped, but Toshiyo barely leaves her office as it is. And Starla grew up on a space station: all tight spaces, everyone living practically on top of each other. Sure, it's nice to have her own apartment now, shared only with her —

Shit.

"Pepper and Mango," she signs to Toshiyo and El. "They'll have to come out here with us, which means we need to make sure this place is cat-proof." Those little bastards love to try to escape, but despite their belief in their own immortality, they wouldn't last a minute outside Starla's Bulari apartment — let alone out here in the desert with the dziva hounds and velvet adders.

"Copy that," signs El.

Toshiyo glances over her shoulder at the murder-copters. "I like it," she signs. "I think it works." She trails off, her expression says there's a "but" coming.

"But Jaantzen is going to hate it," signs Starla.

"And Manu." Toshiyo sighs. "They're both going to be insufferable out here."

She's right. Starla can already see Jaantzen crouched at his desk in one of the bunkers, tense as an overwound spring at not being in the center of the action. And Manu will wear down a path with his pacing, rangy energy in every movement, smile too bright and jokes too sharp.

"Then we make sure they're not stuck out here for too long," she signs. She takes a deep breath. "All right. I'm going to call Jaantzen and let him know we're gonna buy this deathtrap. Wish me luck."

# PART 4

---

# EPHEMERA

# RECIPES, ESSAYS, AND FREQUENTLY ASKED QUESTIONS

This section contains a number of oddities related to the Bulari Saga, which I hope you'll enjoy.

First up are a handful of recipes — cocktails and mocktails from Phaera's cookbooks, and Jade's famous chicken in black bean sauce (which is Manu's favorite takeout dish).

I had a ton of fun experimenting with these recipes, and can't wait to hear how they turn out for you!

(If you want to print the recipes out, I've formatted them on cards you can download at: *jessiekwak.com/ bulari-saga-recipes.*)

I've also included a couple of essays that add a bit more context around what it's been like to write the Bulari Saga — one on worldbuilding, and one on writing villains in a morally gray world, which I originally published to my newsletter a few years ago.

Finally, one of the Kickstarter stretch goals for this project was a Frequently Asked Questions section, where I solicited questions from backers. That resulted in some very fun questions, and I tried to answer them all to the best of my ability!

# JADE'S FAMOUS CHICKEN IN BLACK BEAN SAUCE

---

*I've always imagined Jade's famous chicken in black bean sauce as having a flavor profile similar to mole negro: smoky and earthy, with lots of complex spices. I love mole and have made it on multiple occasions — but it takes forever, and I hate cleaning up my kitchen afterwards. I wanted this black bean sauce to scratch my mole itch without requiring 30 ingredients and an entire day's labor.*

*In the Bulari Saga, Manu always orders the fried yucca to go along with his chicken — but I have no idea where one acquires yucca outside of specialty restaurants, and I don't have a deep fryer at home. So I chose to substitute one of my favorite treats as a side dish: tostones. Tostones are savory fried plantains, which I continue to prepare the way my friend*

*Jorge taught me in Venezuela so many years ago. I've included Jorge's instructions here.*

*I've written this recipe to serve two people, though you'll have plenty of leftover black bean sauce. If you're cooking for more, plan for a half pound of chicken and half a plantain per person. The black bean sauce can be made ahead of time. It can be stored for 5 (ish) days in the fridge, and it freezes well.*

---

## Black Bean Sauce

### INGREDIENTS

olive oil

1/2 onion (roughly chopped)

6 cloves garlic (roughly chopped)

1/3 cup golden raisins

1 teaspoon cumin

1 teaspoon oregano

1/2 teaspoon coriander

1/2 teaspoon garlic powder

1/4 teaspoon cinnamon

1/4 teaspoon clove

1/4 teaspoon cayenne

1 (15 ounce) can black beans

1/2 teaspoon salt

1 cup water

1 Tablespoon apple cider vinegar

## Instructions

1. Heat a drizzle of olive oil in a medium saucepan until hot. Add onion, garlic, and raisins and sauté until onions are browned and raisins are puffy and golden, about 10 minutes.

2. Add dry spices and sauté until fragrant, about 1 minute.

3. Pour onion mixture into food processor along with 1/2 cup of the black beans, salt, water, and vinegar. Process until smooth, then return to the saucepan along with the rest of the can of black beans. Simmer for 10–15 minutes, stirring frequently, until the beans are soft and the sauce is thickened.

Grilled Chicken

## Ingredients

4 cloves garlic (minced)

handful of cilantro (chopped)

1/2 teaspoon smoked paprika

1 pound boneless, skinless chicken thighs (about 4 thighs)

1 orange, divided

1/3 cup sliced almonds

## Instructions

1. Combine garlic, cilantro, smoked paprika, and juice from half the orange, in a large bowl. Add chicken thighs and marinate for 30–60 minutes.

2. Grill chicken on high for 16–20 minutes, turning every 4 minutes (or until chicken is cooked through). Remove from grill, cover, and let rest for 5 minutes.

3. While the chicken cooks, toast sliced almonds in a dry skillet until browned, and slice the remaining half orange for garnish (see serving instructions).

Tostones

## Ingredients

olive oil
1 green plantain
3 cloves garlic (finely minced)
salt

## Instructions

1. Cut the plantain in half crosswise, then cut each half lengthwise into 4 slices.

2. Heat olive oil in a heavy pan, and fry the plantain slices until lightly browned, approximately 3-4 minutes.

3. While the plantains cook, finely mince the garlic and spread it out over your cutting board. Sprinkle salt generously over the garlic.

4. Remove the cooked plantains from the pan. One

by one, lay a plantain piece across the minced garlic and salt mixture and, with the flat of your knife, press it until it's about 1/8 inch thick.

5. Return the flattened plantain pieces to the olive oil and fry until crispy and brown, approximately 3-4 minutes.

6. Remove the tostones from the pan and set on a paper towel to drain and cool.

## To Serve

Serve grilled chicken thighs over rice. Top with black bean sauce, toasted almonds, and a sprinkling of cilantro. Garnish with orange slices and tostones.

# DEVIL'S TEARS (COCKTAIL)

---

In Crossfire, Jaantzen and Manu visit Phaera at the Devil's Table, where she serves them a cocktail called Devil's Tears. I wrote the scene with no real cocktail in mind, so I just described something that sounded fun. In trying to recreate it for this book, I've run into several problems. One is that I describe her as using jienja, which I totally made up, so I wasn't sure which real-life alcohol to replace it with. I decided to go with mezcal, since that's Phaera's go-to anyway.

If you've never had mezcal before, it's a Mexican spirit made from agave (just like tequila), but the agave is coal-roasted beforehand, which gives it a nice smoky taste reminiscent of the peat-smoked flavor you find in many Scottish whiskies.

*Just like tequila, mezcal comes in a range of ages.*

*- **Joven (young):** Unaged mezcal bottled straight from the still. (Often called "silver" in tequila.)*

*- **Reposado (rested):** Aged in oak barrels for a few months to a year. (Often called "gold" in tequila.)*

*- **Añejo (aged):** Aged for a minimum of 1 year.*

*The younger the mezcal, the more intensely the smoke flavor will come through. The longer it's been aged, the more mellow the flavors will be. If you like that smoky flavor, go for a joven. (They're also less expensive.) If you want your cocktail a bit mellower, go for a reposado. You could also simply substitute tequila if you want to avoid the smokiness altogether.*

*The second problem I came across was that I describe a milky pearl that is dropped into the drink as a garnish, "dissolving in a stream of tiny ruby bubbles." In consulting with my friend Melissa Flitsch, who is one of the best bakers and cooks I know, she suggested replicating the effect with "food caviar." I then went down a huge rabbit hole watching Chef Majk on YouTube (www.chefmajk.com) make these fascinating little spheres, and ultimately decided that I was never going to spend the time making them myself. And that delivering a cocktail recipe for this book that required hours of prep work was a big ask. Instead, I opted for a drizzle of hibiscus simple syrup to create that same sparkling ruby color. Where do you get hibiscus flowers? If you have a Latin grocery nearby, look for jamaica flowers (pronounced "ha-MY-aca"). Otherwise, many US grocery stores sell hibiscus tea.*

*Finally, Manu mentions that he tastes sage in the cocktail, so I decided to throw in a handful of sage leaves — which turned out to be a delicious addition!*

---

## INGREDIENTS

1-1/2 ounces mezcal (or tequila)
1/2 ounce St-Germain elderflower liqueur
1/2 ounce lime juice
1/4 ounce hibiscus simple syrup (see recipe)
5-6 sage leaves
ice

## Instructions

1. Fill a cocktail shaker (or mason jar) with ice. Add sage leaves and muddle.

2. Add mezcal, St-Germain, and lime juice. Shake

for 30 seconds, then strain into a rocks glass and fill with ice.

3. Float hibiscus syrup around the outer perimeter of the liquid so it will drip down inside the glass like tears

4. Garnish with a dried hibiscus flower, a sage leaf, or both.

# SIREN SONG (COCKTAIL)

*Because the Devil's Table has a signature cocktail, it seemed only fair to come up with one for the Lorelei.*

*When my husband and I go out, I tend to get a hoppy IPA, and he tends to get something sweet that comes with an umbrella. Even better if it comes in one of those ridiculous tiki glasses that are shaped like pineapples or Easter Island statues. When Robert asked a bartender in San Diego for "a pirate drink," she made her version of a Three Dots and a Dash, and it turned out to be his personal siren song.*

*I've been trying to recreate the drink ever since — however, a Three Dots and a Dash requires a laundry list of specialty ingredients* we had trouble finding even in Portland, Oregon, and I wanted the drinks in this book to be more accessible. I did end up falling in love with the main ingredient, rhum agricole.

Rhum agricole is made with sugarcane rather than molasses, and is specifically made in Martinique. It has an earthy, grassy flavor which makes it quite interesting, and I wanted a cocktail that would bring out those herbaceous flavors. I decided to go with a twist on a basil gimlet, which is normally made with gin. The result is a bright, refreshing cocktail. (And you can absolutely make this with a white rum if you have trouble tracking down rhum agricole.)

## INGREDIENTS

1-1/2 ounces rhum agricole (or white rum)
1/2 ounce lime juice
1/4 ounce agave nectar or simple syrup
8-10 medium basil leaves
ice

## Instructions

1. Fill a shaker with ice. Add basil leaves and muddle.

2. Add rhum agricole, lime juice, and agave nectar (or simple syrup). Shake for 30 seconds.

3. Strain into a martini glass and garnish with a basil leaf.

# RUBY LAGOON (MOCKTAIL)

*This is a twist on a drink we call, at our house, "Rob Soda." My husband loves spicy water (sparkling water), and his favorite way of drinking it is with the juice of half a lime and half a lemon. I thought it would be nice to add a touch of sweet, slightly tart hibiscus syrup to make it even more fun.*

### INGREDIENTS
1 lemon
1 lime
1-2 ounces hibiscus simple syrup (see recipe)
sparkling water
ice

. . .

## Instructions

1. Fill a glass with ice.

2. Squeeze the juice of half a lemon and half a lime into the glass, then add hibiscus simple syrup and top up with sparkling water.


## Notes

I like the tartness of 1 ounces of hibiscus simple syrup, but my husband prefers his Ruby Lagoon on the sweeter side, with 2 ounces.

Also, here's a trick for choosing limes at the grocery store, which I learned from my supervisor at the Seattle Repertory Theater when I worked at the bar there in college. My supervisor's lime-picking mantra was "dark green in color and heavy for its size." That'll help you get the perfect juicy lime every time.

# HIBISCUS SIMPLE SYRUP

*This is a simple recipe useful for many cocktails and mocktails, including Devil's Tears and Ruby Lagoon.*

**INGREDIENTS**

1 cup sugar

1 cup water

1/2 cup dried hibiscus flowers

## Instructions

1. Bring sugar, water, and hibiscus flowers to a boil, stirring, until sugar has dissolved.

2. Remove from heat and allow to cool, then strain

out the hibiscus flowers. Refrigerate the syrup until needed.

3. This simple syrup will keep refrigerated in a sealed container for around 2 weeks, but if you have extra, you can also freeze it in an ice cube tray.

## Notes

This is a fun recipe to experiment with! Add sliced ginger, a cinnamon stick, or even a dash of cayenne pepper when simmering the sugar and water.

# THE STRANGE ALCHEMY OF WORLD BUILDING

---

*This essay was first published in Mad Scientist Journal in 2019.*

---

I'LL BE THE FIRST TO ADMIT THAT I'M LESS THAN scientific when it comes to my science fiction.

In fact, the reason that I create science fictional worlds isn't usually because I want to explore a strange alien universe or technological idea. Rather, it's because I want to build a specific type of laboratory that I can put characters into and watch how they react.

Characters are my corked vials full of alchemical compounds, the world my precisely laid out lab conditions. For me, the fun in the writing process is pouring everything together and seeing what explodes.

In my current series, I knew I wanted to experiment with the idea of freedom. Who has it? What is it worth? What does freedom mean to individual characters, and how far are they willing to go to get it?

To play around with this idea, I needed a world with a variety of interesting constraints for my characters to bump up against.

## An easy life, or the ability to make your own rules?

I've always loved Westerns, and as I began to put together my universe, I knew I wanted it to have that Wild West vibe of civilization vs the frontier.

The civilized part of the system is the planet that was first colonized, Indira. There, life is easy and water-rich and—of course—such freedom to live a good life comes with certain societal expectations and oversight.

Some people are little bit too ornery for polite society, though. Maybe they decided they'd rather take a risk on the harsh desert planet, New Sarjun, because there were fortunes to be made mining minerals. Maybe they were escaping conscription into "polite" society's never-ending wars. Maybe they were running from the long arm of the law.

Whatever the reason, they gave up an easy life for one where no one's looking over their shoulders.

(Although, this kind of freedom still comes with its own rules—and its own cost.)

These two planets aren't just peaceful opposites, of course. Their way of life is also in conflict. Ever seeking order, the more law-abiding planet, Indira, is constantly trying to get to the rest of the Durga System to join with them in an alliance.

The result would be peace—another type of freedom. One which comes with plenty of strings attached.


## A good job, or freedom to live?

Another condition I built into the world has to do with education. I wanted to play with the idea of what it really costs to get an education.

What if, instead of each individual taking out a loan to get a college degree that may or may not land them a job, corporations funded education for the jobs they needed?

That would solve our current problem in the U.S. of a surplus of students graduating with degrees and debts while employees still can't fill certain jobs. In this system, graduates would know that they'll take on a certain level of debt to their employer—but it comes with a guaranteed indenture to a stable job.

It seems like a rational solution. But if reading about it made your skin crawl—yeah. Me too.

Because in reality, there still only a certain number of jobs, and no matter how smart some kid in the slums is, they're more likely to end up indentured to a mining corporation out in the sticks rather than landing a C-suite job at a pharmaceutical company.

Alternately, if your family has money and can pay for your schooling outright? The world is your oyster.

Or, you could do what most of my protagonists have done and turn instead to a life of crime.

## Who can afford freedom?

Layering the idea of an indenture system for employment over this dichotomy of a society—free-spirited versus rulebound—gave me another ingredient to play with. But there's another layer that affects them both.

Who can *afford* to be free?

I wanted to build a world where the usual things people get discriminated against for don't matter: disability, gender, ethnicity, sexuality. I've always subscribe to the idea of "write the world you want to live in," which is why in the Durga System, you can attain an equal level of respect whether you are a bisexual black man, a deaf woman, an Asian grandmother, or an amputee.

(I like to joke that in my world anyone can be a space gangster.)

I didn't want those things to be variables in my exploration of what it means to be free. Instead, I wanted to play with the idea of wealth and social status. Who has money, how do they get it, how does it buy them freedom?

And if it buys them freedom, will it also buy them respect from people who feel like they came from a better background?

If you grew up in an orphanage and on the streets, or in the slums of the capital city, or out in the asteroid belt with a family of space pirates, will you ever have enough money to earn respect from people who were born to wealth?

## Pour it together and watch it explode

That sketches out the limits of my laboratory, the constraints of the world designed to force my characters to continually grapple with what freedom means and what they're willing to pay to get it.

For my protagonist, Willem Jaantzen, fleeing the orphanage rather than taking on an indenture bought him freedom to make his own choices—but the price was life on the streets. And now that he's built his own successful business empire, will it buy him the freedom of other business owners' respect?

Meanwhile, his lieutenant, Manu, grapples with the freedom—and the cage—that comes with his work while Manu's partner, Oriol, learns exactly at what price his own yearning to be free and travel has come. And Jaantzen's goddaughter, Starla, grapples with the limits her devotion to family places on her personal life.

And above it all, greater political and social forces

rub together like thunder clouds—and trouble is defi-nitely right around the corner.

Let's see what sparks fly, shall we?

# ON VILLAINS

---

*I wrote this series of essays in 2021, after coming back from Sirens, a feminist science fiction and fantasy conference in Denver, CO. The theme of the conference was "Villains," which led to lots of delightful programming and conversations about the role of villains in our stories.*

*As someone who's always been fascinated by the concept of "right" and "wrong" and the complicated spaces in between, spending a weekend talking about villains sparked my curiosity about the role of the villain in my own books.*

*There are a few clear villains in the Bulari Saga, and a few who are less clear. And, fun fact, Jaantzen and his crew originally started out as the villains in a long-dead version of the novel that finally became* Double Edged.

*These essays were originally published to my newsletter. Part 1 of the series contains no spoilers for the Bulari Saga, but I do delve more deeply into the events of the book in parts 2 and 3.*

*Enjoy!*

---

[Part 1] Who gets to be a villain?

As a child, I loved the Disney movie Sleeping Beauty — but probably not for the reason I was supposed to.

I suffered through Aurora's sappy yearning for love. I yawned at the Prince (. . . um, Erik?) and his earnest escapades.

I loved Flora, Fauna, and Merriwether of course — who doesn't appreciate a gaggle of adorable witchy aunties who are just doing their best at adulting?

But I watched Sleeping Beauty for my idol.

Maleficent.

She had power. She commanded minions. She was fierce and strong. She did whatever the hell she wanted.

Yes, cursing a baby to die is pretty terrible — especially when her beef was actually with the parents. But as a child I remember feeling awed by her strength, confidence, and casual assumption of power.

She was a boss bitch, and she was amazing. I'd rather be her than boring, sappy Aurora crying on her bed any day.

As a girl, I felt like I was offered two choices in Sleeping Beauty: sit around waiting to be saved, or turn into a literal dragon and set some shit on fire.

I wanted to be the dragon.

### Cue Sirens...

A few weeks back, I attended Sirens Con, the feminist SFF convention in Denver, CO.

The theme of the conference was villains: Who gets cast as villains in our media? How are straight, cis male villains treated compared to female, nonbinary, and LGBTQ+ villains? What does a villain need to do to have a redemption arc? What does it mean to be morally gray?

Nearly every panel and talk touched somewhat on the theme. As a writer of sci-fi crime stories about space gangsters and pirates, you can bet I have a LOT of thoughts on how these topics relate to my own work.

My attempt to sit and write a quick recap of Sirens turned into a multi-part series of essays.

Shall we dive in?

. . .

**Maleficent didn't become a villain by accident.**

(And, no, I'm not talking about her character back-story, or the recent retelling with Angelina Jolie.)

Her character design in the animated film was deliberate, influenced by a Prohibition-era set of rules called the Hays Code — which we learned about at Sirens in a fascinating keynote talk given by Sarah Gailey.

The Hays Code was provided in 1927 by the Motion Picture Producers and Distributors of America — it listed things that should not be included in movies, such as profanity and nudity, but also things like relationships between people of different races, scenes of childbirth, and the positive portrayal of sexual depravity.

The idea is based on something I completely agree with: stories expand our experiences and help us empathize with other perspectives. Stories teach us, whether we're aware of it or not.

What the Hays Code said, though, was that we should only be teaching audiences to empathize with certain people.

As Sarah Gailey pointed out in their talk, the Hays Code wanted audiences to empathize with "model citizens." White, Christian, straight, and hard-working.

Anyone who didn't fit that box could only be portrayed in a negative light. They got to be villains.

No one empathizes with the villains, right?

Well, no one except for us misfits.

You'll notice sexual depravity on the Hays Code no-no list, of course. Loose women and women who are confident in their sexuality obviously fall into this category — hence the trope of the femme fatale, or the voluptuous vixen who gets a humiliating downfall.

And, of course, the gays. Start listing off old movie villains in your head, and just notice how many are butch women and effeminate men.

Sticking with Disney villains for a moment, take Ursula the sea witch, another of my Disney favorites. Sarah Gailey pointed out that Ursula's character design, expressions, and movements were literally based off the famous drag queen Divine.

The Hays Code was generally abandoned by the 60s for the rating code we use today (at least in the US), but the reverberations linger.

Imagine it.

- Think of the gay kids who are only ever allowed to glimpse themselves in Scar or Ursula or Javier Bardem's depraved Bond villain.
- Think of the Muslim kids who are only ever allowed to see themselves as terrorists.
- Think of ambitious girls who are only allowed to see themselves as psychotic, power-hungry madwomen.

**As a girl, I wanted to be the dragon.**
In real life I've actually become more like Flora,

Fauna, and Merriweather, the witchy aunties just doing their best at adulting — but Maleficent still inspires me.

I have a figurine of her on my desk, a gift from my sister. Every time I catch a glimpse of it, I remember that it's okay for a woman to be a bit monstrous if it means advocating for herself and fully coming into her power.

And it reminds me to pay attention to the worlds I'm writing, and the implicit lessons I'm sharing about who can and cannot be a hero.

## [Part 2] Morally gray worlds

One of my favorite talks at Sirens was by Fonda Lee, author of the phenomenal *Green Bone Saga*.

Fonda's talk was inspired by a discussion she had earlier this year on Twitter, where she wrote:

---

> *I've noticed that a lot of people think I write morally gray characters. Personally, I've never thought of it that way. I write morally gray "societies." There's a difference.*
>
> *(And let's face it, all societies are morally gray, aren't they?)*

---

In her talk, Fonda broke society into a 2x2 matrix

to demonstrate how a character's morality relates to the world.

- On the Y axis, we have whether a character is fighting to uphold the society, or to destroy it
- On the X axis, we have whether a character is acting selfishly or for the good of others

Think about our own world for a moment (meaning, the world whose morals we are familiar with/agree with). Looking at each of the four quadrants you get:

- Hero: A character is fighting to uphold this "lawful" world for the good of others
- Villain: A character is fighting to destroy this "lawful" world for selfish reasons
- Anti-hero: A character is trying to do the right thing for the wrong (selfish) reasons
- Sympathetic villain: A character is doing the wrong thing for the right (selfless) reasons

Anti-heros and sympathetic villains might be considered morally gray. But where things get more interesting — and where the world of the Bulari Saga comes in — is when the society itself is morally gray. That is, when its moral code is different from our own.

It's in these morally gray societies when things start to go wobbly like a funhouse mirror, where "right" and "wrong" aren't so clearly defined. Destroying a planet full of people is wrong. Destroying a planet-sized Death Star full of people is . . . right? Supporting the rebellion to save others is heroic. Supporting the rebellion to make a quick buck is . . . morally gray.

That's the sandbox I wanted to play in when I wrote the Bulari Saga.

(Spoilers from here on out.)

Fonda Lee has said her own clan organizations in the *Green Bone Saga* (which are based on real life syndicates like the Yakuza and the Triads) aren't criminal organizations because in the world of Jade City, the clans are legitimate governing bodies.

In the world of Bulari, Willem Jaantzen and co fall squarely into the realm of the illegitimate and illegal. However, the border between the criminal underground and the legitimate business and governing spheres is very, *very* porous. The underground is a violent place ruled by force and leverage, while the legitimate realm is . . . the same, just less physically violent.

Bulari's morality isn't that different from our own world, and that was part of the point to me. My characters aren't working to tear down a big, evil Empire like in Star Wars. They're just trying to succeed in a society whose rules look a lot like ours: Be born privileged — or at least look the part, work hard, make the right friends, and pay off the right people.

Of course, there are some key differences. For

example, we don't ask people to take on indentures in order to pay for their education. (Or do we?)

In the first book, *Double Edged*, the reader is immersed entirely into the point of view of Willem Jaantzen and his crew of plucky criminals. In later books, we start to get outside perspectives that give the reader glimpses of Jaantzen's crew through other lenses.

- Oriol as an outside mercenary who's deciding whether to finally shift his mostly selfish reasons for helping out to more selfless ones
- Timo Cho, as the detective who's long tried to take Jaantzen down — only to realize he'll have to reconsider his own ideas of right and wrong if he wants to take down the bigger bad
- And, of course, Phaera — who comes from outside the underworld, and repeatedly has to decide if she's comfortable with her new allies

People tell me all the time how much they love my characters — and I love them, too. But as Jaantzen says to Gia at the end of *Crossfire*:

---

*"You can tell yourself I'm doing the right thing in a world of people who aren't, but don't lie to*

*yourself and pretend I got where I am clean, Giaconda. Tevi's the one saving the world. Not me."*

---

I didn't want to simply hand-wave away some of the actual bad shit Jaantzen and co do in order to reach what feels like a noble goal.

And although I didn't know she was going to sweep in and steal my heart (and Jaantzen's), Phaera ended up playing the role of the audience stand in, constantly checking in with how Jaantzen fit her own moral compass.

If this was a traditional mafia story set in our world where we generally equate "lawful" and "unlawful" with "moral" and "immoral," the tension would be whether Phaera can redeem Jaantzen, or whether Jaantzen will corrupt Phaera.

When you remove the connotations of legality = morality, the story becomes different. After all, the abuse Toshiyo suffered during her indenture was perfectly legal. The villages Oriol helped destroy while quelling the New Manilan bid for independence were razed legally. It's perfectly legal to remove voting booths from the Fingers to repress voters.

Is that the society Phaera wants to uphold?

At first, Phaera steps into her flirtation with Jaantzen and the Bulari underground boldly. She's a woman who knows what she wants, and she's out to get it.

Eventually, she begins to realize the extent of her blinders — and gets to decide if she wants to take them off. She asks Jaantzen for his help dealing with Levi Acheta, but at first she doesn't let herself acknowledge what "deal with Acheta" actually entails. She allies herself with him against Geum-ja Leone, but she tells herself it's to help root out corruption in the government.

What she realizes instead is that she's not fighting to replace corrupt power with non-corrupt power. This is just the way the system works.

She's not helping change the system, she's helping change the people who are in charge.

Will these people govern better? I certainly hope so.

But as Jaantzen says, we can't pretend they got there clean. (And neither can Phaera.)

In *Heat Death* (Bulari Saga 4), Phaera has one of several "face the truth" moments when she asks Oriol if Manu killed Timo Cho; Oriol tells her (truthfully) that he didn't.

---

*"You were with me," Phaera says. "You can't know for sure."*

*"It wouldn't make sense."*

*"It wouldn't make sense, or it wouldn't be right?" He's silent, and something shifts at her core, a deep fracture that has nothing to do with this charade and everything to do with the*

*truth of the world as she knows it. "Tell me, Sina," she murmurs. "Tell me Jaantzen's not the kind of man who'd order Manu to kill a police officer."*

*Oriol takes a deep breath, but he can't tell her no — Phaera knows that, with the sickening dizziness of realization that she may be putting on a show, but every word she's said here is true. She's long been wondering what skeletons Jaantzen might have in his closet. But maybe the better question is, how long will she keep fooling herself he doesn't?*

Another "face the truth" moment is in *Kill Shot* (Bulari Saga 5):

*She's lying to herself if she pretends Willem Jaantzen's just another successful bootstrapping story with a rough past that's far behind him, but she can't decide if that matters to her.*

*It should.*

*But she saw the "honest" Bulari business owners and politicians lining up to pledge their loyalty to Liatris Yang at Julieta's funeral. And despite Jaantzen's reluctance to talk about what he actually did for Julieta, she knows smuggling isn't bloodless. She loved Julieta. And has heard plenty of whispered* stories about how ruthlessly the woman ran her business, and the role a young enforcer named Willem Jaantzen played.

How ruthlessly is Phaera willing to run her own business?

Of course, she already has an answer. When Levi Acheta started demanding protection payments from the business owners in the Casino District, she could have paid him like the others. Instead, she went to Jaantzen for help. Acheta ended up dead, and her problem went away. She might not have admitted it to herself at the time, but wasn't that the result she'd hoped for?

She didn't go to Jaantzen because she wanted to reach a friendly agreement with Acheta. She went to him for help because she wanted the bastard gone and she knew Jaantzen could make it happen.

Maybe Jaantzen and Acheta would have clashed in the end, but it doesn't change what Phaera fundamentally asked Jaantzen to do.

If Acheta's death sits uneasy on her conscience, though, that fades as her cab pulls up in front of the Lorelei.

The Lorelei's facade has been repaired seamlessly since Acheta's people shot it up, the cascading holograms flowing to create the illusion of walking through the veil of a waterfall into a mystic cavern beyond. There's no sign

> *left of the bodies of her people, her patrons, who bled out on the sidewalk and in the lobby.*
>
> *Acheta deserved what he got, and Phaera's chin is high when she walks through those doors, Oriol and Mel at her back.*

---

And of course, there is the ending of the Bulari Saga — which my husband Robert and I argued about passionately.

After defeating the murder cultists, Jaantzen does what the "legitimate" society of Bulari would say is the right thing. He makes a deal with Leone, cementing his own power and proving himself an equal in the upstanding business community. He has a long-term plan of political machinations that will eventually lead to her downfall, but he is nothing if not a patient man.

Except that leaving Leone to keep her power without consequences would have been extremely unsatisfying to the reader — and completely crushing to Phaera, who's born the brunt of Leone's villainy.

Jaantzen had already proven that he can move beyond past wounds and work with an enemy (we'll talk all about Coeur in the next part of this essay). But working with Coeur almost destroyed his relationship with Manu.

Working with Leone would have destroyed his relationship with Phaera.

What Jaantzen ends up doing instead is handing Leone off to Thala Coeur to be dispatched. Fully in cold blood, Jaantzen sits down with Leone for coffee, tricks her into recording a confession, and puts her in a car with Coeur. He then walks away, his hands technically clean and soul completely unburdened.

When Robert first read this scene, he said, absolutely not. Killing supreme court justices in cold blood is not what heroes do.

Jaantzen isn't a hero, I argued. And letting her live would be unsatisfying.

So have her get killed in the final battle, Robert said.

But that felt very untrue to the world. Sure, she'd be gone — but that would also remove any hard choice Jaantzen or Phaera would have to make.

It's pretty rare that Robert and I argue so strongly over a plot point in one of my books, but when we do, it's because it's something I fully believe needs to happen, and I just haven't sold it well enough in the writing. Eventually, Robert sighed. "At least make sure we know Phaera is okay with what he did," he said.

At that point, I'd already written the final scene in *Kill Shot* where Jaantzen goes to visit Phaera, but I'd cut it off when she invites him in. After the conversation with Robert, I realized that in leaving her acceptance of the underworld rules unsaid, I was missing the landing on her character arc, too.

This is the scene as it was published:

*Phaera pulls one of a set of mismatched coffee mugs out of a cupboard and pours him a cup, then turns wordlessly to sit on the red leather couch, leaning back against the arm with her feet up on the cushions, knees bent to give him room to sit. Her bare feet are a handsbreadth from his thigh, yet he doesn't know how to touch her again.*

*She's watching him expectantly.*

*"You're going to say I should have told you what I was planning," he finally says.*

*Phaera sips her coffee. "And you're going to say you don't want me thinking of you as the kind of man who could carry out a hit on the chief justice of the Supreme Court." She slides her feet forward until her toes are wedged under his thigh, and heat sparks electric from that point of contact. He lets his hand fall to rest on her calf, sliding under the loose silk of her house trousers.*

*"But you are," Phaera says.*

*"Does it bother you?"*

*She considers it a moment. "I wanted you to. So it makes me a hypocrite that it bothers me."*

*"Or it makes you human."*

Phaera found her own path through the morally

gray society of Bulari. I can't say if she's right or wrong, but I can say she was one of my favorite characters to write because of that journey.

Thanks for sticking with me on this discussion of morally gray worlds. In the next part of this essay series, I'm going to do another deep dive inspired by the Sirens conference. We're going to talk about what makes a good villain.

Yep, that's right.

We're going to talk about the woman who is the worst — yet who's also secretly my favorite character in the entire Bulari Saga.

Thala Coeur.


## [Part 3] Blackheart's gonna Blackheart

I can't remember the exact moment I decided not to kill Thala Coeur.

Maybe it was when she convinced Manu to give her the knife at the end of *Double Edged*.

Maybe it was the defiance in her bloody smile the first time we meet her when Jaantzen is breaking her free.

But most likely it was the scene in the hospital room the night of her rescue, when she lands barbs on Jaantzen with surgical precision — and they're exactly the thing he needs to hear to get him to make the right decision.

She's just such a good villain.

What do I mean by that?

A good villain should push the heroes to be better people — and not just in the sense of doing good deeds to counteract the villain's bad deeds. A good villain should be a furnace specifically calibrated to the temperature the hero needs to forge themselves into a better person.

A good villain should transform the hero.

Killing Coeur at the end of *Double Edged* would have felt justified — and more than a few reviewers have let me know how angry they are that she didn't get her "proper punishment." But it also felt so easy. So predictable.

I knew that if I kept Coeur alive and followed through with the plan to put her in power, she would either destroy Jaantzen's relationship with his family, or transform it into something infinitely stronger.

Maybe I could even redeem her, I thought.

But when I was writing *Pressure Point*, though, I was starting to wonder if I'd made a terrible mistake.

Jaantzen makes his own peace with Coeur early in *Crossfire*, not exactly forgiving Coeur for the death of his wife and children, but actively deciding to begin healing the wound he's guarded so tightly all these years.

But Jaantzen isn't the only person Coeur hurt, and the others aren't able to forgive that easily.

The first real fight Jaantzen and Manu have is directly after the hospital room scene in *Double Edged*, when Manu is frankly betrayed by the fact that Jaantzen would consider putting Coeur back in power. Manu slowly comes to terms with the fact that Coeur is their best bet for keeping the peace in Bulari, but the internal tension of trying to pretend he's fine with it almost tears him apart in *Pressure Point*.

Writing that book was a struggle — I didn't know how Manu would manage to forgive Jaantzen.

I remember driving back from a convention in Spokane, WA with my friend Jon; I spent quite a bit of that 6-hour drive laying out the tangled web of emotions and betrayals Manu felt towards Jaantzen, and trying to brainstorm how to heal their relationship.

Finally Jon shook his head. "I don't know how you come back from that."

A good villain forces the hero to face their darkest demons. So I decided to add another one to the mix.

Manu might have torn himself to pieces trying to reconcile his loyalty to Jaantzen with his feelings of betrayal if another villain in his life hadn't shown up: his father.

Because Manu may be a badass, but in his heart of hearts, he's still a kid nobody protected. A kid who's grandma looked away when she should have stepped in and stopped the abuse. A kid who was taught early that he was expendable.

Jaantzen working with Coeur had triggered those feelings of expendability in Manu once more, but when Manu's father arrives on the scene, it forces Manu to understand truly how far he's come over the years.

Because, of course, Jaantzen doesn't see Manu as

expendable at all. There is deep, powerful love between those two men, and although Jaantzen may be fairly stoic, he's also not afraid to show it.

He does so in this scene in *Crossfire* where Manu is about to leave to drive Coeur back to her crew.

---

*Jaantzen catches Manu's wrist before his lieutenant can rise, leaning close as the others begin to disperse. "No unnecessary risks," he murmurs. "The most important thing tonight is you coming back in one piece."*

*Manu's dark expression softens, and he reaches his other hand to clasp Jaantzen's jaw and neck, drawing him closer until their foreheads touch. He's silent a moment, breath even and calm. "I'll see you tonight," he says, then releases him, a smile pulling at his lips.*

---

Even so, the combined pressures of Coeur and Manu's father trigger old patterns — and the main villain of *Pressure Point*, Victoria Tierren, is a master at forcing heroes to face their fears. As she does so in this scene near the end of *Pressure Point*.

---

*"Why do you stay with him?" she asks finally. "That's what I don't get."*

*He frowns at her. "Jaantzen?"*

"Blackheart almost kills you once, shame on her. But twice?" Tierren laughs. "You need to find an employer who actually gives a shit about you."

"Someone like Leone?" Manu keeps his voice level, but his mind reels, searching for what she means. Twice?

"Kaboom." Tierren smiles, sly. "You didn't know? You didn't wonder why Jaantzen didn't come visit you in the hospital?" Her gaze sweeps past him once more as another set of footsteps pass the mouth of the alley. "Nice that he can still feel shame — I think Leone's long past that."

Manu wants to say, Coeur didn't set the bomb. He wants to say, And if she did, Jaantzen didn't know about it.

But he's having trouble forming those words of denial. Because it's absolutely the sort of thing Coeur would do, and absolutely the sort of knowledge Jaantzen would protect Manu from — and destroy himself with shame over.

A slow smile is forming on Tierren's lips as she watches him — and with an effort, Manu shoves the feeling of realization aside. That dizzying sense of pieces falling into place isn't epiphany; no one thinks clearly at knifepoint. Jaantzen didn't let Coeur try to kill him. Not the first time, not this time. No amount of *adrenaline-spiked false-revelatory euphoria is going to make that true.*

*"They made the plans together," Tierren says, and now she's thoroughly reaching, the uncanny verisimilitude of her previous lie melting to glass.*

*Manu breathes deep against the prick of the needle.*

---

A good villain asks the hero to face their fear so they can see clearly past it.

Manu knows in his core that Jaantzen — his chosen father — is nothing like his biological father. But it's not until the moment Tierren invites him to name his deepest fear — that Jaantzen doesn't care about him — that Manu understands he's been letting it live rent-free in his mind.

Tierren, his father, Coeur — they all lose their hold on Manu in that moment. Manu is never going to forgive Coeur, and he doesn't have to in order to move on. He just needs to forgive Jaantzen.

---

In the end, I'm not sure if Thala Coeur had a redemption arc.

We understand her better. She understands our heroes better. She's learned to be a bit less rash, and she has genuine regret for (some of) her past.

I don't know what the future holds for the characters of the Bulari Saga, but I trust that Coeur will (probably) do the right thing. Maybe even for the right reasons.

In the end, though, Blackheart's gonna Blackheart.

As Mizal Seti says in *Heat Death*, "Being angry at Blackheart is like being angry at an earthquake." Which is why she was absolutely perfect when it came to forcing our heroes to grow.

A good villain teaches you how to defeat them by exposing your weaknesses to the light. A good villain teaches you to be stronger by forcing you to become a better, healthier person.

You can't really blame an earthquake — or Coeur — when it rouses the demons you need to deal with. You just need to do the work on yourself if you want to win.

# FAQ
## YOUR BURNING QUESTIONS, ANSWERED

**WHERE DID YOU FIRST GET THE IDEA FOR THE Bulari world?**

The seed of the Bulari Saga came from a short story I wrote for the inaugural Bikes in Space anthology from Microcosm Publishing.

I'm a natural novel writer, and the craft of writing short stories eluded me for quite some time. For a while, every short story I wrote was just the first chapter of another novel. This one was no exception.

I did what I normally do when writing a new piece, which is to think of a character, put them in a situation, and then follow for a while to see what happens. The main character of this short story turned out to be a schoolteacher who found a strange object smuggled in with a shipment of bicycles that she had ordered for her students. The strange object attracted the unwanted attention of a local crime lord and his crew — and that's where all the trouble began.

That first short story is wildly different from the books that eventually became the Bulari Saga. When I first expanded it into a novel and turned it in to my editor (Elly Blue at Microcosm Publishing), her feedback was that it felt like I had written two books: one socially conscious book about disadvantaged students and systematic oppression, and one shoot-'em-up space gangster book.

In truth, I'd quickly become obsessed with Jaantzen and his crew, and the schoolteacher/bikes plot had gotten sidelined.

Because I was originally writing this book for Microcosm Publishing (and most of what they publish is very socially conscious), I went back to the drawing board and attempted to extricate the space gangsters from the schoolteacher storyline. I got about halfway through that second draft before realizing I was deeply bored.

I couldn't stop thinking about the book I was *really* interested in writing, about Jaantzen and Starla and Manu and the alien — and all the seedy underworld stuff.

So I went back to my editor with an apology. I wouldn't be able to write the book she wanted.

Elly didn't seem surprised. "When I read that last draft, it seemed like you were having way more fun with the space gangsters anyway," she told me. "That's probably the book you should write."

And so I walked away from that publishing contract and started working on a third draft, which eventually became *Double Edged*.

**How did you decide the astronomy and politics, the particular mix of planets and moons and asteroid belts, and how the populations of each interact with one another?**

The very first version of that short story was set on Mars.

I'd written most of it when I told my husband about the story, and that one of the key features was this shipment of bicycles for the students.

"You can't ride a bike on Mars," he told me. He launched into a discussion of gravity and physics and started talking about how I could change the bicycles to something that would work with Martian gravity.

I cut him off. "Can you ride a bike on New Sarjun?"

He looked confused. "I don't know where that is."

"It's where my story is set," I said. And off I went to make up a new world.

One of the reasons I enjoy writing science fiction and creating my own worlds is that I'm much more interested in the story and the characters than I am in coming up with complicated scientific explanations for things or fact-checking whether or not there's actually a parking lot on the corner of Sixth and Pine.

Because that initial story had been set on Mars, the version of the Durga System that had started to settle into my brain was fairly similar to our own solar system. I liked the interplay of major habitable planets closer to the sun, with a more tenuous civilization living in the asteroid belt and beyond. It seemed like it would offer some interesting societal tensions.

I've always been very interested in South American history, and how layers of colonialism intersect there. There was the original wave of colonizers from Spain, Portugal, the Netherlands, and others. But there was also a secondary wave of colonial interference from the United States, which continues to this day.

I wanted to explore how the influence of an overbearing country that feels both entitled and protective of its neighbors can turn into resentment and violence, and that question informed the idea of the Alliance and the general political structure of the Durga System.

I also wanted the story to be set in a closed system, where humans were forced to figure out their problems because they couldn't just zip off to another galaxy if they didn't get along.

Zooming in to the politics of Bulari, specifically, I was very interested in the interplay between ostentatious displays of wealth and abject poverty.

I've seen this in cities throughout the world. The dusty sprawl of ramshackle temporary housing outside Lima, Peru. The hillsides packed with brightly painted slums surrounding Caracas, Venezuela. The tent cities in Seattle and Portland.

The cognitive dissonance of luxury high-rises within sight of makeshift homes that don't even have running water is incredible.

We used to hide that more in American cities — but these days most of us have learned to live with the mental and moral disconnect of stepping past a man without shoes sleeping in a doorway in order to meet friends for happy hour at a rooftop cocktail lounge.

If you don't have money, you're forgotten. So it shouldn't come as a shock that Bulari is a city where money buys security and communities without it are left to police themselves. If you're going to ignore a slum like Altamira, is it any wonder someone like Blackheart will be able to take it under her wing? And, since she turned out to be the only one lifting a finger to help the slums, is it any wonder that they rose up to put her in power over the whole city?

I wanted to explore the interplay of wealth and morality. Could you be moral and have wealth? Could you be moral if you were scraping the bottom of the barrel? What defines right and wrong, when legal and illegal are just concepts put in place by an entity whose job is to keep the poor poor and the rich rich?

In Toshiyo's deleted scene (where she meets Jaantzen for the first time), she wonders what legal and illegal even mean. She grew up indentured, and the company she worked for did whatever they wanted. There were rules and there were consequences, none of which were governed by this sense of moral or immoral, right or wrong, legal or illegal.

When she was finally free to make her own choices in the world, why would she care that the life Jaantzen offered her wasn't strictly law-abiding? She had no association between the concepts of law and justice.

Anyway, all that to say that the inspiration for this world was to create a messy political and socioeconomic system that would provide a good backdrop to ask those kinds of questions.

But also because you apparently can't ride bikes on Mars.

### Are there any real locations that inspired locations in your books? If so, which ones?

I describe my approach to worldbuilding as a magpie collecting shiny treasures and hoarding them until the time is right. When I start to write, shiny details drop out of my magpie brain and onto the page. Sometimes I know where they originated, sometimes they're just ideas that have been tumbling against each other in my subconscious for years.

But there are a few locations which I can definitely pinpoint the origins of!

Julieta's greenhouse was inspired by my grandma's husband, Doug, and his love of orchids. He had an incredible greenhouse — though not as huge as Julieta's. But I took heavy inspiration from it when writing those greenhouse scenes in *Double Edged*. (I also have one of his orchids on my desk as I write.)

A lot of locations are influenced by my travels in South America. Surquillo Market (where Manu and Oriol meet for lunch once Oriol gets back in touch) is literally lifted from the market with the same name in Lima, and the safehouse that Starla goes to with Ximena is inspired by a hotel my husband and I almost inadvertently stayed at in Lima, which had mirrors on the ceiling and rooms probably rented by the hour.

Alusina, which isn't actually in the books but shows up in the short story "Holiday," was inspired by my home in the lower Yakima Valley, in Washington state.

The Tamarind District is loosely based on Las Ramblas in Barcelona, which is one of my favorite cities.

And Jaantzen's restaurant, The Jungle, isn't specifically inspired by a real-life location. But it is 100 percent the restaurant that I would build! I've often said that I might open a restaurant or coffee shop purely as an excuse to have more room to buy enormous indoor plants and to allow the ones that I currently have to grow to their full potential.

**Of all the places in the Durga System, where would you retire, and what appeals to you about that location?**

I'm not sure I want to live in space, because the

thought terrifies me — which means I'm limited to Indira or New Sarjun.

I'm also a city girl, and despite its many, many problems, I do actually love Bulari.

Plus, there are parts of it that are quite safe if you have enough money — like the Tamarind District, which is full of art and delicious restaurants and quaint buildings. I might enjoy a charming townhouse on a quiet side street in the Tamarind, within easy walking distance of all my favorite restaurants. I might open my own cafe there, with floor-to-ceiling windows filled with enormous monsteras and too many hoyas.

On Indira . . . I'm not sure I would want to live in Arquelle, because it sounds too constricting. But I have an inkling that the techie island nation of Teuça might be a nice spot to get away from troubles and sip a margarita on the beach. I'll have to explore it in an upcoming book.

**What's some of your favorite lore you haven't managed to fit into a published story?**

The thing about the way that I write is that I tend not to know much more about the world than what I've written.

Essentially, I only fill in details as I need them — sometimes so haphazardly that I forget I've made up a particular detail until my editor catches it and reminds me that I already contradicted myself several books ago.

This is why hiring a good editor is so incredibly important!

But there are a couple of threads that I am dying to pull on and learn more about. In fact, I think they could be connected.

I really want to learn more about the Zmiya organization that Mel was a part of. (Mel is the mercenary that Oriol hires — she shows up in his short story, "Trouble," as well as later in the Bulari Saga series.) I also want to learn more about the artifacts that supposedly belong to the Tisare cult that the crew of the *Nanshe* keep finding in the Nanshe Chronicles.

I wonder if those two threads might be connected, in part because of Deyva, the mechanic Starla knew as a kid on Silk Station. He also had the Zmiya snake wrist tattoos, and I assume he'll wander into the Nanshe Chronicles in the next few books . . .

I suspect we'll find out together, starting around book seven of the Nanshe Chronicles. ;)

### How old were you when you decided to become a writer as a profession?

I'm pretty sure my mom still has one of those journals from elementary school where you talk about what you want to do with your life. Mine says that I want to be a writer.

(I also wanted to be a doll maker and a veterinarian at one point.)

By the time I was in high school, though, I was telling people that I wanted to write novels. My senior year, I actually got one of my English teachers to sign off on a special projects period where I just sat in the library and wrote a fantasy novel the entire year. I turned it in to him at the end (and got an A in the class).

I shudder to think that he might still have a copy!

It took me a lot longer than that to figure out how to make "writing as a profession" work, but the desire to write stories more or less full time has been a driving force for basically everything I've done in my life.

### How did you get started writing sci-fi crime stories?

I really enjoy reading thrillers and detective stories, and watching Mafia movies and shows. My favorite parts of Star Wars were the bits in the seedy cafes and the smugglers' dens. And so when I started writing science fiction, it's probably only natural that I kept turning my attention to the underworld instead of hanging out in the shiny lawful spaces.

### How are you avoiding being a "starving artiste?"

My strategy has always been to have something

other than writing that earns a reasonable amount of money and takes the pressure off my work. I'm slowly building up my fiction catalogue to a place where it's making some money. But most fiction writers I know who are making a full-time living either got major book deals with a traditional publisher or wrote a lot of indie books very quickly.

I admire my friends who can write both fast and well, but I can't quite write at the pace they do and get the level of quality that I want (and that they manage to do).

So I've sought out other ways to earn income that gives me creative freedom. For a lot of years, I waited tables in order to have the flexibility to write. Eventually I started working as a copywriter, and sometime after that went freelance so I could have more time to write fiction.

These days, I ghostwrite business books for coaches, consultants, entrepreneurs, and other business types. It's super enjoyable work, and it pays the bills well as I continue growing the fiction business.

I'm also lucky that for the past eight-ish years, my husband's company has offered me a nice healthcare package instead of me having to pay for my own. That's extra money I can invest back into covers, editing, and marketing.

**How do you flesh out characters? Do you get an idea of the type of character you need and go from there?**

I often feel like my characters show up fully formed, and I'm just getting to know them as I write about them. The annoying thing about this is that they don't always do exactly what I need them to do for the story.

When I do need a character for a specific role, I tend to start with my first assumption of who that person would be, then shift it 90 degrees to find something different.

A good example of this is Calanthe Yang. In an earlier version of *Double Edged*, Jaantzen got called to the police station for questioning, and he called for his lawyer.

We all have a stereotype of who a crime boss's lawyer might be. And so I asked myself, what's 90 degrees to that? A woman, sure. She could be dressed in a sharp, dark, serious suit so people take her seriously. Or, like Calanthe, she could favor a palette of rose gold and pale pink that catches people off guard and gets them to underestimate her before she goes in for her kill.

Another small detail showed up as she first walked into the interrogation room in her rose-gold sheath dress and heels: the bulge of her very pregnant belly straining against the dress.

Letting my mind add in these little details always makes for so much more interesting characters, I think. Because you immediately ask, "Why is a pregnant woman in a rose-gold dress the first person this hard-ened crime lord calls?"

It becomes clear the minute Calanthe starts talking just how competent she is. And, of course, a lawyer who is also a mother of three is guaranteed to be one of the most no-nonsense badasses you'll ever meet.

Another tool I use for character development is the tarot.

About halfway through writing the Bulari Saga, I started experimenting with doing character spreads with tarot cards. By the time I started writing the Nanshe Chronicles, I was doing that with nearly every major character, including my villains.

I use a nine-card spread I found online:

1. Character
2. Dominant outer characteristic
3. Dominant inner characteristic
4. Goal
5. Motivation
6. Stakes
7. Flaw/Need
8. Source of the Flaw/Need
9. Effect of Flaw/Need on achieving the Goal

I've found this to create a really interesting jump-ing-off point for exploring characters, and when I've drawn tarot cards to explore plot points (I like a three-card Situation-Action-Outcome spread for this), it often creates interesting resonances with cards that show up in a particular character's spread.

I'll write more about this with concrete examples when I do a special Nanshe Chronicles Kickstarter book, since that's where I used this technique the most.

## What kind of research do you do before you start writing?

Honestly, I do just as much as I need to jump-start me on the story.

I tend to require a lot of input and intellection (if you know your CliftonStrengths) before my creative juices get flowing, and because I'm not writing things that are set someplace requiring historical accuracy, I normally retain only as many facts as I need to flavor whatever I'm writing.

(This is another example of how my magpie brain works when it comes to writing.)

Sometimes I seek out specific research ahead of time, like when I read an 800-page biography of Che Guevara to inspire me to write about Lasadi's abusive ex-partner in the Nanshe Chronicles. Sometimes I just go exploring when I'm stuck on what might happen next.

That's what happened with *Deviant Flux*. I was stuck about halfway through, so I started noodling around on Wikipedia and listening to history podcasts. I can't remember the trail I took, but I ended up going down a rabbit hole of labor movements and historic strikes, and suddenly the rest of the plot clicked together for me.

### Are you a plotter? A pantser? Something in between?

For those of you who aren't writers and don't know this parlance, a plotter is someone who outlines their books in detail, while a pantser is someone who writes "by the seat of their pants" and just sees where the story takes them.

I wrote the Bulari Saga by the seat of my pants, which was terrifying when I got through about book five and still didn't know exactly how it was going to end.

With the Nanshe Chronicles books, I've been meticulous about outlining them. Because they're all heists and cons, they have to be a bit more structured. So I spent a lot of time studying that specific plot structure, as well as studying television scripts to figure out how much story and backstory and character development and all of that could fit into a 44-minute TV episode.

(Which, side note, feel free to pass my name on to all your TV executive friends! The Nanshe Chronicles is already set up with the right structure!)

But even though I outline more now, I still have a lot of issues with my story wandering away from me until I know my characters well.

Because of that, I don't outline the full book in

detail. I rough out all of the acts so that I know what the major beats are going to be in each act, and outline the first act in a lot more detail.

I write that act, revisit my outline, write the next act, revisit my outline, etc.

I basically realized that if I was going to end up throwing away the second half of the outline anyway, why bother to do more than outline the first part and roughly sketch in what would happen for the rest of it.

### How long does it take you to write each book?

The first book of the Bulari Saga took me three or four years. Part of that was because, as I mentioned, I wrote it three times from scratch. But also, as I was trying to figure out how to write it, I started working on character backstories that turned into *Starfall*, *Negative Return*, and *Deviant Flux*.

Later books of the Bulari Saga took me about six months each. And that's about how long most of the Nanshe Chronicles books have taken. Because of my eye injury last summer, the fifth book of the Nanshe Chronicles ended up taking almost a year and a half — but now we're back on track.

### I'm guessing it's like picking a favorite child, but do you have a favorite character in the Bulari Saga?

That's definitely a super hard question!

I love each member of Jaantzen's crew for different reasons.

Manu might edge into the lead because I love his energy and enjoy being in his head.

But I also love Starla because she's so well-adjusted and non-traumatized — even though she's been through plenty of hard things in her young life, she's always been loved and she's always felt safe. Which means she hasn't developed the same arsenal of messed-up coping mechanisms everyone around her seems to have. She's a nice breath of fresh air.

And it's hard not to love Phaera after she just steamrolled into my story and took over. I like her no-nonsense attitude, her backbone, and her sense of humor.

Outside the crew, I really love Detective Cho — and I wish that he had been able to keep his mouth shut instead of asking too many questions and getting himself killed. But that's how the best detectives are, I suppose.

And I know it's awful of me to say, but I really do love Thala Coeur. I want to believe that she's learned to stop flying so close to the sun and how to play better with others by the end of the Bulari Saga . . . but I wouldn't put money on it.

**Which character is most like you and which is most different? Which was harder to write?**

Phaera is probably closest to me, in that she is ambitious, used to be a waitress, and is fairly well-adjusted. Her ambition and desire to succeed politically far outshines my own, but I can see the spark of it in me. In a way, writing her was a thought exercise of what Super-Ambitious Jessie would look like if I cared about going Phaera's route instead of chilling and writing stories instead.

It also made her hard to write, because there were times when I was aware that too much of my own self was bleeding onto the page. I had to be careful to ask what Phaera would do in a situation, rather than what *I* would do.

Manu might be the character who's least like me, in that he's flashy, he's a performer, he enjoys taking risks, and he believes that rules were made to be broken.

He's also a total workaholic, so we have that in common. And it was actually very easy to write him, because I felt like I could just sink into his point of view without wondering where the edges mixed with my own. I always knew what Manu would do — and it was almost always the complete opposite of my first impulse!

### What about the "bat" aliens? Where do they come from? What's their story?

Well, that is a fantastic question! I look forward to answering that in future books. ;)

## FREE BOOKS!

Want more stories? Don't miss the free Nanshe Chronicles prequel novella, *Artemis City Shuffle*.

You'll find all that and more at *jessiekwak.com/nanshe*.

# ABOUT JESSIE KWAK

Jessie Kwak has always lived in imaginary lands, from Arrakis and Ankh-Morpork to Earthsea, Tatooine, and now Portland, Oregon. As a writer, she sends readers on their own journeys to immersive worlds filled with fascinating characters, gunfights, explosions, and dinner parties.

When she's not raving about her latest favorite sci-fi series to her friends, she can be found sewing, mountain biking, or out exploring new worlds both at home and abroad.

(*Author photo by Robert Kittilson.*)

*Connect with me:*
www.jessiekwak.com
jessie@jessiekwak.com

 facebook.com/JessieKwak

instagram.com/kwakjessie

# THE NANSHE CHRONICLES

*Haunted space stations? Puzzling totems? Cursed relics? No job's too bizarre for the crew of the Nanshe.*

Lasadi doesn't like strangers on her ship, but she'll need a bigger crew if she's going to steal a mysterious artifact from a dead pirate's long-lost space station. She takes a chance on a charming grifter named Raj, along with a skilled hacker and her genius little brother. And it's . . . nice? If Lasadi isn't careful, she's going to start enjoying having a crew aboard.

Raj's last bit of luck capsized right before he ran into Lasadi, and this job could finally get his life back on track — as long as Lasadi never learns the truth about his past. Raj isn't the only one on this crew with secrets, though, and Auburn Station holds more than long-dead ghosts. Unless this fledgling crew can learn to trust each other, none of them are getting off this station alive.

The Nanshe Chronicles is set in Jessie Kwak's Durga System, where humans have managed to populate the stars, but they haven't left behind their vices. And that's very good for business. Perfect for fans of Cowboy Bebop, Firefly, and Leverage.

*Start the adventure today: jessiekwak.com/nanshe*

www.ingramcontent.com/pod-product-compliance
Lightning Source LLC
Chambersburg PA
CBHW030551020726
47494CB00005B/1565